SLAVE TRADER

Slave Trader

Caroline King

Publisher's message

This novel creates an imaginary sexual world. In the real world,
readers are advised to practise safe sex.

First published in 1999
by HEADLINE BOOK PUBLISHING

A HEADLINE LIAISON paperback

10 9 8 7 6 5 4 3 2

ISBN 0 7472 6167 9

Typeset by CBS, Martlesham Heath, Ipswich, Suffolk
Printed and bound in France by
Brodard & Taupin.
Reproduced from a previously printed copy.

HEADLINE BOOK PUBLISHING
A division of Hodder Headline
338 Euston Road, London NW1 3BH

Slave Trader

Chapter One

Sophie Jenner leaned back into the deep tan leather swivel chair and shut her eyes against the glare from the computer screen which had claimed her undivided attention for the past two hours. After a few moments' respite she opened her eyes again and frowned accusingly at the VDU. There was definitely a problem behind the mass of figures she had been reviewing, of that she was certain. But right now, she was having the devil's own luck trying to get a handle on what precisely that problem was.

'Turner!' she called, shifting her gaze briefly towards the open door of her glass-panelled office. 'Do you have a minute?' Within seconds, Sophie's PA appeared at the door to her office, eyebrows raised in anticipation. 'I need some detail on the company's preliminary capital flow into South America,' Sophie said. 'I'm interested in money transfers of say, two to three hundred thousand dollars.'

'Small change!' protested Turner.

She ignored the interruption. 'I want to know where the cash call originated, where the money was destined, who authorised the transfer. That sort of stuff.' She gave an apologetic grimace to ward off any potential complaints.

'Okay, but give us a clue where to start, Sophie. South America is a big place.' Turner wrinkled his forehead in a plea for clemency.

Sophie thought for a moment, her eyes returning to the flickering computer. 'Columbia and Peru,' she said decisively, as her PA turned on his heel to leave her room. 'But if you don't come up with the goods by the end of the week, you can tackle the rest of the sub-continent!'

Her voice followed Turner as he retreated into the general office with a dismissive wave of his hand. Sophie allowed herself a small smile and found her spirits lifting slightly. She knew that the figures she had requested would be on her desk well within any deadline she chose to set. With any luck, Turner might dig up that extra little elusive detail that would allow her to bottom out the South American project funding jigsaw.

Dragging herself away from the computer, Sophie stretched up her arms and arched her back. She had had enough number crunching for one day. There must be a simple explanation for this pattern of transactions and at least she'd amassed some concrete facts and figures for Turner to start chasing in the morning. What she needed right now was some heavy R&R.

After a few moments' contemplation of her options, Sophie picked up the phone and jabbed four digits into the base set. She listened impatiently to the single ringing tone of the internal telephone system until, with a snort of annoyance, she slammed the handset down. Damn him, never there when she was desperate. Probably out having a good time with one of his girlfriends.

She glared back at the screen which glowed green and red, the lights winking back at her, irritating and unusually impenetrable. She had simply been running regular sample audit checks on money flows around the business; they were all established transfers into recognised eco-friendly operations in the South American sub-continent but as she picked through the numbers something had started to feel wrong.

She couldn't complete the audit trail for a small number of transfers that were apparently making their way through accounts via normal banking routes. She kept telling herself that the numbers involved were hardly significant; as Turner had said, small change. But even so, as she continued her sampling, a worrying pattern had begun to emerge. Several cash calls from a rainforest conservation project in Peru had been authorised using a management code which she didn't immediately recognise and narrowing the focus of her searches she had finally come upon one which had been routed, against normal company practice, to a Swiss bank account where the trail had gone cold.

None of it made sense. But given time it would. Sophie jumped up and reached for her kitbag. Exercise was what she needed, something to break the stale sensation and the monotony that came from staring at a computer screen for too long. The gym in the Broadgate Centre, where she enjoyed the benefits of Deschel Chesham's corporate membership was always on hand to offer various alternative forms of exercise, sometimes even the lewd one which had been uppermost in her mind.

As she stepped out of the glass-fronted corporate office, Sophie's senses were assaulted both by the stifling heat of a late summer afternoon in central London and by the cacophony of bells from St Paul's Cathedral. Musing on some of the advantages of working in an air-conditioned and sound-proofed atmosphere, Sophie turned onto the cobbled street and walked quickly down towards Moorgate and the Broadgate Centre above Liverpool Street Station. She made her way up to the third floor and, ignoring the few remaining commuters scurrying about on the platforms far beneath her, passed into the cool green interior of 'The Gym'. Half an hour on the running machine and the services of her favourite masseur would sort her out.

Revelling in the sensation of his hands on her body, Sophie allowed herself the luxury of a small groan of pleasure.

'That is exquisite, Rani,' she murmured, giving herself up finally to the rhythm of his well-oiled strokes along the length of her back. As her muscles relaxed, Sophie willed her mind clear of the tensions of the day, lulled by the repetitious motion of his hands, the faintly pungent aroma from the oils he was slowly rubbing into her skin and the dull beat of music from a distant room.

But try as she would, the thoughts which had been running through her head since leaving the office came crowding back and, as usual, Sophie gave in to their temptation. As she began the, by now, familiar consideration of her problems at work, she barely registered Rani's hands moving from her back to begin lightly kneading her buttocks; each circular movement becoming deeper, more pronounced and gently easing the rounded cheeks apart. A finger slipping slyly between the cleft in her buttocks shocked Sophie back to the present and she tensed her bottom while wriggling to ease the pressure of lying on her breasts.

'I thought that would bring you back to your senses,' he said, with a quiet laugh. 'Turn over and stop thinking about work or you'll be sorry.'

'Yes, sir,' Sophie murmured as she obediently twisted to lie on her back and resolutely closed her eyes again. She heard him moving around the couch on which she was placed, smelling the fresh wave of aromatic oils as he lubricated his hands afresh. Starting on her shoulders, Rani began his ministration to her body once again and Sophie breathed deeply, knowing there was pleasure and relaxation in his touch if only she would give herself up to it.

With a continuous movement, he extended his massage down her body, passing fleetingly over her breasts to her stomach and returning again to her shoulders. Sophie felt her mind slipping away once more and let out a sigh of contentment.

'Raise your arms above your head,' he commanded, and as she complied, Rani focused his attention on her now taut breasts, kneading the mounds of flesh gently but insistently and ending each stroke with a slight pull on both nipples. Sophie felt his stimulation of her breasts translate into an erotic tingle between her thighs.

'Spread your legs a little,' Rani said, and she responded to the gentle pressure of his fingers on her inner thighs without demur. As he began to work on the firm flesh of her upper legs and pelvis, Sophie fantasised about the effect of her abandoned posture on any red-blooded male. She imagined how his eyes would be devouring the sight of her breasts, pulled high by her raised arms; how he would want to spread her legs even further apart to open the pink lips hidden beneath her golden bush; how he would massage her secret place with oils before mounting the couch and pushing his own engorged sex into hers . . .

Finishing his massage with an almost vicious tug on each of her big toes, Rani stepped back and surveyed his work. 'That's all I can do for you,' he laughed. 'I suggest you go and find yourself a straight man to finish the job.'

'No chance tonight, I'm afraid,' Sophie laughed back, swinging her legs off the couch and reaching for her robe. 'But who needs a man, anyway?'

'Speak for yourself,' Rani quipped, flicking on the lights of the cubicle and pulling aside the curtain. 'See you soon.'

Promising herself the luxury of something chilled and sparkling when she got home, Sophie took a quick shower at the gym, reluctantly washing Rani's perfumed oils from her skin. The taxi home across central London to South Kensington took less time than she anticipated and as darkness began to fall, Sophie finally turned the key in the door of her tiny house in Cranlow Garden Mews and let herself into the cool, silent interior.

Tossing her kitbag into the hall cupboard, Sophie flicked on the living-room low-lights and padded through to the kitchen. A chilled bottle of Janissen-Baradon champagne rested close to smoked Scottish salmon and wholewheat blinis in the fridge and Sophie placed the makings of her supper on the tiled worktop alongside ingredients for a herby green salad.

'But first, to finish the job,' Sophie murmured, opening the

5

champagne with a satisfying pop and pouring a glass of the sparkling nectar into a tall-stemmed glass. Taking a sip and savouring the bubbles on her tongue for a second, Sophie walked upstairs, past the bedroom and onto the top floor, picking up the handset from her cellular phone on the way. She flung open the glass doors of her roof terrace and stood at the entrance for a long moment listening to the muted sounds of the city floating up from below. Taking another sip of champagne, Sophie plugged a number into the handset only to be rewarded with an answerphone message which she didn't allow to run to completion before switching off her phone.

'So much for the straight man,' she sighed ruefully, dropping the phone onto a low table and sitting down on a lounger. She drank heavily from the glass and lay back to stare at the night sky for a moment then, giving in to her growing desires, Sophie shrugged off her leggings and ran one hand down her body, pushing an exploratory finger into the waist of her lace panties. Now where had she been when Rani had so rudely finished his massage? Oh yes, she remembered, thinking about what a 'real' man would do to her.

Sophie's fingers pushed further between the lips of her sex as she recalled the face, body and strength of her fantasy lover: he was pushing her legs apart and, this time, stroking her open sex backwards and forwards with one hand while the other maintained a steady rhythm up and down his shaft which was growing in length and thickness at each stroke. Her arms were now tied at the wrist to a fixture at the head of the couch so that even if she wanted to, she would be powerless to stop his erotic stimulation of her body.

Sophie pushed her panties down below her hips and started to rub her clitoris rhythmically with the palm of her hand while dipping her fingers into her sex which was glistening with the juices of her arousal. In her mind, the fantasy man positioned himself between her legs, pushing them even further apart with his thighs as he directed his engorged cock at her hole. With a

6

long look at her swollen sex flesh, he raised his head and pierced her body with one practised stroke of his shaft.

The tremors of Sophie's orgasm flowed through her body from her clitoris and she moaned with pleasure as she slowed the motion of her hand against her sex. With a sigh of relief, she lay supine for several moments, recovering her breath before opening her eyes and reaching for her champagne. As she did so, Sophie caught a movement from the corner of her eye and turning to scan the buildings which overlooked one side of her terrace, she thought she caught the shadow of a figure against a heavily curtained window, but the light behind was dim and the vision was distant. Raising her glass and taking a swig of cool champagne, Sophie stared directly at the window before pulling on her panties and making for the kitchen to finish preparing supper. She hoped whoever it was had enjoyed the show.

It was ten-thirty. Sophie slipped into bed, pulled out her diary and switched on her notebook computer to have another look at the figures. Now was not the time to have any outstanding queries in any part of the business, certainly not with an official PR launch only three days away and a raft of interviews set up to advertise everything about the fund. Once again she quelled the nervousness that simply thinking about the launch seemed to induce; this was the first time she had ever had to take such an upfront position in a business and it was enough to make her feel sick to her stomach even if it was what she had been working towards.

Maybe it wasn't the business, she told herself, maybe it was just thinking about the effect her good fortune was having on other people that was making her nervous. After all, her working life was about to have a radical change of direction and an opportunity like this was enough to make a lot of people store up a great deal of jealousy. They didn't know why she should get the job, and in a place like the City she didn't need anyone else to tell her that the gossips were out there with their knives already raised, ready to stab her in the back without a second thought if they saw an opportunity.

Looking back on her career to date Sophie could hardly believe how quickly time had gone by. When she originally graduated from college she wanted to work as trader, however tough or aggressive. What she wanted after three years in the quiet of a provincial red-brick university was to feel the buzz and the excitement of a trading floor in a big City bank. But despite interning in one of the oldest merchant banks in London over the summer after graduation, then sending her CV to everyone with any power in the business, it seemed that no-one was willing to take a chance on a nice girl with a degree in history and a real desire to do a man's job. She was five years too late, they told her, far too old. She should have started straight out of school, and in any case it wasn't a job for a woman, certainly not a Brit. The American women were different; they were tougher, they could cope, but she was too fragile and she'd get trampled on in the hard, 'succeed or you're out' environment. Anyway, they said, why did she want to do a job like that? She'd be much better in research or marketing, or maybe on a graduate training programme in a high street bank.

It was crap of course, all of it, but there was no chink in the armour that Sophie could see, so she took the first decent City job she could, working as a research analyst in a huge Japanese bank. It was there that she realised her first mistake had been to focus on developing a relationship with the women in the business. They were the ones who were really difficult to work with and the more powerful and well paid, the less they were interested in having an attractive upstart come into their midst.

Stuck in a cubicle with a PC and a library card she spent three months making coffee and having reports taken out of her hands by her boss, the vicious and bitchy Sally, before she could even complete them, and certainly before she could get her name on them. But set-backs just made Sophie more determined; she stuck at it, she played the game and slowly she tried to get some bargaining chips stacked on her side. She organised temps to make the coffee and made herself available for running errands and taking notes, concentrating intently on the content of any meetings she was able to sit in on; she learnt about business systems and made herself indispensable through her expertise in managing and interrogating electronic information databases; she toughed it out with some of the men and flirted with the rest, but didn't sleep with any, no matter what everyone in the office thought, and after a year, by the time a chance for a promotion appeared, Sophie had hardened up a great deal. The job was completely out of her league, but Sophie pushed everyone she knew, and talked to anyone who might feasibly support her advancement, for a move into Philip Blakemore's team.

Pip Blakemore was the golden boy of the bank; he'd started as a dealer in his youth and made a lot of money for himself as well as everyone on the Board. Then he disappeared and went to college, only to come back to storm through Mergers and Acquisitions before making a side-step into fund management. He worked his team half to death, but he was a 'star' both as a trader and a fund manager, and his big ideas had made the right people rich. However, though he was successful, handsome and charming, he was also mysterious and could be very aloof. The rumours about his private life were legend and unsubstantiated: he lived in a vast mansion off Regent's Park; he was a loner, asexual and uninterested in anyone except for himself and money; he was a sexual deviant who cruised the streets looking for girls and boys to toy with; he was secretly married to an exotic Brazilian artist and heiress. The fewer facts anyone knew, the stranger the stories became.

Sophie was rather nervous of meeting the famous Pip Blakemore, and by the time she actually got into an interview with him she was shaking in her boots, but set against the other, more qualified applicants, Pip seemed to find Sophie's gall rather amusing, and to everyone's surprise, including her own, he'd taken an interest in her, although he didn't give her the job. Instead he had her moved from research and into sales and marketing, devising new products for the institutional clients of the bank. He advised her to focus on one area. Perhaps, he said, emerging markets, or more specifically, South American debt would be a good idea. Her time, he told her, would come. Then, a year and a half later he 'suggested' that she get into banking operations, controlling the back office of the trading floor, completing deals, making transfers and money approvals, taking responsibility for the completion of deals. She went abroad, first to Frankfurt and then, in a big step, on secondment to the US, in the New York offices working on NYMEX and then Chicago, working with the team on the Chicago Options Exchange. Then, finally, he'd sent for her, offered her a way out of the bank and taken her with him as part of his team when he moved to Deschel Chesham, bringing her into the fund management business. She had been working there ever since, but now things had changed.

Pip was still a big name in the business and his bosses were happy to indulge him and his rather unorthodox ideas, but in truth, Sophie knew that Pip was bored with work and wanted to do something different. Even she was surprised when he started talking about ethical investments and eco-friendly funds, and the Board were stunned, to say the least, although now he had them completely convinced that he was entirely converted to eco-projects. Sophie knew perfectly well that he didn't give a damn about the environment – he was amusing himself convincing everyone this was a mission – but really saw this as just another means of making a great deal of money. The idea was to create a new fund that would invest in profitable ethical businesses, not completely unheard of in the City, although in this case the business would work with an almost completely flat structure, run by and through local people 'on the ground' in South America, Africa or wherever it might be targeted. No management layers, no costs. No people siphoning off profits along the way; no dumping of chemicals and effluent to make a quick profit; complete transparency of action; a link from the rainforests of South America to London, with nothing in between.

Or at least that's what the marketing slogans were telling everyone. In fact there were lots of people in between, brokers, lawyers, accountants and clients, but who cared? They were all foreigners, as Pip pointed out dismissively, just a bunch of South Americans in some backwater country.

Whatever their initial misgivings the Board had stumped up their support at the sight of Pip's analysis and business projections, a superb concoction of marketing hyperbole and over-optimistic figures. Sometimes even Sophie was a little alarmed at how optimistic Pip was about the returns. But he didn't care, and the biggest surprise of all was that he wanted Sophie to front up the business alongside him.

She let out a great sigh as she studied her diary. Philip's idea of sharing the PR work seemed to be to let her answer all the questions; she had seven interviews lined up for Thursday, all following a PR lunch and launch at the Deschel Chesham offices. Essentially it was an opportunity to sell the idea to the media by giving them information, food and copious amounts of alcohol.

Sophie groaned at the thought. She switched her computer off and put it back on the night-stand; she wasn't getting anywhere going over work at this time of night, she could get back to it tomorrow. She threw her diary on the floor and switched off the light, snuggling down under the sheets. Right now she was knackered, she needed sleep, she knew the pressure was just going to get worse, and where the bloody hell was Pip anyway?

Sophie's day normally started at six o'clock, sometimes making her way straight to the office and her desk, but quite often going via a warm-up trip to the gym. Today she got up early, packed her clothes, pulled on her running shorts and T-shirt and made her way out of the mews and into a taxi, whizzing through Knightsbridge, Westminster and central London with only a few solitary joggers to see her on her way.

The gym was already fairly busy, with a variety of lean, tanned bodies warming up on the running machines. Some were people she knew, early risers and lots of Americans, all getting their exercise fix before the first meeting of the day. Sophie's favourite way to get some exercise at this early hour was to use the pool; the water was warm, and it was usually very quiet, with perhaps just a couple of other swimmers joining her in the lanes. And sometimes only one.

She stopped at her locker and pulled on a plain one-piece swimsuit before making her way through to the pool. The gym had various pools; a warm one for swimming, an ice-cold plunge pool for closing the pores after a sauna, and several hot, bubbling Jacuzzi baths for lounging and luxuriating. She headed towards the swimming pool with an irrational sense of excitement; he would be waiting for her, she was sure.

His name was Andrew and over the past couple of months they had been meeting up and racing together, two, three, sometimes four times a week. At first it was by accident then casually on purpose and now by an unspoken agreement. In the past month Sophie had invested in a new array of sportswear and she had taken to making herself look presentable before she left the house, just in case. She wasn't disappointed; Andrew was there already, diving into the clear deep water, his lean body visible beneath the rippling surface, his tan enhanced by the gleaming white tiles around the pool and the lights beneath the water line, a sheen of water glistening across his face as he bobbed up in front of her. He was very dark-skinned with jet-black hair and intensely deep brown eyes and he had the most stunning body she could imagine; tall, well-built, a firm chest, washboard stomach, muscles not bulging, but solid and rounded, sitting beneath the surface of his skin, growing when he flexed his arms. He was handsome enough, she had decided, to be a model, although the location of the club probably meant he was just another banker. There was, however, no way he was gay; she had worked that one out from his reaction when they were swimming alongside each other. They had been silently and innocently flirting ever since they met, but neither had made a move, not yet anyway.

Andrew smiled up at her from the pool, slicking wet hair back from his face. 'Hi.'

'Good morning. How is it in there today?'

'Great, same as always. You're early.'

'Got a busy day ahead.'

He smiled almost coyly. 'Just so long as you weren't trying to avoid me.'

She laughed. 'Why would I want to do that?'

'Afraid of the competition.'

'No way.'

'Okay, your funeral.' He pulled himself fully out of the water, droplets running lazily down his chest, a few clinging to the sleek line of dark hair that ran from his chest to his navel, and beyond. Sophie had to force down the urge to stroke the line down to its natural conclusion. He wore tiny European-style swimming trunks, black and shiny; no baggy figure-obscuring shorts for Andrew. She could see almost everything inside the trunks, and the bulge looked invitingly substantial to say the least.

He turned to face the water and Sophie got into position alongside him; with no one else around they were able to dive and race as much as they liked. She glanced across at him. 'One, two three, go!'

Of course he beat her, he always did. Except when he let her win their little race. But Sophie didn't care. They were towelling off their hair when he dropped his bombshell.

'I'm leaving town,' Andrew told her. Sophie stared at him. 'I'm going back to the States.'

'Oh.' She was surprised at the immediate sense of

disappointment, of an opportunity missed. And at the same time by the realisation of how much she had grown to enjoy this morning flirtation.

'In a way I'll be glad to go home, but I haven't lived there for a long time.'

'New York?'

'Actually no, although that's where I'm from. I'm going to Chicago.'

'Nice place.'

He nodded. 'I guess. Though I'll miss London.' They turned to walk towards the changing rooms.

'I don't even know your last name, and you're leaving.'

'Jameson.'

'Or what you do for a living.'

'I'm a corporate lawyer.'

'Ohhh.'

Andrew laughed. 'What? Wasn't it obvious?'

She smiled back. 'Maybe. I thought you might be an actor, or a model.'

'God no! I was a terrible actor at school, I'd never get a job or eat.' She laughed. 'I'm flattered though. How about you, Sophie?'

'I'm in banking.'

'Oh?' He seemed impressed. 'What sort of banking?'

'Emerging markets.' She blushed. 'I'm just about to launch a new fund, eco-investments.'

'A banker with a conscience.' He said it with a smile, but it was just a trifle patronising.

'You know,' Andrew went on, walking towards the exit, 'if you're about to do your launch and I'm going away we won't be meeting here again.'

'I suppose not.'

Andrew took her hand, and as Sophie looked up in surprise he pulled her towards him. He kissed her. 'Let's make out.'

Sophie laughed but his face had grown serious.

'We've been dancing around for weeks now and this is

14

unexpected. I have to go very soon, so this could be our last chance.'

'Maybe.' As she spoke Sophie could feel the blood rising in her face, a flush spreading across her chest. 'How far do you normally go on a first date?' she teased.

'All the way. Don't you?'

Sophie looked quizzically at Andrew. 'Interesting question. What on earth did you have in mind?' she said, raising her eyebrows and placing one hand on her hip in mock offence.

'Well, I don't have to be in work until later on this morning and I rather thought that half an hour in a relaxing Jacuzzi would be the thing to finish off my early morning swim.' Andrew cocked his head on one side and adopted a look of innocent pleading. 'Will you join me?'

Sophie looked around. The pool was still empty and the chances were it would stay that way. No-one need ever know. 'A farewell Jacuzzi then,' she said, adding 'but it had better be good.' A broad grin on his face, Andrew treated her challenge with disdain and holding out his hand, led her up the steps to the deep Jacuzzi which overlooked the swimming pool. The bath lay silent and tranquil amongst several mature pot palms, waiting for the first customer of the day to bring it to life. Stepping in ahead of Sophie, Andrew gave her an impish smile and turning his back on her, pushed his trunks down over his hips, letting them rest around his upper thighs. His buttocks were firm with a fine covering of dark hairs and Sophie started to smile. This could be fun.

'Turn round and let me see what you've got,' she said, making no move to follow him into the water.

'I'll only show you mine if you promise to show me yours.' Andrew glanced over his shoulder, threatening to pull his trunks back up.

'Okay, okay,' Sophie laughed. 'Get a move on, some of us do have to get to work today.'

Slowly, Andrew turned round to face Sophie, bending

15

slightly to ease his trunks below his knees and kick them off at the same time. Straightening up he opened his arms wide and looked Sophie straight in the eye. Sophie pursed her lips and narrowed her eyes as if weighing up his attributes against a mental checklist. He had a thick bush of pubic hair from which his penis protruded, of medium size but quite thick even in its semi-erect state.

'Well,' Andrew said. 'You promised.'

Smiling widely, Sophie pulled the strap of her swimsuit from her shoulder, lifting one heavy breast free. Andrew's cock gave an appreciative twitch and Sophie noticed it begin to grow in length. She repeated her action with the second shoulder strap, letting Andrew have his fill of the sight of both her breasts before pushing the swimsuit to her hips and wriggling it down past her buttocks and hips. Andrew's cock was now proudly erect and Sophie noticed that his balls had been pulled high as the skin of his penis stretched to accommodate his arousal.

'Aren't you coming in?' Andrew held out one hand to encourage Sophie down into the bath, at the same time using his other hand to stroke the length of his shaft enticingly. Sophie reached to push the start button on the wall and the Jacuzzi instantly sprang into life, causing Andrew to step back in alarm and fall briefly beneath the bubbles. Surfacing immediately, he roared with excitement and grabbing Sophie's ankle, pulled her into the water. They jostled for a few seconds, invisible soft and hard flesh passing tantalisingly through their grip. Then, panting, they flung themselves apart and sat laughing helplessly at opposite sides of the bath, the water churning between them.

'You're gorgeous,' Andrew murmured, moving slowly towards Sophie with his body submerged to the neck. 'And there's no time to waste. I have an incredible stiffy and I want you to try it out. Why don't you kneel up on this ledge, show me your ass and let me have my evil way with you?'

'Andrew!' Sophie grimaced, at the same time doing exactly

as he suggested. 'Is this the way you speak to all your female friends?'

'Only those I'm going to shag silly,' Andrew laughed and, reaching his hands between Sophie's legs, pushed her thighs apart, his fingers finding her hole. Sophie giggled with the sensation of the water jets on her sex as Andrew parted her labia.

'Here we go.' Andrew bent his knees and butted his cock against Sophie's sex cleft. Arching her back so as to give him easier access, Sophie dipped her breasts beneath the thrashing water and closed her eyes to revel in the feel of the stinging jets on her tender flesh. At once, Andrew entered her hole with one long stroke of his penis and Sophie gasped at the energy of his thrusts in and out of her body.

'Uuh,' Andrew rutted beneath the water, his penis long and thick and his balls banging against Sophie's clit adding to the sensations of the Jacuzzi jets. Suddenly pulling away, he stood back and panted. 'Got to slow down a minute. Sit here and spread your legs.'

In a daze, Sophie followed his order, turning over and sitting down on the ledge. Andrew had chosen a prime spot for one of the underwater jets to be directed straight between Sophie's spread legs into her cunt, aroused and swollen by his recent intrusion. She let out a moan of pleasure at the stimulation of her sex by the pulsing jet. Moving between her legs, Andrew pushed his fingers into her pussy and with the expertise of an experienced lover, located her clit and began to rub it rhythmically. Sophie leaned her head back against the rim of the Jacuzzi and gave herself up to the sensations.

Suddenly, Andrew stopped his masturbation and stood up. Sophie opened her eyes to see him peering through the fronds of the palm, down into the swimming pool.

'Shit,' he hissed as he turned back to Sophie and gave her a long stare. 'There's someone in the pool.' Sophie looked in panic towards her swimsuit which was well out of reach where she had discarded it in what now seemed like indecent haste by the side of the Jacuzzi. 'It's all right.' Andrew was continuing to monitor the innocent intruders. 'They're swimming. Now, where were we?'

'Are you quite mad?' Sophie squeaked unbelievingly. 'They could come up here any minute and we'd be done for exposing ourselves in public.'

'The way I'm feeling, we'll be through in a couple of lengths.' Andrew's eyes glinted as he turned round and allowed Sophie a full frontal view of his huge erection. 'Come here.'

With a wave of bravado entirely fuelled by the sight of Andrew's hard-on, Sophie decided to take the chance and waded over to where he was now sitting on the lower ledge. Andrew grinned as Sophie knelt astride him and slowly lowered her cunt onto his waiting cock. As she sank his full length into her hole, Andrew reached around her buttocks and pulled her bottom cheeks apart so that she was suddenly being pounded along her tender cleft by the powerful jets of water. Sophie set up a fast rhythm, squeezing Andrew's cock with her sex muscles, her breasts jiggling in front of his eyes. Over his shoulders, she could see the two swimmers intermittently passing up and down the pool.

Andrew let out a groan as he rapidly approached his climax and Sophie closed her eyes against the distraction of the swimmers to concentrate on her own orgasm. With a series of sharp, suppressed cries, she let go of the tension in her cunt and allowed the release of a sharp climax to rush through her body. Andrew came at almost the same time, excited beyond control by the sight of Sophie's pleasure and the feel of her tight hole around his cock. Sophie slowed her thrusts and slumped against him, only opening her eyes to see the two swimmers climbing out of the pool, clearly intent on investigating the source of the noise emanating from the Jacuzzi.

'Quick, they're coming,' she hissed, pulling herself off Andrew's rapidly deflating cock and clambering out and going in search of her swimsuit.

'I rather think we beat them on that one,' Andrew laughed as he scrabbled for his trunks in the churning water. 'Where the hell are my pants?'

Chapter Two

It was the day of the launch and the City analysts and journalists were all gathered in Room 2000 on the top floor of the building; the presentation room. Sophie paused before she went in, studying them on the video panel in her desk; there were about thirty of them and, typically enough, most were men. In any case, it was easy to separate the analysts and the press people, the press weren't as well dressed, that was for sure. The analysts, economists and banking representatives were in dark bespoke suits and white shirts, the uniform of American banks in particular, whilst the press were more casual, in off-the-peg suits, jeans and chinos.

She switched off the video as Pip came into the room. Pip smiled and she responded automatically; he was so very sexy. Tall and blond, with a good strong body underneath and a very trim bum, she would do anything to get him to take his jacket off and turn around, just to get an eyeful of those cute, round cheeks. Pip seemed to have everything and he attracted a great deal of envy in the business, not to mention amongst his competitors, but so long as he kept making money, his position was safe. He was experienced and smooth, always coming up with a reasonable answer to a question, however stupid he might really think it was, and she suspected that, whatever he said, he was probably going to take most of the questions from the floor.

'So,' she said, 'do you think we're ready to face the wolves?'

'Not exactly wolves, Sophie,' he told her, 'just a bunch of sheep.'

'Sheep with teeth?'

He laughed at that. 'Look, don't let them bother you. Just remember, you're smarter than they are, and you know all about the business. They're dying to hear from you, they want something good to tell their boss and you're going to give it to them.' Sophie grimaced. 'And I'll be there to field questions if they do start getting rough.'

'Hey, I can handle it!'

Pip laughed again. 'I know you can, I just want you to believe it.'

'I wish you hadn't set up those one-on-one interviews . . .'

But Pip was shaking his head. 'It's just what we need. You're the face of the fund.' She grimaced again. 'Accept it. It's good PR.'

'Having a woman in charge?'

'Having a strong, sexy woman with great tits.'

'Philip!'

He laughed again. 'Just teasing. Come on, let's go and face those sheep; like I said, they're just dying to meet you.'

Pip closed the office door and Sophie sat back down at her desk opposite the last reporter, a woman, Daria Williams. A smart redhead from a very glossy magazine, armed with a tape recorder, a notebook and an extremely slimline computer at one side. Sophie smiled across the desk, but Miss Williams was busy making a big deal of letting Pip help her out of her jacket, allowing her eyes to catch his and flirting wildly. Not a surprise, Sophie thought to herself. All the women did it.

'So, Mr Blakemore,' Daria Williams crooned, shifting in her chair to expose as much cleavage as possible and crossing and uncrossing her legs as casually as she could, her skirt slowly riding up her thighs to expose the top of her stockings. Sophie cast a glance at Pip; he was smiling in the wolfish, sexy way he did when he was in pursuit of something, or someone. The reporter was still gazing up at him with an encouraging smile across her face and Pip sat down on the edge of the desk. 'Perhaps we could set up a meeting for a chat as well?'

He raised his eyebrows in mock surprise. 'You want to interview me?' She nodded. 'What about?' She shrugged.

'We could see what develops.'

Enough, thought Sophie, just about fed up with this blatant flirting. She gave a little cough to interrupt them. 'Ahem. Miss Williams?'

Pip gave her a sidewards look and stood up. 'I'm afraid I have to go. I know you don't have that much time and I have a meeting.'

The reporter nodded, whisking a card from her chic little black handbag. 'This is my number, call me if you want to discuss an interview.'

'You can count on it.' Pip took the card, pocketed it and left the room, nodding to Sophie as he went. Daria Williams' eyes followed him to the door, returning to focus on Sophie only when the door clicked shut.

'Wow.'

'I beg your pardon?'

'He is rather fine.'

'Oh?'

'Oh come on,' Daria said, 'you can't have missed it.' She gave Sophie another, more curious look. 'Not of course, unless you go the other way.'

'Thank you,' said Sophie stiffly, 'but I don't think my personal life is any of your business.'

Daria wasn't put off in the slightest. 'I like to know all about my interviewees, but I'll take that as a no,' she said smoothly. 'Still, that's a shame.' Sophie narrowed her eyes but Daria didn't seem to notice. 'So in which case, you must have realised that he's gorgeous. And what a body.'

Sophie shifted in her seat, which seemed to be getting hotter with each passing second. 'He's my boss,' she said simply. 'That's our relationship.'

'Very sensible, I'm sure,' said Daria, 'if rather boring.' She glanced down at her papers. 'Of course,' she went on, 'the rumours are that he's completely unprincipled. Were you aware of that?'

'I most certainly was not and I don't believe in listening to unsubstantiated rumours.'

Daria raised her eyebrows in surprise. 'Really? I find that hard to believe. Still, that's the word on the street.'

Sophie glared at her. 'I think you'll find the City has the utmost faith in Philip Blakemore. If you look at the reports in the paper tomorrow morning concerning the eco-fund you'll find that confirmed.'

Daria shook her head. 'Actually, I wasn't talking about the City.'

'Then who are you talking about?'

The reporter paused and studied her notebook. 'Oh, people.' She looked up brightly across the desk. 'But I digress. I'm here to interview you today, not Pip Blakemore.' Sophie nodded. 'Do you know I really admire you being in a job like this.' Sophie stared at her, amazed at the sudden change in tack. 'No,' Daria went on, 'I mean it. It must be very difficult having to work so hard, knowing about the glass ceiling, wondering when you're going to hit it.'

'I've been very fortunate to get where I am,' Sophie said carefully, 'and yes, I've had to work very hard to get promoted above women as well as men.'

'So how do you feel about your rise to the top, heading up a business like this? Being the new face splashed across billboards and on the advertising campaign. Does that make you nervous at all? And tell me, what do you think about the competition?'

'Other businesses?'

But Daria snorted with laughter. 'Of course not, I mean the men. I bet they just love watching you move up the ladder and, as for getting this job, what do they say? That you're screwing your boss to get on?' Sophie flushed. 'Sorry, I didn't mean to be offensive, but it's the sort of thing everyone wants to know about.' Daria smiled persuasively. 'I know what it's like. I've been there.'

Sophie clearly didn't look convinced and Daria made a decision and stood up. 'Look, we've both had a tough day. Let's not piss about here any more, let's go and get drunk.'

'What?'

She shrugged. 'Sophie, I'll be honest with you, I'd like a good piece to put in the magazine. It would be good for me and for you too.'

'So?'

'Listen, we're the sort of people who really should get on and do a bit of networking. We're both in competitive jobs and we're both just trying to get ahead of all the others with the connections and the background.' Sophie raised her eyebrows. 'I know your background and I know for a fact you don't have a rich daddy to run back to. Neither do I, we're both just ordinary girls who've worked our butts off to get this far without any help from anyone.' Sophie continued to study her, not really sure whether to believe the speech or not and Daria sighed.

'Well, whether you believe my sisterhood angle or not, you deserve to celebrate this launch. It can't be much fun being stuck in here with me asking you searching questions that you clearly don't want to answer.' She grabbed her jacket and started putting it on. 'If I get you a bit drunk I might get more information out of you! Come on, Sophie, give me a break. The champagne's on me!'

Sophie crawled out of her taxi feeling like death. She paid the fare and caught a sight of herself in the window as it whizzed off and groaned. God, she really did look like death, completely knackered. Still, it had been a very long day.

Daria Williams and her bloody questions – and her bloody champagne. A few drinks had turned into a long session and the worst of it was that they got on really well. God knows what she'd told Daria that she could use in her article. Sophie

25

walked in through the hall and towards the back of the house, pouring herself a large glass of water as she went through the kitchen and up the stairs onto the terrace. Here at the top of the mews she was high above almost everyone else, looking down and across rooftops, down into the cobbled street below, the city skyline ahead of her, the stars above and the roar of the city all around. A small conservatory opened out onto a deck that covered the entire roof space and was crammed with bushes, herbs and shrubs, climbing plants and rambling rosebushes at the edges, all making their way up an ironwork trellis on the only exposed side of the terrace. At this time of year, with the clear skies and flowers in bloom, it was like being in a botanical garden, with its scents and hot summer colours. Oranges, pinks, crimson and violet contrasted with softer creams, scented white 'Iceberg' in pots and blue 'Zephirine Drouhin' roses draped around the trellis.

She inhaled, breathing in an intoxicating mixture of aromas; flowers and herbs, lavender, rosemary and thyme. It was delicious and almost immediately relaxing. Stretching her arms, Sophie turned back into the glass conservatory and the counter there which hid, amongst other things, a fridge for emergency night-time recuperation. She pulled out a bottle of white wine and reached for the corkscrew; as she did so she heard a rustle behind her, but before she could move a hand had snaked around her mouth and held her tightly.

'Don't move,' a voice whispered. 'Don't turn around, and don't scream or I'll gut you where you stand, right here and now. Understand?' She nodded and the hand slowly withdrew. 'Now light those candles.' She obediently reached out for the matches and the large church candles sitting on the counter above the fridge. 'Better,' said the voice, as she lit them, and with a click the downstairs light went off, leaving her standing in semi-darkness, the soft candle glow casting shadows of her body onto the floor and reflecting her image back from the glass panels of the conservatory.

'You know what's next, I expect.' She shook her head. 'I

want to see what's under that shirt. Start by taking off that jacket.' She shrugged off the crisp black jacket and held it out.

'Let it drop.'

'It's silk,' she argued.

'So what?'

'It'll crush.'

'Tough.' She gave an exasperated sigh. 'God, you're whiny, princess,' the voice snapped. 'Get your boyfriend to buy you a new one.'

'I don't like to get things dirty,' she complained again.

'I told you, stop whining and get on with it.' With a sigh Sophie let the jacket slip onto the floor. 'Now let's get rid of that blouse.' Sophie unbuttoned the blouse, pulled it out of her waistband and stretched out a hand, ready to drop it on top of the jacket. 'Not too fast.' She stopped, holding the blouse. 'Silk too?' She nodded. 'My, they must be paying you well. Now the skirt.' She obediently unbuttoned the waistband and unzipped her skirt, letting it drop to the floor; it rustled as the tight-fitting lining slid down her legs and lay crumpled at her feet.

She stood there, silent. 'Very nice lingerie,' said her voyeur, studying her semi-naked body. 'But then, it should be, it cost enough.' It was true, her lingerie was the most expensive La Perla design, a fantasy of deep cream and coffee; soft lace and delicate hand-embroidered bra and matching panties, a coffee-coloured suspender belt and sleek stockings, smooth and almost glistening in the candlelight. A hand slid around her buttocks, feeling them carefully. 'Very nice,' he said again, then the hand slid around the front, stroked her tummy and drew a soft line from her panties up to her breasts.

She turned slowly around; Pip Blakemore was standing in front of her, fully clothed and carrying a gun. He squeezed the trigger and a stream of water spurted out.

'Oops!'

Sophie put her hands on her hips, ignoring the water dribbling down her waist. 'You are a bastard,' she said.

'Did I have you fooled?'

'For about a nanosecond.'

'So why didn't you stop me?' He smiled. 'Perhaps you thought your boss would fire you if you complained.'

'Perhaps I did. Or perhaps I was wondering if my boss was wishing I'd brought home a certain reporter.'

'Reporter?' he said vaguely. 'What reporter?' Sophie glared at him again. 'Well, she was cute, in a rather obvious sort of way.' Sophie raised her eyebrows. 'Anyway,' he went on, 'redheads aren't my type, I prefer blondes.'

'Really?' she asked with heavy sarcasm.

'Absolutely, and of course, nothing is cuter than you, not when you're standing there in two bits of lace and some very nice stockings. Now, why don't you take off your bra and come over here like a good little girl?'

'I don't know if I want to, not when you're being patronising as well as lecherous.'

He smiled and backed away, beckoning her to follow. 'You have to. I'm your boss.'

'That's sexual harassment.'

'I know,' he replied, 'don't you just love it?'

Sophie shook her head in despair. 'You really are such a bastard.'

'Me?'

'Yes. You.'

Sophie stalked out into the night with as much dignity as possible when she was dressed in her lingerie and high-heeled court shoes. Pip picked up the two glasses and followed her outside to join her on a wide lounger in a corner of the roof, Sophie sprawled there, ignoring him, looking out across the city with the sky stretching away for ever.

Pip put the wine down. 'You don't really mind me being a bastard. It's what turns you on, knowing I'm going to screw people.'

'That's different. I mind you being a unfaithful bastard, that's for sure,' she grumbled. 'And as for checking out that reporter

28

whilst I was still sitting there, that was a bit much.'

He chuckled. 'You didn't really mind, did you? She was rather putting a few signals my way.'

'And mine as well actually.'

'Was she?' He seemed interested, more than surprised. 'You know, that could be fun.'

'Forget it,' Sophie scoffed. 'You are not getting me in some sordid little sex triangle.'

'You are a spoilsport,' Pip crooned. 'Couldn't I persuade you?'

'You'd do better to keep your hands off her,' Sophie warned him. 'I can think of more stupid things than screwing a reporter on the side, but not many!'

Pip just laughed and leaned back onto the lounger. 'So how was it?'

'Okay, I guess. I think I did all right on the questions. I just didn't realise you were going to have quite so many photos of me kicking around.'

He chuckled again. 'Yes, I saw your face when the screens lit up and the posters came out.'

'You could have told me,' she pointed out.

Pip shrugged. 'I thought you might enjoy the surprise.'

'I don't like surprises, you know that, I like to know what's going on around me.'

Pip studied her carefully. 'I'm not so sure that's what you really want.'

'What are you talking about?'

He smiled. 'Nothing, just thinking. Drink?'

She nodded and he poured her a glass of chablis. They lay side by side, staring up into the open spaces above them. 'It was a good launch,' she said absentmindedly.

'It was excellent.'

She rolled over and faced him. 'And don't forget, I'm going to be in charge, so there's not going to be any messing around taking decisions out of my hands.'

'Would I do that to you?'

29

'I mean it, Pip, it's all signed and sealed, but I don't trust those buggers on the Board. I don't want to be some little marketing ploy.'

'What? Our girl Friday?' He was gently mocking. 'Why would they do that?'

'I don't know, but I do know not everyone wanted me in charge. They just wanted a figurehead, and for you to pull the strings.'

Pip looked quizzically at her through the gloom. 'And just how did you come to hear something like that?'

'It's common gossip,' Sophie said casually. 'But it's true, isn't it?'

Pip sipped his wine and topped up their glasses before answering. He had his efficient work-face on. At length he nodded. 'I didn't realise you knew.'

'Pip,' she sighed, 'no-one my age and with my sort of experience gets a job like this. Not so easily. I know what people say.'

'And what's that?'

'That I'm a little fluffball, that I'm on your chain. That I should stay in operations and stick where I belong, in the back room.' She scowled. 'And that you're fucking me and that's how I got the job.' Pip smiled. 'Well, that's true, isn't it?'

'That I'm fucking you? Yes.'

'That that's what they're saying.' He nodded. 'I'm not stupid you know.'

'I know,' he answered. 'And that's why you got the job, and not because you look good in a photo, which, by the way you do, but because I know you can do it.'

She smiled up at him. 'Thanks, Pip.'

'Of course, fucking me got you on the list even if it didn't get you the job.'

'Pip!'

He shrugged. 'Well, I wasn't going to give it to someone who couldn't give me a good blow job.'

'Pip!' Pip laughed and dropped to his knees, crouching next

to her. In the twilight the temperature was dropping and she shivered involuntarily. 'Goose bumps,' he muttered absently, letting his fingers trail on down her body, stroking her breasts lightly, and running a forefinger down a line below her breasts and then across her navel.

She glared at him. 'Stop trying to seduce me when I'm trying to have a serious conversation about work.'

'Now why would I do such a thing?' Suddenly Sophie looked up, and around the terrace. 'What's the matter? Gone shy?'

She shook her head. 'I thought I heard something. Somebody moving about.'

Pip laughed. 'Not that again.'

She glared at him. 'I'm serious! I told you, I'm sure someone's watching me, us, up here. I thought I saw him yesterday.'

'Just tell me how there could be anyone up here without us knowing.' He smiled and pinned her gently against the lounger. 'Anyway if there is someone here, good luck to them.' Gently, Pip reached down and stroked Sophie's belly once again. He let his fingers trace the near-invisible line of pale hair from her pubis to the space between her breasts and kissed her softly on the lips. In one of his lightning switches of character he had become sensual and gentle, teasing out each moment with delicate kisses over her body. Nothing was too much for him; he stroked her breasts and removed her bra with the greatest of care; then he rolled her over onto her front. He caressed her body and massaged her shoulders, working his way down from her neck, easing away any remaining tension and moving slowly down her spine, exciting every inch of skin as he went, carefully stroking her, setting fire to her nerve endings. Moving on to another spot he made his way down to the base of her spine, leaving her supine and completely relaxed. She exhaled slowly as he reached her buttocks and eased her panties away, then started to caress her flesh again, moving down to her thighs, stretching and toning each muscle and tendon beneath the

31

skin, knowing her so well that she felt she was almost floating with sensory pleasure.

At last Pip came to the base of her feet; he stretched her toes and began to work his way back up her body, rolling her over to face the skies above. With her eyes closed every touch became more intense, each new portion of skin that he caressed burned with desire, and it was only with difficulty that Sophie kept herself from holding him close. Carefully avoiding all the obvious erogenous zones, Pip returned at last to her breasts. By now Sophie was breathing hard, knowing he was near, feeling him very hot and tense, the occasional touch of his hard penis, obvious even through his clothes as he caressed her breasts then her belly, the brush of soft hair from his arms as he leant across her and the butterfly touch of his tongue on her skin were slowly, very slowly, bringing her to a sense of climax.

For a long time Pip left her lying there, her eyes closed, her trusting body posed on the lounger beneath him. Tiny beads of sweat were on her belly, and at the apex of her legs her golden pubic hair was darkened with sweat, moisture and juice. Unwilling to break the silence, Sophie's tongue licked her dry lips gently, waiting for him. Pip smiled and knelt down between her legs, letting his tongue slip between her thighs; Sophie trembled and in the silence around them he clearly heard her gasp and then exhale, a faint moan of pleasure accompanying the breath as it left her lungs.

Sophie felt Pip's tongue as a burning hot presence on her clit, and she gasped with pleasure, letting her legs slide apart to ease his passage. He gently licked her sex in a long smooth exploration of her body, then worked his way inside her, deigning to touch her clit, stroking the damp pubic hair out of the way. She shivered and wrapped her legs around his neck, drawing him even further into her, feeling each lapping motion in her sex. Pip started to stroke her clit, first gently, as if to reacquaint himself with the swollen mound of flesh, then he began to move more quickly, deliberately masturbating her with his fingers and probing her sex with his tongue.

Sophie could feel the waves of orgasm starting inside her, pulling her to the point of pleasure then, as his fingers eased off, falling back again. Each time the sensations grew in intensity, working their way deeper inside her until she could hardly feel his touch any more; they were rolling waves of pleasure, each time denying her a final release, but each moment of disappointment was followed by another stronger wave of pleasure. Without realising she was groaning and panting, her back arched off the lounger, her legs spread apart, utterly abandoned to the sensations inside.

Her groans grew and she thrust her pelvis towards him, begging him for more and, almost reluctantly, Pip left her sex. When she sank back down he replaced his tongue with his cock, and joined her on the lounger, crushing her down with his weight, grinding his groin against her clit. It was the final impetus to bring Sophie to climax and, as he thrust into her sex, his own senses were also close to fulfilment. She gave the first in a series of gasping, panting moans; half pleasure, half stunned release, all poise and dignity lost beneath the cumulative effects of his care and now his near-vicious pounding into her body. She was almost insensible to his thrusts and seeing and hearing her orgasm was the final stimulus to Pip; he too was incapable of restraining himself and he came with an intense grunting orgasm, their sweat and juices mingling as they cried and groaned into the night.

The following weeks were full of work: solving problems, instructing staff, preparing reports and promoting the business as much as possible, in addition to which there was the usual caretaking of systems and the all-important money transfers both to keep their established third-world businesses running and to set the new ones up. For Sophie it was exhilarating, if exhausting. She had never been so much in demand or in such a high profile job and, quite aside from work, invitations to corporate hospitality events were flowing into her office;

Glyndebourne, the races, first night galas, cocktails with bankers who would previously have hardly known her name and dinner invitations to make 'relationships' with other companies, traders, analysts and the like.

Everything was going well. Or so it seemed. Tonight she was due to meet Pip at the Gordon Hotel in Knightsbridge for the Swiss Trading Partnership's Summer Party. The Partnership had taken over a square outside the normally restrained hotel, and the party, Pip had assured her, would be stupendous. Admission was by presentation of the invitation card, a personally inscribed CD-ROM, which had listed the entertainment, such as the rodeo bull, laser quest, the dodgems and the tarot and palm readers, the bands, the dinner menu, and all the other side-shows, like the sushi bar, the teriyaki bar, the jugglers, stilt walkers and hula dancers and, at the bottom, the breakfast menu for the hardy souls who made it through to six o'clock the next morning.

Sophie had already changed out of her business suit, since it was a black tie event, and sitting at her desk she looked ludicrously out of place in her evening gown. She had arranged to meet Pip in the hotel lobby at seven-forty-five, but she hadn't been able to stop herself from taking five minutes to check over a few reports, and that had been half an hour ago. Sophie checked her watch, it was seven-thirty. Damn. She looked back down at her screen; those funny transfers were showing up again. She had dismissed them as irrelevant before, but now there were definitely more odd numbers cropping up in the reports. She accessed another level and started to get even more worried. Numbers were jumping around, but she couldn't actually make sense of it. She shook her head; she must be wrong, there was no way that money would be moving between those accounts, it had to be a blip. But she couldn't shake the thought from her head that something was not quite right. Then she realised, there was a delay in the transfer of funds from one account to the other; in the UK transfers were going through fine, but there was a time discrepancy in the South

American systems, something she hadn't expected.

She glanced at her watch again, it was eight-fifteen. Pip would be furious at her for being this late.

She was right. Pip was at the hotel and waiting for her in the lobby, barely acknowledging the people around him. He looked pleasant enough but Sophie knew him better than most people. He was livid. He greeted her politely, took her wrist and, with a smile fixed to his face, he ignored the train of people moving out of the hotel and towards the square and instead half-dragged her into the depths of the hotel, down a quiet corridor leading to the deserted ball room.

He glared at her. 'What the bloody hell do you mean by standing me up?'

'I've been trying to contact you for ages and I left messages. Ow, Pip, you're hurting me.'

He didn't release his grip. 'I don't expect to be made to look a fool by your being late!'

'Pip!' She was furious herself now. 'This is ridiculous. I'm just a bit late. I had a problem at the office.' He continued to glare at her, his face set in hard lines, his fingers biting viciously into her wrist.

At length he relaxed his grip slightly. 'What do you mean there's a problem? Why didn't you tell me this earlier?'

'I've just found out.'

'What sort of problem?'

'Well, it may be nothing.'

'How much are we talking about?'

'Well, not much,' she admitted, 'less than a half a million bucks . . .' She had her mouth open to continue but Pip's eyes were blazing again.

'And you stood me up for that?' He was incredulous.

'Hey,' she began, 'this could be something, or it could be nothing. It's my job to make sure things work, and I didn't like what I was looking at. I can't explain why, not yet.'

Pip grasped her wrist again and pulled her tight. He was,

she realised, close to losing his temper, which she had previously never thought possible with Pip. Certainly not in public. But something had just pressed all the right buttons and now he was far more angry than a simple delay in her arrival could justify.

Pip pushed her shoulders back against the wall and pinned her there. 'Don't you ever stand me up again. You get here on time, no matter what.'

'What's the matter, Pip?'

'I don't want to feel like a fucking idiot, that's what.' He relaxed his grip on her wrist and she breathed a sigh of relief.

'You're the boss.' She tried to lighten his mood, but it didn't work.

'That's right,' he hissed. 'I'm the boss and I'm the one with the power. I'm the one in control.' His expression changed. 'Anyway, at least you look all right now you're here.'

'Thank you very much,' said Sophie in a teasing tone, 'I think I look more than all right.' Her dress was new, a floor-length bias-cut fuchsia satin, with a low neck and back line and only thin spaghetti straps to hold it up. What little of her breasts were covered up were contained within tight satin, whilst below the waist it softened, sliding down to the floor in ripples of soft, flowing fabric. It was very sheer and she had had to dispense with any underwear just to get it on. It suddenly became clear that Pip had realised just that fact when he ran his fingers down her side, and paused around her hips, testing the mild friction of satin against flesh with his fingers.

Sophie caught the change in his face and pushed him away. 'Pip, forget it.'

'Forget what?'

'No, Pip. We are not doing anything, this dress cost a bundle and there are people we need to see.'

She pushed him away again and got the shock of her life when Pip pushed her back up against the wall. 'Don't you try to tell me what to do.' He pulled at the fuchsia fabric and reached underneath for her crotch.

'Pip!' Up until now the hallway had been almost deserted but now behind Pip's shoulder she could see waiters begin to gather beyond the open door. 'Pip, for God's sake!' He turned slightly to see the gathering of white uniforms at the far end of the corridor linking the ball room and the lobby. 'Pip, I think we should go outside and join the party.'

'I don't.'

'Pip!' But it was no good, Pip's mind had turned completely to sex. He grabbed her wrist again, dragging her through the door and into the ball room, empty except for a few tables of equipment; the main party was in the square where there were marquees set up for dinner. He looked about, and they both heard the sound of talk coming from the corridor behind them. 'This is ridiculous, Pip,' she hissed.

He smiled at her. 'I think you're enjoying it. I think you want it.' Deftly he reached for her clit, rubbing it through the satin, making her shudder.

'I didn't say I wouldn't want to do it, but we don't have time,' she whispered, excusing herself and her disobedient body.

'I don't care,' Pip murmured, and pulled her behind him into an alcove. As the waiters came in through the main entrance he reached out and let a heavy drape fall down, hiding them behind a wall of heavy crimson velvet. Pushing the stunned Sophie back into the recess and against the wall he pulled up her dress and started unbuckling his pants.

'Pip,' she hissed, pushing him away, 'stop!'

Pip lifted his head to glare at her and for a moment Sophie hardly recognised him. His eyes were defocused and glazed with lust. Pip ran a finger down the side of Sophie's face and stroked her hair. 'All I can think about is fucking you,' he whispered harshly. 'I've got to have you right now.'

'Pip,' she hissed back, 'we've got people to meet, and there are people outside, can't this wait till later?'

'Why wait? You liked doing it outside, screwing me on the terrace in front of your voyeur. Think about doing it here, now. What if the boys outside heard us, what do you think they'd do?' Pip's fingers made their unerring way across Sophie's nipples and down between her legs, stroking the soft pussy hair at the top of her thighs and sliding between the folds and crevices of sex flesh. His fingers roamed around her body and slid down the firm thighs, to the lace top of her stockings; he pulled her skirt up further and looked down at the view below, long legs spread out and split apart, creamy pale flesh at her groin, darkening gently into tanned thighs, and black stockings above stiletto-heeled fuchsia shoes. 'I think they'd open the curtain and watch me screwing you. I think they'd wank themselves off, watching me doing you, making you beg me for it.' His fingers slid back between her thighs and Sophie's body betrayed her arousal. Even though she was furious with him for dragging her up here, even though she was already sure she was going to get a bruise on her arm from his hard, vicious grip, and even though she really wanted to be outside, working the room and making contacts, a part of her was excited by his behaviour. And by the idea of doing it here, with people wandering about outside, maybe listening to them.

She shook the idea from her head. 'Pip,' she whispered sternly once more, 'come on, get a grip. Think of the embarrassment. The professional embarrassment! I insist we get out of here now!'

Pip looked into her face and saw the expression there, the reflection of his desire. He smiled. 'I'd rather have you wet and wanting me, but I do want you, Sophie. I want you now. And you're going to do what I tell you.'

'Pip,' she began but he was already in place and without any further words he pushed his cock into her pussy and holding her arms apart he started to fuck her. Sophie shuddered and gave up any vague remaining thought of refusing him, of insisting that sense prevail. In the tiny alcove they stood, pressed up against the wall, his lips pressed on hers, his tongue forcing its way into her mouth, the two of them grinding their bodies together. At any moment, she thought, someone would walk by, open the curtain and see them and then the gossip would be everywhere. The thought excited her. Pip was right. 'I don't give a fuck what anyone would say if they see me,' he growled. 'Do you?'

'Yes,' she lied.

'Why?'

'They'll talk about us.'

'They'll talk about you, you mean,' he said, and he pushed his cock in and out, starting up a new rhythm, grinding her hips into the wall.

'Yes,' she hissed. 'God yes.' Involuntarily she let out a groan. 'Ahh, Pip.'

'What?'

'They'll be talking, talking about me.'

'So why are you letting me do this to you?'

'I can't stop you.' She shivered as his hands left hers and gripped her buttocks instead, pulling the fleshy globes apart. 'Oh God, Pip.'

'Do you want me to stop?'

'Yes.'

'Why?'

'We shouldn't be here. I . . . you should stop.'

He smiled. 'But I won't and I'm in charge.' She didn't answer. 'Aren't I?'

'Yes,' she answered back, forcing herself to reply. 'Yes, you're in charge.'

'And I tell you what to do.'

'Yes.'

'When and where to fuck and how to do it.'

'Yes,' she groaned. 'Yes, you're in charge. You tell me what to do and when.'

'You like being dominated, don't you, Sophie?' Pip hissed in her ear. Sophie didn't reply. 'You like being the helpless little girl, with the big bad fucker behind you.' Still she didn't reply. 'At work you pretend you want to be in charge, but outside the office really you want to be the subordinate. You want me to dominate you, you like me being in charge.' Pip

39

seemed tireless, pushing himself in and out of her and Sophie shuddered again, waves of pleasure coursing through her body, listening to him talk, barely hearing the words, knowing what he was telling her was true, unwilling to admit it, even now.

With an effort she tried to reply. 'I like being in charge, I like to be in control.'

'No,' Pip hissed, 'I think you're lying. And I think it goes further than that. I think you'd enjoy being a slave, fucked whenever and wherever I wanted. Wouldn't you?' Abruptly he pulled himself out of her and turned her around, pushing her out of the alcove. With a gasp of alarm Sophie gripped the heavy rope tiebacks at the sides of the entrance, just stopping herself from being pushed through the curtain. Pip chuckled softly and pushed her head down, pulling her long silk skirt up around her waist. He slid a finger from her clit through to her butt-hole. 'You'd better hold on,' he whispered, 'or they'll see you.' Then he was inside her again, holding her buttocks apart to give him greater ease, pushing his cock into her as far as it would go. He stopped for a moment and ran a finger down her back and around her breasts, tweaking her nipples through the silk fabric.

'Don't think I'd care if they saw me,' he told her. 'They'd just see a slut being fucked. They'd just think you were a whore who opened up your legs for me whenever I wanted.' She groaned, desperate for him to continue, unable to believe the intensity of the sensation. Behind her Pip was keeping up his relentless pressure, extracting as much pleasure from his verbal assault on her sexual desires and secrets as from the physical penetrative act. 'Or maybe they'd see a slave, servicing me whenever I wanted.' He paused. 'Would that excite you, Sophie?'

'I don't know,' she murmured. 'Please, Pip, don't stop.'

'I'm not going to stop, Sophie. I've been thinking about this for a very long time. And I think you need to learn about yourself.' She whimpered softly as Pip's fingers moved from her buttocks to slide across the front of her sex, wetting themselves on her juices, and stroking her swollen clit, forcing her into a state of near orgasmic collapse.

'I'm going to come in you soon, Sophie.'

She groaned again. 'Please, Pip, don't stop.'

'I'll stop when I want to. And you'll come when I want you to.'

She shuddered again as his fingers stimulated her clit, masturbating her hard, forcing her orgasm ever closer. Inside her she could almost feel Pip's cock swelling, readying itself for his own climax. 'Beg me for it, Sophie.'

'Please, Pip,' she whispered, 'please.'

She stopped as a murmur of voices filtered through the curtain from outside. Pip stopped as well, and she almost moaned out loud with the disappointment but they both held still for a moment. The voices, indistinct behind the heavy velvet, spoke to each other. The curtain twitched. 'Not in there,' someone said, 'that one.'

'You sure?'

'Of course. Come on.' The voices moved away, footsteps just audible on the wooden floor. She started to get up but Pip roughly pushed her head back down, standing with his hands on her back. With a sudden sensation of relief she felt his fingers reaching down again, reaching around her to find her clit, and she stood obediently in front of him, all self-control and concern about her position gone, determined to achieve the maximum pleasure from this unexpected rough and ready handling. Her clit hardened again, and she caught her breath whilst, behind her, Pip steadied himself against her hips and with his hands on her clit he started pushing his organ up her cunt, thrusting himself deep inside her, pulling her on and off him with increasing force, his balls gently beating against her. Then she heard him groan as his own climax came to the fore.

'Yes,' he growled under his breath, then louder, 'yes.' His fingers gripped her waist and in a massive thrust he began his final assault into her, forcing himself so far up her she thought his cock would split her in two. With an uncaring howl of

41

pleasure Pip climaxed, drowning out Sophie's own smaller gasps and whimpers as a frighteningly intense climax washed over her, waves of pleasure hitting her senses, her clit swollen and throbbing as the muscles in her pussy and her belly contracted as one.

'Yes,' Pip snarled, his cock pulsing again and again, his come draining out of him until, with a last thrust he was done. He stood for a moment with his hands flat on her back, then he pulled Sophie upright, her dress falling around her as she leant back against him, her breath still coming in shuddering gasps.

'So,' Pip murmured, holding her for a moment. 'You do enjoy being dominated. I thought you would.' As he turned her around to face him, she suddenly felt ashamed of herself and her responses to his outrageous treatment. 'That opens up a whole new realm of possibilities.'

Chapter Three

Sophie arrived at work later than usual the next day but she told herself that she deserved the lie-in after the effort she had made at last night's party.

All evening she and Pip had kept a discreet distance between them while never letting each other out of sight for too long. His domination of her in the alcove had left her bruised and tender but each time she caught his eye, she felt a rush of desire flooding her groin. At his signal, she had made her excuses and left the reception without him, keeping the fiction of their independence alive. She had taken a cab home and thrown her clothes into a mangled heap before dropping into bed to fall immediately asleep.

Arriving in the office, she had only just begun to log onto her PC when Turner rushed into her room. 'Sophie, where have you been?' he snapped, his eyes wide open and a small frown clouding his forehead.

'Turner?' Sophie replied with a quizzical look. 'Calm down. I had a late night at the reception, that's all. I think it was extremely successful. Anyway, it's only just turned eight o'clock and my first meeting isn't until eleven, is it?'

'All your meetings for today have been cancelled,' Turner blurted out triumphantly, 'and Mr Blakemore has been asking for you urgently for the past hour or more. He sounds furious.'

'What on earth are you talking about?' Small butterflies fluttered in Sophie's stomach. 'Why have my meetings been cancelled? And what does Philip want?'

'He wouldn't say.' Turner was clearly starting to enjoy the

situation which promised much for his ability to spread some juicy gossip in the general office. 'All he said was to cancel your meetings and for you to report to him as soon as you arrived in the office. And he's been calling every quarter of an hour since seven.'

Sophie gazed at her PA in exasperation. 'Well, this all sounds very melodramatic,' she said, turning back to her PC dismissively; until she knew what the problem was, there was no way she wanted Turner spreading gossip in the office. 'Tell Philip I'm in and that I'll be with him as soon as I've checked my urgent mail.'

Ten minutes later, Sophie walked down the corridor to Pip's office. She entered the room without knocking and, closing the door softly behind her, she stood for a moment watching her partner as he tapped at his computer keyboard.

'You seem to have something urgent to discuss with me, Pip, if I understand Turner correctly,' she said quietly. Giving no sign that he had heard her question, Pip continued to work for several long minutes, leaving Sophie standing by the door with a feeling of growing indignation. What was he playing at? What had gone wrong since last night?

Eventually Pip spoke. 'You're rather late. Again.'

Sophie frowned. What was the problem? She tried to be humorous; 'Well, you of all people know how hard I was working last night.' She smiled. 'I thought I deserved an extra hour in bed at least. Is that such a crime?'

Finally releasing his gaze from his PC, Pip leant back in his chair and stared hard at Sophie. 'Last night was last night. I told you what I thought of you then.' His eyes glittered coldly in the reflection from the screen. 'You seem to be forgetting that we will not make this venture succeed unless we give it all the hours we can and when I want you here, I expect to see you. If you want time off you can ask me.' Sophie was momentarily stunned into silence by Pip's bizarre stance and the harsh tone of his voice. 'And I did not give you permission to leave the reception last night.'

'What do you mean?' she asked quietly, trying to keep control of her mounting irritation. 'I thought you signalled me to go. You didn't seriously want us to leave together, did you?'

'It seems to me, Sophie,' Pip said, his voice low and threatening, 'that you are making too many decisions based on what you think rather than checking with me first. I thought I was getting the message through. You are the face of this venture but I control the direction. I make the decisions. Is that clear?'

'No, Pip, actually it isn't clear.' Sophie was stung by his words into attack. 'We've talked about this and you know very well that I am not prepared to be a figurehead.' She glared at him. 'I expected this from the Board, not you! A lot of my ideas have gone into making this whole fund a success. And my audit knowledge is a big part of our defence against fraud . . .'

'Ah yes,' Pip cut in. 'Your backroom expertise. My dear, if you think that you can justify one of the best remuneration packages in the City by checking figures you are sadly misguided.' Suddenly, Pip stood up and walked around his desk towards her. Grabbing one of her arms in a painful grip, he twisted it slightly behind her back and tilted her chin up with one disdainful finger. 'I've been very soft with you so far,' he said, 'I thought you realised that last night would change all that.'

Lowering his head, Pip fastened his mouth on Sophie's lips, his tongue forcing its way into her mouth and exploring its inner softness roughly. Sophie could not stop her body responding to the assault on her senses. The proximity of his hard body and the taste of his familiar juices started to work on her arousal. Pulling away sharply, Pip released her arm and pushed her to one side, returning to his desk and sitting down. Sophie stood, breathing heavily and watching for his next move. 'Like a bitch on heat,' Pip said casually, with a satisfied smile. 'You need to learn some control, Sophie, and I'm the one who's going to teach you.' Pausing for a long moment, he held

Sophie's eyes with his own sardonic gaze before turning back to his PC and starting to tap at the keyboard. 'Take the rest of the day off and meet me tonight at my flat. Eight o'clock sharp.'

'What do you have in mind, Pip?' Sophie tried to calm the pounding of her heart.

'You have a few lessons to learn, Sophie, and the first one of those is who's the boss in this relationship. I told you so last night, now you need to prove to me that you have what it takes.' He looked up at her. 'Do as I say or the whole thing's off. Now go.'

Hesitating momentarily, Sophie turned on her heel and walked out of the room slowly. Despite her indignation at Pip's treatment of her, she was excited by the tone of his voice and the mystery behind his orders. Well, whatever he had in mind, she would be ready.

Emerging from Regent's Park that evening, Sophie stood for a few moments on the pavement looking across to the tall mansion block where she knew Pip would be waiting for her. A warm breeze stirred the leaves of the trees behind her and she breathed a heaviness in the air which preceded a late summer storm.

Pip's flat was on the penthouse floor and she stared up at the blank windows, wondering if he was watching her. She had dressed carefully for their meeting, choosing a tightly fitting shirt dress in pale mint-green silk. The deep lapels displayed just a hint of cleavage and the clean cut of the dress emphasised the curve of her buttocks. Her underwear was also silk, in creamy flesh-coloured tones; a lacy bra underwired to push her breasts together and high-cut string briefs which would not disturb the line of her dress. Smiling to herself, she felt the string of the briefs chafe slightly between the cheeks of her bottom as she stepped off the pavement to cross Prince Albert Road, still busy with late commuters heading out of the city. It was unusual for Pip to invite her to his home and the unfamiliar territory left her feeling slightly out of control, heightening the sexual tension which had been building in her body since her bizarre interview with him in the office that morning. The urgency in Pip's voice as he gave her instructions for their rendezvous had added to her excitement and a shiver of anticipation about what he had planned for the evening ran down her spine as she strode up to the grand front door of the mansion block and pressed the buzzer for his flat. She had a strong suspicion this would not be a typical business meeting.

Sophie waited impatiently for several interminable minutes, expecting to hear the click of the automatic door release, and she reacted with a jolt of surprise when the door swung open just as she reached to press the buzzer again. A well-built man in his twenties dressed in a dark, sharp-cut suit suggestive of a gentleman's valet emerged from the building.

'Ms Jenner?' he said quietly, and without waiting for her response stepped back into the shadows of the hall. 'Mr Blakemore is waiting for you, please come with me.'

Sophie felt her heart hammering at the unexpected turn of events. She could not recall Pip ever saying that he had a manservant and her mind raced to understand the significance of the clean-cut young man now holding the door open for her. Telling herself that all would doubtless become clear very shortly, she gave a backward glance at the busy thoroughfare behind her and, taking a deep breath to steady her nerves, stepped into the cool interior of the tiled Victorian hall. Letting the door fall softly shut on the sounds of normality outside, the man walked slowly to the wrought-iron gates of the lift and indicated with a wave of his arm that Sophie should enter ahead of him. Obediently, Sophie walked into the lift and stood silently as the man followed and turned to close the double gates. Staring at his back, she noticed subconsciously how broad his shoulders were beneath the fine material of his jacket. The space inside the lift was cramped and she was acutely aware of his clean male aroma beginning to work on her senses.

'Excuse me,' he said softly, meeting her eyes with a long stare as he reached to press the button for the top floor of the block. Sophie gave herself a mental shake; she was minutes away from a major business meeting with Pip and apparently in danger of creaming her pants over a complete stranger. As she told herself to cool it, the lift jerked suddenly into upward motion and, almost imperceptibly, the man's hand brushed her chest as he straightened his stance. Sophie felt her nipples harden with the fleeting touch and she lowered her eyes, suspecting that he must be aware of her arousal as her breasts pushed forward through the thin silk of her dress. Glancing at his crotch, her suspicions were confirmed as she saw the bulge of a developing erection. In her heightened state of anticipation, she found herself wondering about the size of his cock and how, as it hardened within the confines of his trousers, he would need to adjust himself for comfort, his hand reaching down to reposition the thickening member.

Flushing as her fantasy took hold, Sophie raised her eyes from his crotch to find that he was staring at her with a faintly sardonic smile on his lips. Their eyes stayed locked for a long moment until the lift juddered to a halt at the top floor and, with a slight nod, he turned his back on her once more to open the gates. The door to Pip's flat was directly across from the lift and Sophie flushed even more deeply as she realised that Pip was standing on the landing watching them arrive, his eyebrows slightly raised as he noticed her discomfiture.

'Good evening, Sophie,' Pip said, his ice-blue eyes scanning her face as she stepped out of the lift. 'Bang on time for once. I see you and Charles have been getting to know each other already.'

'What's going on, Pip?' Sophie demanded, ignoring his outstretched hand. 'I assumed we were going out to dinner together.'

'All in good time, Sophie.' He stood to one side of the door, guiding her inside. 'All in good time.' With a sigh, Sophie strode inside.

As she entered the huge living room Sophie was struck once again by the simple elegance of the decor which managed to combine an essential masculine austerity with an aura of expensive luxury. The deeply cushioned ivory sofa and armchairs were positioned to one side of the highly polished mahogany parquet floor, whilst to the other a glass-topped dining table had been set with a blue and gold Limoges dinner service and a magnificent display of deep red roses had been placed in the centre. Sophie's eyes were drawn to the large Georgia O'Keefe original hanging on the main wall of the room, the erotic suggestion of the pale pink tulips producing a responsive tingle high up in her groin.

She sat down. 'Well,' she asked. 'What now?'

'Sophie, you know that I have been having serious doubts about your attitude lately and I decided I had to satisfy myself that you have what it takes to be my partner in this, and other ventures. What I have in mind calls for complete privacy and so I thought we would have dinner at home tonight where there would be no distractions.' He paused. 'To make the evening run smoothly I called an agency to hire some help and Charles comes highly recommended, as far as paid servants go. He's been busy arranging things in the flat all day, haven't you, Charles?'

Sophie was faintly surprised. She could count the number of previous visits she had made to Pip's flat on the fingers of one hand; invariably they were en route to some expensive restaurant or theatre date. She realised now how little time they had spent alone together when they weren't making love or working and the suggestion of an intimate dinner à deux with only the enigmatic Charles for company was certainly a novel one. She was also increasingly intrigued both as to how Pip was going to test her abilities and what he meant by 'other ventures'. She smiled her acquiescence to his suggestion. 'That would be lovely, Pip.'

'Will I serve cocktails, Mr Blakemore?' Charles's impassive gaze was at odds with his still evident erection and Sophie wondered that Pip seemed so unaware of the man's arousal.

'Yes please, Charles. We'll have them on the balcony.' Charles

49

turned away in the direction of the kitchen and, offering his hand to Sophie again, Pip said, 'Come along, Sophie, let's look at the view of the park.'

They walked hand in hand to the panoramic windows which lined one side of the room and stepped through the patio doors onto the large, private balcony. Dusk was falling and the perfume of night-scented stocks was heavy on the humid air. Leaning on the balustrade, Sophie let her eyes adjust to the gloom, eventually making out the vague shapes of figures in the park below, hurrying to reach the street before the gates were locked for the night.

As if reading her thoughts, Pip pointed at the park warden cycling slowly towards Gloucester Gate. 'Once he's gone it becomes a different place,' he said in a low voice, his mouth close to Sophie's ear and his breath suddenly hot on her neck. 'You can see a lot of night life from this balcony. All the coupling that goes on under cover of darkness; lovers taking their pleasure in the open air; prostitutes selling their bodies for the highest price; sex slaves giving relief while their pimps stand by and watch the show. And of course, no-one knows you're watching from up here. It's perfectly safe.'

Sophie stared into the deepening gloom and could almost see the naked, copulating bodies as she listened to the hypnotic tone of Pip's voice. She felt his hand fall from encircling her waist and start to caress her buttock, rubbing the sheer silk material of her dress in a circular motion around the firm mound of flesh.

'Do you promise to do exactly as I say, Sophie?' Pip whispered again in her ear. 'Will you promise to obey my every command and let me teach you how to succeed?'

Turning towards him, Sophie searched his eyes for a clue as to his intentions. His eyes were dark, the pupils wide in the gloom of the balcony. 'Whatever you say, Pip,' she said, turning back to the balustrade with a laugh. 'Within reason!'

'Good.' He stared outside and silence fell. 'I want to see you, Sophie,' Pip said suddenly, turning her roughly round to face him again so that she leaned back against the balustrade of the balcony. 'Undo your dress, I want to look at you.'

'Pip, don't be silly, Charles will be walking out here any minute with drinks, remember!' Sophie laughed lightly and half-turned away to continue scanning the park below.

'Do as I say,' Pip insisted, pulling her back to face him. 'Command number one. Now undo your dress.'

Glancing into the living room, Sophie checked that Charles was not approaching before shaking Pip's hand from her arm. 'You are out of your mind but if it means that I'll get my dinner on time, here goes.'

Keeping her eyes on his face, Sophie started to slowly undo the buttons of her shirt dress one by one from the top. As she reached the waist Pip snapped, 'Stop there and show me your tits.'

With another glance into the living room where the coast was still clear, Sophie drew the lapels of the dress apart and provocatively thrust her chest forward. 'Good enough for you, big boy?' she whispered. Pip moved towards her and placed a hand on each of her breasts, encased in the lacy flesh-coloured bra through which her large dark nipples were clearly visible. After a brief massage of each breast, he lifted the material of one cup and gently reached in to lift the heavy breast free from its halter. Repeating the action on the other side, he stepped back to admire his handiwork. As she watched him staring eagerly at the sight of her exposed flesh, lewdly displayed outside the restraints of her bra, Sophie felt the throbbing of sexual arousal begin between her legs. Her nipples hardened as the cooler evening breeze flowed over her naked skin and she wished that the two of them were alone in the flat.

As if by telepathy, she heard the thwack of the swing door to the kitchen as Charles emerged into the living room carrying a tray of drinks. Instinctively, Sophie reached to pull the lapels of her dress together but she was stopped in her tracks as Pip snapped, 'Leave your dress alone. I want you to stay on display.' Stunned by his command, Sophie's hands froze and she stared back at Pip who was smiling faintly. 'Thank you, Charles,' he said calmly as the waiter walked out onto the balcony and placed the tray of drinks on a mosaic-topped table. 'We'll have dinner in ten minutes.'

Sophie remained frozen in her position as Charles took a long moment to look at her exposed breasts, passing his tongue over his lips before saying, 'As you wish, Mr Blakemore,' and turning away to leave the balcony.

'Good girl,' said Pip. 'Now why don't you take your dress right off and come and have a seat. You'll be much cooler that way.' As the shock of her discovery in this position by the waiter started to ebb away, Sophie found herself becoming eager to comply with Pip's commands but she decided to test the boundaries in the hope of gaining a little more insight into his intentions. She undid the remaining buttons of her dress and slipped the garment from her shoulders. As she tossed the dress to one side, she moved to place her breasts back in the cups of her bra. 'No,' Pip snapped. 'Leave them hanging out. I said I wanted you to remain on display. Now sit over there where I can see you.' Pip indicated a high-backed chair placed directly opposite the sofa on which he was now lounging. Sophie walked over to the chair and sat down.

'Can I have my cocktail now, Pip?' she asked as demurely as possible.

'Charles,' Pip shouted. 'A moment please.' Then turning back to Sophie, he said, 'Spread your legs and sit up straight, that's a good girl. I said I wanted to see you.'

As Charles appeared again from the kitchen, Sophie opened her legs and thrust her naked breasts forward as she straightened her back. She met the voracious gaze of the waiter impassively and waited for Pip's next move.

'A little wider, Sophie. I need to check whether or not you are presentable for dinner.' Pip signalled for Charles to pass him one of the glasses of ice-cold martini from the table, which he sipped while watching as Sophie opened her legs wider, feeling the lips of her cunt parting beneath the slinky material of her panties. 'Mmm, not bad, but I think we could make a few improvements here and there. Charles, I have changed my mind. Put back dinner and take Ms Jenner through to dress. She will need to be thoroughly prepared before putting on the outfit I bought for her. You remember the procedures we talked about earlier?'

'Indeed, Mr Blakemore,' the waiter responded as Sophie looked in confusion from one to the other. What on earth were they talking about?

'Go with Charles, Sophie,' Pip said. 'He'll look after you. I'll wait dinner until you get back.' Reaching for the second martini, Pip waved Sophie vaguely in the direction of the living room and she rose to follow Charles, who had stepped inside and was standing politely to one side. 'And remember, when you get back, Sophie, you must be on display at all times, legs apart so that I can see your cunt – and keep those nipples hard.'

Wondering what was in store for her next, Sophie padded after Charles who walked ahead of her through the living room to a door at the far end and then into a bedroom. Once inside the room, Charles closed the door quietly and motioned Sophie to stand still while he passed through to a third room and presently she heard the sound of running water. Whilst waiting for Charles to return, Sophie looked around at the large limed oak wardrobes which lined one side of the room. A pretty vanity table had been placed in front of the window and the heavily embroidered drapes had been drawn tightly closed. In the centre of the room, rather than a conventional bed, there was a flat couch at waist height upholstered in black leather and split into three sections. Then she noticed the leather stirrups hanging from a fixture in the ceiling above the couch; Sophie's eyes widened and she felt her pulse begin to race once more, but almost immediately Charles re-emerged from the bathroom carrying a tray on which was placed an enamel bowl and what Sophie recognised as the paraphernalia of a gentleman barber.

'Up on the couch please, Ms Jenner, lie back and relax. Mr Blakemore likes his females to be trimmed right back so that they have no problem keeping themselves on display for him. This will be quite painless and you may even find some pleasure in the procedure. I have had no complaints in the past.'

Sophie found herself automatically, almost eagerly, complying with the waiter's request. Once she had climbed onto the couch, Charles raised the section supporting the upper part of her body until she was in a semi-seated position. He fastened her wrists by her sides in soft leather handcuffs, then, pulling down each of the stirrups in turn, he secured her ankles in the leather restraints. As he tightened the straps on the stirrups once again, Sophie's legs were raised into the air and spread wide apart. Picking up a knife from the tray, Charles snipped each side of her panties and pulled the material free of her sex before tossing it aside and repeating the procedure with her bra. Dropping a flap at the base of the crotch to enable him to stand directly between her raised legs, Charles smiled and said, 'Here we go, Ms Jenner. Just shout if I nip you with the razor.'

From her reclining position, Sophie watched as the waiter set to work on her cunt. First, an all-over trim with a pair of sharp scissors, after which he covered her sex with a sweet-smelling lather in preparation for shaving. The bristles of his soap brush tickled the tender flesh of Sophie's labia unbearably and she wriggled her bottom as her nipples hardened in response to the sensation. Moving the stirrups a little further apart so that her sex was completely open, Charles picked up his shaving steel and ran the blunt edge of the cold metal along her open slit. Sophie's clitoris sprang into life at the icy touch and she let out an involuntary gasp as he started to work along each of her outer labia in turn, shaving the bristles of her pubic hair away.

Charles was as good as his word and Sophie found the procedure entirely painless; the occasional touch of cold steel against her clit served to tease her arousal along as Charles hummed softly to himself. A tiny arrow of golden hair was left at the top of her slit before he finally wiped her clean of remaining lather with a very cold cloth, leaving Sophie gasping at the sensation.

'Now, to finish you off, a quick rub down with my special depilatory lotion. This will keep you smooth for weeks. It might nip a little but there's nothing to worry about.' Charles dipped his fingers in a jar on his tray and started to massage Sophie's sex with the lubrication. As he worked, Sophie closed her eyes and began to relax into the arousing motion of his hands. Parting her labia, Charles concentrated the pressure of his fingers firstly on the already hardened bud of her aroused clitoris, then, dipping his fingers one by one into her hole, he started to gently stretch her sex flesh. She moaned softly with the beginnings of an orgasm and Charles abruptly stopped his ministrations and stepped back from the couch.

'No need for that just yet,' he told her. 'You just lie there for a few minutes, Ms Jenner,' he said, 'and let the lotion take effect. Then I'll come and wash you down and you can get dressed for dinner. I'll leave this mirror here so that you can see the result of your little haircut if you like.'

Wheeling a long mirror to the base of the couch, Charles pulled on the stirrup straps once again so that Sophie's bottom was slightly raised from the couch, patted her buttocks and walked from the room. Alone, Sophie peered in the mirror at the reflection of her shaven cunt, incredibly aroused by the sight of the pale skin of her outer labia juxtaposed against the swollen pink flesh of her inner sex. She noticed a warm glow spreading from her cunt into the rest of her body and tried to relax, but the minutes until Charles's return to the room passed interminably slowly. The shackles on her wrists and ankles prevented her from relieving the increasingly insistent throbbing between her legs and in her breasts and Sophie began to think that if she didn't get laid soon, she would go mad.

At last Charles returned and, smiling faintly, he washed the depilatory lotion from her skin, immediately applying a musky oil along the length of her slit and in the cleft between her buttocks.

'Your dinner outfit is over by the vanity table, Ms Jenner,' he said, lowering the stirrups and releasing her ankles and wrists from their cuffs. 'Dinner will be served in ten minutes.'

Rubbing the circulation back into her legs, Sophie slipped from the couch and ran an exploratory finger along her shaven slit. She felt strangely bare and exposed, but there was no time to waste before dinner and she walked quickly over to the vanity table to see what Pip had bought for her to wear.

With a sense of growing excitement Sophie surveyed the erotic lingerie laid out on the table. First, a tiny black bra which was no more than a halter for her heavy breasts, leaving most of the mounds of flesh exposed but raising their weight slightly and keeping her cleavage intact. Then, an equally tiny thong which she found had a split crotch designed to fit around her clitoris. Finally, a strappy black garter belt with sheer fishnet stockings and spiky-heeled court shoes. Picking up some liquid rouge from the table, Sophie painted first her nipples and then her lips, then she strode to the full-length mirror to survey the outcome. She had to admit that a shaved cunt looked much better with this sort of get-up and her fleshy labia poked appealingly around the strap of the thong. As she walked to the door of the bedroom, Sophie realised that the crotch of the thong rubbed on her clitoris with every step, helping to maintain her already heightened level of arousal.

Emerging from the bedroom, she saw that Pip was already waiting for her by the dinner table. 'Sophie, you look wonderful. I hope you like the outfit I chose for you. Now come over here and let me get a closer look at you.' Sophie did as he requested and as he seated himself at the table, Pip motioned her to turn around in front of him, feasting his eyes on her exposed and aroused body. 'Lean over that chair-back, Sophie, and bend you legs a little,' he ordered. Doing as he asked, Sophie felt Pip pull the strap of her panties from her cunt and part the lips of her sex in order to rub his fingers along the length of her cunt. Pushing his fingers into her hole, he commented, 'You are very wet, Sophie. I hope Charles wasn't taking too many liberties with you in there.'

'No, I'm just so bloody hot for it, Pip. Do we have to eat dinner right now?' Sophie peered over her shoulder as Pip continued to work her hole with his fingers and Charles entered the room with two covered salvers.

'Be quiet, Sophie, I did not say you could speak. That was only the first stage of your test. You are doing very well so far and I am pleased with your progress, but don't spoil it now by trying to take control. You know how you have a big problem with recognising authority but tonight you are going to show me that you can change. Now sit down and let Charles serve dinner.'

Pip withdrew his fingers from her sex and allowed the string of her thong to snap back into place, working it backwards and forwards a little in order to ensure it was safely ensconced in her slit and bottom cleft. He gave her a sharp slap on her bottom and Sophie reluctantly turned to the seat opposite Pip's and lowered herself onto the chair. As Charles moved to uncover the salvers she was startled by Pip clapping his hands together and standing up abruptly. As he strode round to her side of the table, Sophie noticed the bulge of a huge erection in his crotch.

'I told you, Sophie, that you must always be on display for me yet what do I find but that you are calmly sitting there hiding yourself from my eyes!'

Stifling a word of protest, Sophie stared down through the glass-topped table and realised that she was sitting with her legs crossed at the ankles. She immediately spread her legs wide, even pulling her labia apart to expose the swollen flesh of her inner sex to Pip's view. But it was too late.

'Punishment, Charles, is the only way this girl is going to learn her place. Please take her away and teach her what will happen when she is disobedient. I will watch on the video whilst having my dinner. When you are satisfied that she has learnt her lesson, you will bring her back to me.'

Turning to flick a switch on the video, Pip settled back down at the table. Sophie watched as the video screen came to life, offering a full view of the couch on which she had just been strapped while having her cunt shaved and depilated. Taking hold of her wrist, Charles led her back to the bedroom.

'And feel free to use the crop on her if necessary,' Pip called after them as Charles shut the bedroom door and turned the key in the lock. Going to one of the wardrobes, Charles opened a drawer and extracted a long crop with a leather switch at the end. Flicking it experimentally against his hand, he indicated the couch which was now back in a horizontal position.

'Up on the couch again, Sophie. But this time on your hands and knees.'

Noting the change in Charles's demeanour towards her, Sophie judged that is would be better to play along for the time being. She climbed onto the couch and squatted on her hands and knees, her breasts hanging freely and the cleft between her buttocks slightly spread. Charles secured her hands back in the cuffs at the side of the couch and ordered her to bring her knees towards her chest where he placed a strap around each knee and fastened them to the same cuffs as her wrists. Lowering the flap at the base of the couch once more, Charles ran the handle of the crop between her now well-parted buttocks to her cunt and pushed the cold metal a little way into her sex hole.

'Squeeze onto the crop, I want to see how tight you can get,' he said, turning the handle round so that she could feel the size of its intrusion into her body. Sophie gripped her sex muscles tightly and Charles tugged slightly on the end of the crop. 'Very good, now keep yourself tight while I get changed. If you let the crop fall out of your cunt, I will be very angry.'

Leaving the crop hanging out of her cunt, Charles disappeared into the bathroom and Sophie could hear him pissing into the toilet bowl. She was reminded that she had not been able to pee for some hours now and the growing pressure in her bladder was adding to her chronic state of arousal. Keeping her sex muscles tightly gripped around the handle of the crop was almost unbearably exciting and Sophie imagined what her exposed cunt and bottom must look like to Pip as he watched on the video in the next room. For his pleasure, she flexed her muscles slightly, allowing the crop to ease out a little with each relaxation before tensing her muscles again. If the sight of that didn't make him want to get her out of here and into his bed as soon as possible, she didn't know what would.

After a few minutes, Charles returned to the room and came to stand directly in front of her face, now wearing only a jockstrap made of some sheer material through which she could clearly see his semi-erect cock. She could make out that his pubic hair was also completely shaved away and she parted her lips involuntarily at the thought of taking his naked phallus into her mouth.

Satisfied that she was becoming extremely excited at the sight of his body, Charles moved to the base of the couch again and tugged on the crop. With relief, Sophie relaxed her sex muscles and let it slip out of her hole. Laying the crop down by her side, Charles began to rub his fingers up and down her slit, bringing on the flow of her juices and Sophie could hear the slick movement of his fingers as he alternately dipped his fingers into her hole and tweaked her hardening clitoris. The scent of her arousal became almost palpable in the room and she started to pant slightly as she felt an orgasm beginning to build.

Abruptly Charles stopped rubbing her cunt and picked up the crop again, stroking it faintly across her buttocks. Without warning he raised the crop and brought it down smartly across Sophie's bottom. She flinched at the sharp stroke and braced herself, clenching the muscles in her buttocks as she heard him raise the crop again. 'Relax,' he said harshly and, against her will, Sophie found herself obeying his instruction, letting the pain from five more stripes flood through her lower body, much like the sudden freedom of an orgasm. 'Six of the best,' Charles said, laughing softly as he placed the crop back on the couch. 'And now for your real punishment.'

Peering over her shoulder, Sophie watched as Charles pushed the jockstrap to his thighs, revealing his hugely erect cock. Moving between her legs, Charles started to rub himself along the length of her slit, occasionally pushing the head of his cock a little way into her tight hole. Sophie started to rock backwards and forwards in an attempt to entice him into her cunt, straining at the ties on her wrists and legs, but Charles only increased the frequency of his strokes, breathing heavily as his orgasm approached.

Suddenly pulling away from her cunt, Sophie watched with dismay as he finished off his orgasm with a few swift strokes of his hand, spurting his come in a perfect stream onto her back. 'Your punishment,' he said with a smile, as Sophie slumped against her restraints, aching with desire and needing desperately to relieve the swelling of her sex flesh. Charles pulled his jockstrap back over his semi-flaccid cock and released Sophie from her ties. Unlocking the door, he led her back into the living room where Pip was sitting in front of the video massaging a healthy erection.

'Quite enjoyable. I hope you've learnt your lesson, my dear,' he said. 'Take her through to the bedroom, Charles, and make her ready. It's time she gave me some after-dinner pleasure.'

With a firm push against her shoulder, Charles guided Sophie towards the main bedroom. One wall of Pip's bedroom was lined with mirrored wardrobes and Sophie glanced over her shoulder and, with a gasp of surprise, saw the welts across her firm buttocks from the six strokes of the crop she had just received. Noticing her reaction, Charles patted her bottom again.

'A timely reminder of your lesson, little bitch. There are some even more interesting punishments hidden in these drawers if you seem to be forgetting it. Kneel on the bed on your hands and knees. That way the master will be able to view my work.'

Casting Charles a vicious look, Sophie did as she was told,

bringing her knees up to her chest but making sure they were spread apart so that her whole sex was on full display from behind. Charles placed several large cushions beneath her belly and then, just as she thought she would be allowed to remain untied, he reached over and clipped her wrists into a pair of leather cuffs. The cuffs were attached to a silken rope fixed to a ring at the head of the bed and as Charles shortened the rope, Sophie's arms were stretched forward and her chest flattened against the bed, while her butt remained raised on top of the pile of cushions. It was displayed in this inelegant mode that Pip found her when he sauntered into his bedroom several moments later.

'Thank you, Charles, that is very pleasing to me,' she heard Pip murmur. 'You may stand to one side for the moment but I will need your services again shortly.' Sophie sensed the bed sink as Pip climbed onto it behind her and straining her neck round she caught a glimpse of him undoing the flies in his trousers and pushing them to his hips. He was wearing no underpants and his engorged phallus sprang forward immediately. She felt the touch of his fingers stroking the welts on the cheeks of her bottom and then her whole sexual being tensed in anticipation as he began to stroke the full length of her cunt and ass backwards and forwards. She moaned with the intense pleasure of his forefinger teasing her hardened clitoris, now completely freed from its fleshy hood by her outstretched position.

Behind her, Pip began to repeat the actions of his fingers with the shaft of his cock and Sophie started to rock her ass up and down to intensify the action of his strokes on her sex. 'Tell me what you want, Sophie,' Pip grunted. 'Tell me that you want my shaft in your cunt. Beg for it, Sophie.'

Frantic with the desire for the feel of his cock inside her body, Sophie had no hesitation in begging for release. 'Give it to me, Pip. Please. Let me feel your shaft inside me. I need it so badly.'

With a sudden pause in his strokes, Pip repositioned himself between her legs and drove his cock into her tight, wet hole with one long movement. Sophie let out a groan as her flesh stretched to encompass his size and she pushed her chest further down into the bed so that her cunt was raised even higher towards the male behind her. Leaving his cock buried deep inside, Pip moved his hips in a circular motion to ease the entrance to her hole even further open, knowing that the pressure of Sophie's full bladder would add to her arousal. Sophie's whole being seemed concentrated on the wet, swollen flesh between her legs; she could think of nothing else but the growing throb of her orgasm as Pip worked at her with his cock. Then, withdrawing his cock from her hole up to the head of his shaft, Pip began to pump his member in and out of her body with a strong slow rhythm which made Sophie pant at each stroke. As his rhythm became faster and harder, his balls began to bang against her clitoris and Sophie's orgasm finally gained hold. Her sex muscles spasmed against the hard flesh of Pip's cock and he let out a shout as he lost control of his own orgasm with her touch. Shooting his come into her with a massive flood, Pip slumped forward against her now prone body. They lay for a few moments together, panting with the effort of their frantic coupling then Pip pulled himself away and climbed off the bed.

'Turn her over, Charles, and get her ready again. I'm not finished yet,' Pip said, as he stepped out of his trousers and walked to the bathroom. Once again, as Charles removed the cushions from beneath Sophie's belly and twisted her round onto her back without untying her wrists from their cuffs, Sophie heard a male releasing his urine stream into the toilet bowl next door and was reminded, now almost painfully, of her own need to pee. Telling her to raise her buttocks from the bed, Charles replaced the cushions beneath her bottom and, pulling her legs apart, attached each ankle by means of a cuff and rope to rings at the corners of the bed base. With a cold, wet towel, Charles mopped the sex juices from between her spread legs; Sophie tensed at the cold sensation but was almost immediately surprised as she felt the warmth of Charles's mouth licking her sex from back to front. She closed her eyes with the luxurious sensation and knew that her first orgasm had only taken the edge off her arousal. For the next few minutes, she gave herself up to the feeling of a second orgasm mounting in her body as Charles continued his stimulation of her cunt, sucking and nibbling her clitoris back to hardness and pushing his tongue deep into her hole.

A movement to the side of the bed caused Sophie to open her eyes. Pip was standing watching the display, his cock semi-erect. 'Carry on, Charles,' he said, holding Sophie's gaze with his own. 'Ms Jenner will get me up again while you bring her on.' Kneeling on the bed, Pip squatted over Sophie's face and pointed his cock towards her mouth. 'Take it between your lips, Sophie,' he said softly.

Obediently, Sophie opened her mouth and Pip pushed his shaft between her lips. With a few shallow strokes, his cock sprang back into life and Sophie flicked her tongue eagerly around the smooth velvety head of his member, tasting the salty drips of his pre-come as they were squeezed from his tiny slit.

Pip grunted with pleasure, letting her continue until he was hard again, then, pulling away, he told Charles to stand aside. Without preamble, he knelt between Sophie's raised sex and, pushing his cock hard into her open hole, he started to shaft her. Sophie's breasts jiggled with the onslaught of his body's movement against hers. Now desensitised from his first orgasm Pip was able to luxuriate in the feel of her sex squeezing around his own without losing control of his ejaculation and he continued to thrust while feasting his eyes on her prone body restrained beneath him. Sophie moaned with pleasure. This was what she had been waiting for and, knowing that there was plenty of time, she allowed herself to relax as she waited for the slow growth of her own second orgasm.

After several minutes, to her surprise, Pip withdrew and ordered Charles to take his place; Charles's cock was thinner than Pip's but what he lacked in girth he made up for in enthusiasm. Pushing her legs further apart with his thighs, Charles set up a fast, thumping rhythm and Sophie clenched her sex muscles hard around his slender cock as it thrust in and out of her hole. Just as she felt his rhythm become jerky with the onset of his orgasm, Sophie saw Pip pull Charles from her body. Taking a long look at her swollen flesh, Pip sank his own member back between the folds of her cunt. The unexpected size of his member forcing its way back between her clenched muscles broke Sophie's control and she felt waves of pleasure and release breaking from her hole into her sex and onwards throughout her body. Pip ejaculated with a low groan of satisfaction as he watched her skin suffuse with the flush of her orgasm, her eyes tightly shut and her breasts thrust forward.

Pulling his semi-flaccid cock from her cunt, Pip climbed from the bed and allowed Charles back to add his own come to the juices between Sophie's legs and then, finally releasing her from her bonds, Pip escorted an exhausted Sophie through to the bathroom.

When she emerged, dressed in her own clothes once more, Charles had disappeared and Pip was sitting in the living room, just as if nothing had ever happened. He smiled up at her. 'I told you you wanted to be dominated.' He passed her a glass of champagne. 'Congratulations, Sophie, a very good initiation.'

She took the champagne and stared at him, somewhat nonplussed at the complete reversion to normality, as well as his near-lightning change of character.

'Why?' she asked at last.

'Didn't you enjoy it? I was sure you would.'

'That doesn't answer the question.'

Pip smiled again, 'I think it does.'

'And cancelling my meetings, bringing this into the workplace – our office?'

Pip shrugged. 'It rather put you on edge, didn't it, Sophie? And that was quite entertaining.' He stood up and walked to the window. 'And after all, would you have come here if I'd warned you about the evening's enjoyment?'

Sophie shook her head and joined him. 'I don't know.'

Pip stretched out his hand and pointed down into the park. 'See, I told you, the evening parade is starting.' In the distance, just visible in the dim glow of a street lamp, two lovers were embracing. Pip glanced back at her. 'The real show will start later. Will you stay and watch?'

'Have you done this before, Pip?'

'What?'

'Taken someone from work? A woman? Done this with her? Made her . . .'

'Made her a slave to my whim?' he finished lightly.

'Well?'

Pip ran his finger down her shoulder and paused before answering. At length he turned back. 'You know I never let work intrude on my private life, or at least not until now.' He laughed. 'Do you really think I'd be able to keep something like this secret from my colleagues, not to mention my enemies, if I brought my female assistants here on a regular basis?'

'So why me?'

He stopped laughing. 'You're different, Sophie. And my plans for your future are quite different as well.'

Chapter Four

Heathrow's Terminal 3 was noisy and rowdy, seemingly filled with screaming children and fraught parents, and it wasn't until she got inside the executive lounge that Sophie was able to find any peace and quiet. The chaos wasn't improving her mood; the last few days had been a total bitch at work and Pip was nowhere to be found. He had left a message at the office to say he was going off on a business management retreat, whatever the hell that might be, and turning off his phone, his fax and failing to reply to any e-mails, simply disappearing into thin air, was just too much! Sophie pulled out her phone and tried Pip's numbers again. Nothing. Damn him.

Well, she told herself, there was nothing else for it. The office would have to take care of itself for a day or two; she simply had to go to the US and sort this problem out. She sat down in the lounge and tried to relax and concentrate on some papers, but she had left her arrival to the last possible moment and barely had time to drink a cup of coffee before the five o'clock flight to Chicago was being called and it was time to get on the plane. Sophie pulled herself to her feet and made her way through the fast-track club-class zone, marching along the walkways with a determined look on her face. Against the hard floor her high heels clicked aggressively, and as she passed other travellers they scattered out of her way, wary of this preoccupied-looking woman in a well-cut but severe black suit, all angles and business style, hair drawn back into chignon, dark red lips set in a hard line, her mind clearly on other, more important things.

Sophie sat down in her usual seat up in the bubble of the 747 and tried to relax. She summoned the air hostess and curtly demanded a large gin and tonic, 'Immediately,' before dismissing her and returning to her work. She let her head rest against the back of the deep airline seat and once again started to make her way through the papers and files that she had already spent so much time studying.

Those odd transfers and cash calls weren't going away and although they continued to fall below the 'significant number' level of materiality which would have alerted other systems, she was more and more concerned about it. And she still couldn't trace them. As a last resort Sophie had turned everything over to India James, her best 'hunter', a computer investigator par excellence. If India couldn't solve the mystery no-one could, but all India had done was to send e-mail requesting, no, insisting, that Sophie come to the US to 'review' the issues with her. She wouldn't discuss them on a secure line, on the phone, by fax or e-mail, nothing but a meeting in person, with Sophie. That couldn't be good.

Sophie swigged down the gin; it was strong, at least a double, and icy cold, the sour alcohol biting against the sharp tang of lemon. Dammit, why couldn't Pip have managed to connect with her instead of disappearing without a word? Bastard! Added to all her other problems she was dying for a good, satisfying fuck; even if it wasn't on the level of last week's little excursion to Regent's Park at least it would ease away some of the tension inside.

There was a cough behind her and Sarah looked up; a man was standing expectantly beside her seat. 'I'm sorry?'

'I think I'm in the seat next to yours,' he said in a soft nasal twang. 'Twelve B, that's me.'

She looked up and groaned. 'You're right, hold on.' Irritably she switched off her computer and started to pack up and stand up to let him in.

'I'm sorry about this,' he told her, moving back to give her some space. 'I'd sit somewhere else but –' he looked around expressively – 'well, it's pretty full up here. And I'm afraid I'm rather late.'

'I know,' she grumbled, 'it's not your fault, hold on a minute.' She closed the computer, slid it back in its case, closed the shelf in front of her, picked up the computer case and stood up, going into the gangway in front of him, allowing him to get into the window seat. He crawled in with another apologetic look and she sat back down. 'I just hope you're not planning to go to the bathroom for a while. I'm not moving again, you know!'

He smiled. 'No, you're going to have to turn that off soon though, aren't you?'

She nodded, dismissing him. 'But at least I can get on with some work for a bit.' . . . If you will just sit there, shut up and let me, was the other half of the sentence she didn't enunciate out loud. She returned to her report, carefully angling the computer so her neighbour couldn't see the screen; she didn't want anyone else reading her notes.

It was infuriating. Every time she went through the reports it all came back to the same conclusion: whether Pip wanted to believe it or not there was definitely something very dodgy going on in South America. The ring fencing constraints she had put in place, the checks and balances that she designed specifically to prevent anyone else getting the money out of eco-friendly projects and into something else just didn't appear to be working. That was the only answer, but the question was how could they not be working? She had been so careful, and the fund had been designed for this, to make sure eco-friendly investors could be happy that the money was completely clean. But what was really going on? Why were there these gaps and spaces in time, money going on to the accounts, then reversed out, all the mistakes corrected, yes, but why the mistakes in the first place? What was that about? Could it really be just a small regional South American bank screwing it up and correcting their mistakes? Or was that what she was supposed to think?

She sighed heavily; what a mess. And nothing tangible; maybe it really was her own paranoia, and with a bit of luck by tomorrow she'd be regretting pissing about and wasting time in the US when she could have been doing a bit more on the organisation at home. There was a cough at her shoulder and she looked up, surprised to realise that whilst she had been fighting through numbers, e-mails and bank account details the rest of the plane had been getting ready to depart.

'Yes?'

'I'm sorry, Ms Jenner,' the hostess said apologetically, 'you need to turn off your personal computer now, we're going to take off soon.' Sophie nodded shortly and obediently turned the power off. She packed it away and handed it to the hostess to put in the rack above. 'Can I get you another drink whilst we taxi to the runway?'

She shook her head, then changed her mind. What the hell? Two drinks wouldn't hurt. 'I'll have a glass of champagne.'

The hostess nodded. 'And you, Dr Silver?'

The man sitting next to Sophie nodded. 'I'll have champagne too.'

The hostess smiled and went to collect the drinks; Sophie closed her eyes. She was tired and fed up and now she just wanted to sleep for the next ten hours, at least until they reached Chicago. Unfortunately her neighbour seemed to have other ideas; he coughed politely and when she opened her eyes and looked at him he put out his hand with a winning smile.

'Ms Jenner, is that right?' She nodded. 'I'm Paul Silver, I saw you on the posters coming in to Heathrow.'

She shook his hand, wishing he would just let her get some rest and clear her mind, but Dr Silver wasn't put off. 'You know,' he said, 'I work for a very large computer company, perhaps you've heard of us . . .'

Four hours into the flight most people were either eating or watching a movie on their personal video screens. Sophie stood in the bathroom and looked at herself in the mirror. Damn Pip and damn India for making her do this stupid bloody trip. She prodded her face; standing under the fluorescent lighting, looking at her shimmering reflection bouncing off the stainless steel walls she felt knackered. And frustrated, very, very frustrated. God, she thought, she would love a man right now, just to ease the tension.

Sophie pulled her skirt up and slid her finger into her panties. She slid her finger further in, through the damp and into the wetness of her hole, then pulled off her panties and looked at herself in the mirror. Not some sissy steward either, a proper man. She slid her finger further and dragged it back out over her clit; the nerve endings screamed for some release.

Then there was knock at the door and she sighed. Just as well, she told herself, this is completely pathetic, and there's no way you could do yourself justice here. She breathed a long regretful sigh. You will just have to wait until you get to the hotel, she told herself. Stop whinging and get on with it. Get back to those bloody reports. She pulled her panties back on, opened the door and came face to face with her seating companion, Dr Silver. He smiled politely and backed away to let her out.

'Sorry,' he began, 'I wasn't sure there was anyone in there. I didn't mean to disturb you.'

Sophie smiled equally politely in return. 'That's okay.' For a moment they shuffled from side to side, each trying to let the other out, and as they brushed against each other she was almost overwhelmed with a desire to be reckless, to do what she shouldn't to release the tensions that had been concentrating in her body through the last weeks. Dr Silver would do; he might have been a bit irritating but he would do all right. He would be better than that; he was a man, he was actually quite good-looking, and if he had a cock that would make him ideal. She almost giggled out loud as she thought of the conversation: Do you have a cock and do you fancy a quickie? You do? Then come in here . . .

Dr Silver gave her a funny look and pressed himself against

71

the side of the wall. 'Sorry,' he said. 'Again.'

'Actually, can you help me?' she asked instead. 'I think I have a problem.'

'Oh?'

'Please?' She gave him an appealing look and backed herself into the stainless steel cubicle. Dr Silver glanced around as if to call for a stewardess but there was no-one there.

'Well . . .'

'Please?' Sophie was ready to beg him if he held off any longer, and she backed further in to encourage him. Dr Silver swallowed carefully, followed her inside the cubicle and stood there. 'You'll need to lock the door to get the light on.' Obediently he slid the door shut behind him and the light clicked on. He was staring straight at her and he was clearly aroused. He was tense and he was breathing fast; in fact he was so obviously trying to restrain himself just in case he had misread everything that she almost laughed again.

'What do you need me to do?' In the silence of the enclosed cubicle his voice was loud and clear, reflected off the walls, like the light.

'I think you know.'

There was silence.

'I'm not sure what you mean.'

Sophie leaned against the sink and gave him a sexy look from under her lashes, pushing out her breasts. Yes, Dr Silver was clearly susceptible to her charms, he was almost panting for her. 'I need some help, Doctor.'

'I'm not that sort of doctor . . .'

'You're the sort I need.' She leaned further back and unbuttoned the top of her blouse, letting her fingers run around the edge and down towards her cleavage, as though over-whelmed with heat and desire. 'I told you, I need some help, I can't do this for myself, or rather I could, but I don't want to.'

Sophie balanced on the sink and spread her legs apart. Still in his suit, Silver reached out and gently touched the front of her damp, sweaty panties and Sophie's eyes flickered closed for a moment. He swallowed, not quite able to believe this was happening.

Sophie smiled to herself. Pip was wrong, she realised suddenly; she loved the power, the being in control, as well as the submission. She liked it both ways. Or maybe she had seen what he got out of his control. After this she could walk away from the doctor if she wanted to and if she decided she wanted him again she could make the decision and have him. He wouldn't say no, that was for sure. In any case, right now she wanted him.

'It's all right,' she whispered, 'think of it as a daydream. Something out of time. It doesn't matter. It's just for now.' He nodded, his eyes glazed. 'Can you help me?' He nodded again. She leaned further back, her breasts jutting out against her blouse, her nipples hard against the soft lace of her bra and her own breathing quickening. 'Then let's do it.'

Silver reached out and touched her panties tentatively, as if he was scared he was going to be scorched, and then he dropped to his knees. He slid his fingers around her thighs and Sophie stretched out her legs for him to take away the scrap of satin from between her legs. He gasped at the sight of her naked pussy.

Her high heels tapped against the steel wall and Silver pushed her skirt up further, towards her waist. Beneath her skirt, glistening stockings were stretched to the top of her long legs, crisp apricot lace threaded around the tops, indenting the firm, slim thighs. Silver glanced up at her face and reached out tentatively again. This time he stroked her, gently running his fingers along her sex. Sophie groaned with the unexpected pleasure; she had more than half-expected him to simply get his cock out and start screwing her. After all, she was sitting in front of him with her fanny out, that was all she was asking for, not a long seduction. But clearly some woman had trained Dr Silver in what to do for her.

Her eyes closed and as she leant back his tongue slid around the edge of her pussy, licking her like a cat licks at cream, tasting her delicately before reaching in and drinking her up. Sophie pushed her arms out to hold herself in place, her body shuddering with pleasure. 'That's very good, Doc,' she whispered. 'God yes, that's good.' Dr Silver gripped her thighs, his fingers biting into her flesh as he held her in place. She groaned with pleasure at every sensation. 'That's amazing.'

In response, the silent Dr Silver withdrew from her sex, and she eagerly reached out to undo his tie, letting it hang around his neck whilst she unbuttoned his shirt. When she finally started on his belt, his hands reached out to undo the last buttons of her blouse. He didn't slip it off her, but reached inside and around her back, embracing her briefly, his face and lips suddenly very close to her own. Then he undid her bra and eased it slightly loose, stroking her breasts gently as he released them and let them hang over the edges of the apricot lace and silken brassiere. He was still very close and she leaned forwards to kiss him; his mouth was warm and soft, his fingers touching her gently as her tongue explored him. He tasted sweet, and slightly salty, the taste of her own juices almost gone already. Kissing him again, she silently unzipped his trousers, letting them fall to the floor, to be followed swiftly by his conventional dark blue boxers.

Their mouths separated and Sophie looked down to study his cock.

'Okay?'

She nodded. It was solid, very erect, not surprising in the circumstances she told herself, circumcised, with the head exposed, reddened and shiny under the fluorescent light. She stretched out a finger to take the glistening fluid at the top off and gave her finger back to him to lick. He let his lips run to the base and back and then leant down to her nipples, sucking hard at them until Sophie whimpered, at which point he sucked even harder and she gasped as his teeth bit into her. Finally then he stopped and Sophie leaned back against the mirror and spread her legs apart, wrapping them around his back.

He ran his fingers up and down her thighs, pushed them further apart and then, quite methodically, placed his cock at the entrance to her sex and pushed himself inside her. Sophie exhaled. 'Yes,' her voice sounded low and grating, like a whisky drinker after a couple of stiff ones. 'Yes, harder.' He started to move faster, still silent, pounding her against the mirrored wall behind her, pushing his cock in and out of her. 'Yes,' she begged, 'but harder. Do it harder. Ahh, yes, yes.' Amazingly he did it harder, and faster too, the pace building, pushing her against the mirror, impaling her again and again, her arms wrapped around him, pulling him closer to her with each individual penetration. Then she was gasping, groaning and whimpering as her orgasm exploded inside her and his own silent thrusting dissolved into panting grunts, only vaguely distinguishable as words. 'Yes, yes, yes.' With a growling crescendo of sound and a hot heavy panting in her ear, Silver's body tensed and then, with a final thrust, he exploded orgasmically into her.

Chicago Airport was cool and air-conditioned. It was also almost completely empty. As Sophie was standing in line waiting to get through immigration some fool tried to light up a cigarette only to be virtually leapt upon by a security guard. She tore the cigarette from his lips and hissed in his face, 'No smoking in the airport, sir,' just as a tannoy detected the smoke and a calmer warning came over the information system.

'Chicago is a non-smoking airport, please extinguish all cigarettes until after you leave the building. Thank you.'

The chastened boy who had tried to smoke stood in line with the eyes of the security people upon him. For a moment Sophie felt rather sorry for him; it was obvious he didn't speak much English, and he didn't look used to the plethora of guns on the hips of the officials. Then she was motioned through the barrier.

She looked at the immigration officer. 'Purpose of your visit, ma'am?'

'Business.'

He looked up at her. 'No pleasure at all?' He gave her a quick smile. She shrugged; surely he wasn't going to hit on her?

'Well, you never know, I might get lucky.' She gave him a starched smile in return, the one that said, 'I am humouring you, but you could never get anywhere near me.'

The officer didn't take the hint, instead he raised his eyebrows. 'I hope you enjoy yourself if you do, Chicago's a great place to have some fun.'

This time Sophie gave him a stony look. 'I'll do my best, but I'm very busy.'

He nodded and handed her passport back, the momentary lapse in officialism dispensed with. 'Enjoy your visit.'

'Thank you,' she replied, and stalked off, carrying her single suitbag. This was a quick trip and Sophie had long ago got used to travelling with hand luggage, loathing hanging around the carousel with all the tourists, desperate to get to her car and get out of the airport, to the meeting and back again as quickly as possible.

She barged through the double doors almost before they had opened and headed outside. As she had expected a limousine was waiting for her.

The drive into the centre of Chicago was tedious in the extreme; the traffic was backed up almost to the airport and the freeway was full of cars, making lane changes near-impossible. Sophie sat in the back, running through her notes and her plans again. Hopefully India James could cast some light on these money transfers, she was the best analyst and investigator they had outside the bank, and even though India didn't really like working in the banking environment she could be trusted, or so Sophie hoped; for what she charged she certainly should be.

India James and Sophie had met years before at a conference on banking practices. In a room full of middle-aged men India and Sophie stood out, and not just because they were females; with Sophie, the men assumed she was simply a blonde bimbo and promptly tried to get her into bed, but India just looked weird, partly because she was dressed in black from head to toe, including her glasses, and partly because she clearly didn't fit in, however much she tried to behave like a normal banking employee.

Nevertheless, on the run from a particularly amorous and rather drunk divorcé Sophie had started up a conversation with her and, although rather disdainful of each other at first, the two women had swiftly realised that, even if they were not destined to be the closest of friends, they had similar ideas about work and an understanding of the other's motivations. India had dropped out of banking some time ago now, indulging herself in her own private passion for computers and cyberspace and setting herself up as a gun for hire; an independent analyst, someone who could be trusted and who could run rings round the competition, whether you wanted to stop them accessing your material, their own material, or investigate something interesting. India had her own rules and ethics; she never told anyone who she was working for and she never did anything illegal, Sophie hoped.

India's business was located in downtown Chicago, out on Lake Shore Drive, in a new tower block with a fabulous view. It stood next to the freeway that crossed the city, running from the Shedd Aquarium on one end of the walkway by the lake, through the downtown area, and heading towards Lincoln Park, by-passing Wrigley Field to the West. Right in front of them was Lake Michigan, a shimmering mass of water that looked as though it went forever into the distance; the weather was very hot and dry, the sun was high and the sky was a deep intense blue, but fortunately inside the building the air-conditioning was working overtime and the office was semi-refrigerated. The two of them were meeting in one of the large corner offices – not India's, she didn't believe in having her own private office, she shared the same space as everyone else – and much to Sophie's irritation she had refused to lock the door to stop anyone wandering in.

Sophie stood up and turned away from India, staring blankly out onto the lake, letting her eyes wander from Navy Pier and its fairground attractions at one end of the road, down to the white aquarium at the other. In between, a myriad little boats were bobbing about on white crested waves. Sometimes the money, the job, the lifestyle, none of it seemed worthwhile. In a way she just wished she could be out there enjoying herself without having to deal with any of this crap.

She took a deep breath. 'So what are you saying? I flew out here for you to tell me that you don't have a bloody clue about any of this stuff?' She waved her handful of paper, the reports she had puzzled over and studied for days, apparently so much waste paper now.

India bridled and ran her hands through her hair irritably. The contrast between the two women couldn't have been stronger. Sophie was, as usual, in a little black suit and high heels; all efficiency, business-orientated and expensive grooming. India had long, lank, dark hair, which always needed a damn good brush, thick dark glasses which she never changed and these days she dressed like something out of the grunge scene, or a late seventies rocker, with very grotty jeans and a tie-dyed T-shirt. But, Sophie reminded herself, India had her own business and could do what she wanted, wear what she wanted and work when and wherever she wanted. India glared across at her now from under the dark bottle-bottom glasses. 'Did I say anything about not having a bloody clue?'

'As near as dammit, yes.'

'I did not.'

'Then what are you trying to tell me, India?' Sophie threw herself into the ratty fabric armchair. India didn't seem to believe in updating her furnishings either.

'Simply that there's more to this than meets the eye. It's difficult to trace the money trail. It's been put together very well.'

This was bad news. 'You told me that already.' She paused. 'It's definitely deliberate then?'

India stared at her as if she was a total idiot. 'Of course it's deliberate.'

'I just wanted to check.'

'Crap, if you thought it wasn't, would you be here now?'

'Still . . .'

'Look, someone who knows what they're doing and is better than most of the geeks you employ, is moving the money around and into private accounts.' She paused and watched Sophie's desolate expression.

'Private accounts?'

India nodded. This was news to Sophie. 'This is getting worse. Is there no way we can work out who it is?'

'I didn't say that.'

Sophie glared at her. 'India, you bugger, stop mucking me about and get on with it.'

India paused. 'This is important to you, isn't it?' Sophie nodded. 'Why?'

'It's illegal, immoral and it could ruin the eco-fund before it even gets properly off the ground.'

'And the real reason?' she asked cynically.

Sophie threw up her arms. 'Isn't it obvious? I'm the head of the fund, in public at least. I need to know what's going on. If it all goes pear-shaped it won't be just the fund going down, it'll be me as well. There won't be any second chances.'

'Look,' India said, 'as near as I can tell so far, the money is being diverted in various ways; that's why it's taking a long time to work out. Automatic transfers to Lima aren't going through as quickly as they should.'

'I know that,' Sophie interrupted her, 'that's why I called you.'

'Yes,' India went on with barely concealed impatience, 'and I can trace that back to some clerk in Lima.'

Sophie gave a sigh. 'Is that it? Some small-time embezzlement? Jesus, that's a relief. I was worried.' She started to get up, suddenly tired, realising what a strain she had been putting herself under for the last few weeks. 'I am a stupid cow, though I wouldn't let anyone but you hear that.' She smiled over at India, but India wasn't smiling back. 'Come on,' she tried again. 'Cough up the details, India, and let's have a drink. If we know who it is we can get the money out of wherever the little toad's been stashing it away. I don't know why you needed to be so secretive about it.'

India gave her a funny look. 'Sorry, Sophie, that's not why I dragged you over from the UK.'

'What do you mean?' Sophie's heart was sinking even as she spoke.

'You missed the other transfers from Lima.'

'What other transfers from Lima?'

India tapped her computer screen. 'I'm sorry to say that the bit you're completely missing is the important part. The money transfers pre-South America are small potatoes. In fact –' she looked up at Sophie across the rim of her glasses – 'I'm not convinced these are being conducted by the same people.'

'Why on earth not?'

India shook her head. 'This other stuff is a lot more sophisticated than the first shuffling.'

'Hang on a minute, you're telling me the money that's disappeared is small change?' India nodded. 'And there's more going out?' She nodded again. 'How much more?'

'A lot. Millions. Lots of millions. And it's going somewhere first, it's going into the economy and then out. Basically it's being very carefully laundered.' Her voice was grudgingly approving. 'It's really been quite well done.'

Sophie was hardly listening to the details any more. 'And I didn't know.' She stared out of the room and over the peaceful lake. People were still boating and windsurfing out there; no cares in the world. How come she was in here? She turned back to India. 'I still don't understand. How did you find out?' She got a hard look for her trouble.

'That's what you pay me for.'

'So who's doing it and what are they doing?'

India shrugged. 'That's the question, and I don't have all

the answers. Yet. But it's very well set-up, the money looks as though it reaches the projects, and it must be a big operation, because no-one's complaining. Best guess, money's moving around from palm to palm, and the bulk gets salted away in Switzerland. Or somewhere.' She looked back at Sophie. 'But I don't think any of it's seeing its way into your businesses.'

Sophie stood and tried to control her sense of rising nausea. 'Hold on a minute, are you telling me there's *no* money going to my eco-projects at all?' India nodded. 'At all?' Sophie ran her hand through her hair. 'How can this be?' Her world was starting to fall apart. 'It doesn't make any sense. This can't go on for long; I mean we've already found it, can't we stop it?' But India was shaking her head.

'Not yet, I wouldn't know how. And if they're greasing everyone's palm then it could go on for a while; the only ones moaning would be the farmers. They could be bought off, or threatened to shut them up, and then the money could actually go into the projects, such as they are, and out again.' She paused. 'You're not involving western aid or supervision, are you?'

Sophie shook her head. 'That's what makes this business special, home-grown in every detail. Me and Pip and a few others to plan things, but it's primarily government driven and the people in charge are local; it works out of Cusco.'

India sniffed. 'You should have kept more control.'

'Not helpful, thank you, India.' India shrugged and Sophie shook her head again as if trying to clear her brain. 'So have you any real idea what's going on?'

'You're not going to like this.' Sophie glared at her. 'Okay, as far as I can tell, and it is only preliminary, it's going into black market activities. The projects exist, they're just not doing what you thought.'

'So what are they doing instead?'

India shrugged and pointed out information in the page of numbered accounts. 'Possibly strip mining. Maybe other things as well.'

'What?'

'Here, the owners of these accounts have been allegedly linked to drugs and prostitution. It's not certain, but I think there's a channel between these and some of your cash calls . . .' She stopped. 'Sorry, Sophie, no point going into detail.' She looked back up at Sophie with an apologetic look. 'I'll cut to the chase. I think your embezzler is mixed up with some sort of South American mafia. Bottom line, you're being stiffed and on a major scale.'

Chapter Five

Pip flicked through the sheaf of computer printouts and then looked back at Sophie, sitting opposite him, perched on the edge of a black leather swivel chair, her expression tense, her body rigid with anxiety.

'You aren't serious?'

Sophie stared back at him, suddenly deflated, unable to believe that he didn't see the implications in the reports that, to her, were screamingly obvious and should have been clear to anyone who cared to study the evidence.

'Of course I am.' She reached out for the papers, but Pip kept his hold on them. Thwarted, she stood and started to pace around the room, her nerves jangling with tension and a suppressed rage at the possibility that anyone should try to subvert the business for their own gain. Her business. And her responsibility. 'I don't understand why you don't see it,' she went on. 'It's obvious.'

'Not to me.'

'For God's sake, Pip!' She was behind him now, leaning over his shoulder to jab a pointed finger at the pages in front of them both. 'Look at these account details.'

'I see money going in, not out.'

'And I see blips that shouldn't be there.' She flicked irritably through pages. 'Look there, and there.' She straightened up again and resumed her pacing. 'Honestly, Pip. India's really been digging into this and she agrees, the money's getting moved around.'

'India?'

'India James, my investigator.'

Pip looked as if he had sat on a cattle prod. 'That harpy.'

'You know her?'

His lips thinned. 'Only by reputation. I haven't used her services myself. A weirdo who couldn't boil an egg.'

'You don't know her. She's very smart.'

'Then just look at the facts, Sophie. The money's getting to Lima and on into the regions. Which means it's going to the people it should. Your precious farmers.'

'Dammit, Pip, it's not! Why won't you believe me? Or at least the evidence?' She hugged her chest, still striding around the room, her head bent, concentrating hard, trying to work out how to best convince him that her suspicions about embezzlement were correct, however tenuous the evidence at this stage. 'Look, someone is subverting the fund, embezzling the money. And the end result will be that they destroy the business; a business I'm supposed to be in charge of. I don't know who or how but I'm sure as hell they're not putting the cash into the environment or the local economy! Not the legitimate one anyway.' She paused. 'This is a sophisticated operation, Pip, it's not some local setting up a pension fund, sidelining a few shekels for a night on the town and a new dress for the wife, it's much bigger than that.'

'But you don't really know what's going on.'

She shook her head. 'Not yet. If I'm being honest I don't know spit.'

'So what do you expect to do about it?'

'I do know that it's going on. And I also know that I'm the one who's going to have to take the rap if this gets out.'

'Well,' said Pip cynically, 'at least one thing's stayed the same. It's not the poor farmers you've managed to develop a conscience about, it's keeping the skin on your own back.'

Sophie leaned across the desk. 'Pip, it doesn't matter why, does it? It matters that it's happening. You must believe me. I know it's not exactly conclusive, but India is convinced . . .'

'Ha!'

84

His voice was very sneering, but Sophie ignored it. 'And I think she's right. It's well covered up but the gaps in transfer times, the inaccuracies before the accounts re-cleared, it all looks like someone's messing things about.'

Pip leaned back in his seat. 'So why don't you just call the banks in Lima and the Madre de Dios and find out if the money's there?' he asked, in a patronising tone that sounded as if he were dealing with a rather stupid, backward child. 'There's the phone. Go right ahead.' Sophie flushed and shook her head. 'What? Done that already?' She nodded. 'No luck?' She shook her head again. 'And why not?'

This time her voice was reluctant. 'They think everything's fine.' Pip raised his eyebrows. 'But they're wrong!'

'Oh come on, Sophie, I've had enough of this. You're wasting my time and yours.'

'No, Pip. It's a local South American bank.' She broke off for a moment. 'Look, I'll admit now that it wasn't one of our better decisions, pushing control all the way down the chain to the small-town operations. It might make for flat structures and lower operational costs but they just don't have the systems to analyse something like this.'

'And you're suggesting that they don't know what's going on in the vault. They can't even count the money they've got?'

Sophie shook her head. 'Very funny. This just makes it more important that I get a better idea of what's going on. I know it sounds fanciful, Pip, but I really believe India and she's convinced there's something wrong.'

Pip sighed and let the report flop back onto the desk. 'And you want to do what about it?'

She stopped in front of the desk. 'I want to go to Lima and out into the regions. To Madre de Dios if necessary. I want to have a look for myself.'

'Absolutely not!'

'Pip, I need to go.'

'No way. You are not flying off to wander about South America on some wild goose chase. We need you here, and anyway, what good do you think you could do?'

'Pip!' Sophie's voice was rising and angry. 'I'm supposed to be in charge of this business. It's my responsibility to go out and sort this out.' She paused and straightened up, keeping eye-contact with him the whole time. 'I need to do this, Pip. And I'm not asking you, I'm telling you.'

There was a long silence.

'Well.' Pip suddenly sounded rather amused, if still a little irritated. 'You have come on in leaps and bounds I must say. Time was you would be sitting there like a scared fawn asking me for permission to do things that were far less contentious.'

Sophie smiled slowly. 'So, do I have your approval?'

He shrugged. 'It doesn't seem to matter, does it?' Then he sighed. 'Qualified approval, Sophie. South America, Lima, yes. The rainforest and the projects, no.' She opened her mouth to argue. 'I mean it, Sophie, not out into the wilds, that's a whole new ball-game and they treat women differently out there.' She opened her mouth to argue again, but Pip held up his hand. 'I've been there, I know. Now, you're in charge of the business –' he paused – 'but you're also my responsibility. I take the buck for what happens to you.' Sophie nodded reluctantly. 'But let me know how you get on and we can see how things go.' She flashed him a big smile. 'I must be mad letting you do this. However –' he leaned forward across the desk and his voice dropped somewhat – 'it raises other issues. Like how I'm going to manage without you.' Pip smiled. 'Shall we have a goodbye dinner tonight?' He paused meaningfully. 'At my house? Charles would love to see you again.' At Sophie's sharp intake of breath he added, knowingly, 'And with you in this mood there could be lots of possibilities . . .'

But she was shaking her head. 'Sorry to disappoint you, Pip, but I'm leaving in two hours. I'm booked on the next flight out of Heathrow.'

'Very organised,' Pip said with a slightly sour note in his voice. 'Then I guess I'll see you at the end of what? This week or next?'

'Not sure yet, I'll keep you in touch.'

'Well, I'll call our agent in Lima. You haven't met Hugo la Torre, have you? No, well, I'll make sure he sends someone to take care of you. Enjoy your trip. And, Sophie, take care of yourself and don't forget what I said.'

Sophie nodded and almost marched through the door with a wave and a smile. Beneath her attempt to maintain a sophisticated exterior was a little girl running off on a jaunt, Pip thought as he watched her go, a rueful expression on his face. Then his expression changed and it was a far harder and colder Pip who picked up the phone and started dialling.

'Hugo? Buenas dias. How are you, my friend? And business? Excellent.' He leant back in his chair and gazed at the ceiling. 'I've just been having a discussion with my associate Sophie Jenner, you recall we discussed her role in any future business plans.' A pause. 'Exactly. She's coming to visit Lima. And she thinks she might need to do some sightseeing. To the National Park in the Madre de Dios. I told her that would be unwise, but sometimes she can be quite headstrong.' There was another long pause. 'I agree. It's her first trip to Peru. I want you to make sure it's her last.'

The journey from Heathrow to Colombia passed with the normal tedium of a long-haul flight. Knowing full well that it was considered unwise to drink alcohol throughout the flight, Sophie nevertheless stifled her boredom with a bottle of Moet served by the attentive staff of Colombia's Avianca airlines. For this flight she was travelling first class, and although, as she acknowledged to herself, the movie was no substitute for the entertainment she enjoyed on her last intercontinental trip, at least there was room to stretch her legs, a fully reclining seat for when she wanted to sleep and a reasonable standard of airline food served on demand during the ten-hour flight to Bogota. However, by the time the plane put down for a two-hour stopover in Colombia, Sophie was beginning to regret the bottle of fizz she had consumed at high altitude.

She decided to take a shower in the first-class transit lounge facilities to try and restore her equilibrium. Although she was rather unnerved by the obvious appreciation of her shaven pussy from the stout Colombian woman who guarded the ladies' powder suite, she felt the benefit of her shower almost immediately and emerged, human again, to board the plane for the final leg of her journey, a three-hour flight from Bogota to Lima.

Sophie spent those three hours contemplating what she needed to do when she arrived in Peru. Her initial contacts with Hugo la Torre in Peru had been made before she got on the plane in London and she had a carefully worked out game-plan to follow. She was determined to travel from Lima into the rainforest border towns from where the farm and development projects should be controlled. Once there she hoped to make more personal contacts with the local managers in the company's eco-projects and push for some real facts to back up her suspicions.

The problem, she thought, would be getting people to talk to her. She hadn't wanted to admit it to Pip but she had a strong suspicion that he was right; a lot of Peruvians wouldn't want to deal with a woman, whatever her credentials might say about her authority in London. At least, she thought, the agent, Senor la Torre should be able to fix things up for her to travel in reasonable comfort. With a bit of luck this would all turn out to be Pip's wild goose chase; she looked out of the window. Even despite India's most recent findings? God, she hoped so.

Landing in Jorge Chavez Airport in the early hours of the next morning, Sophie emerged from the relative quiet of the arrivals lounge into the full glare of the busy public concourse packed, even at this hour, with a babble of expectant porters and taxi-drivers. Becoming an instant focus of Peruvian male attention because of her flowing if now rather messy blonde hair and patently Western looks and clothes, Sophie was momentarily panicked as seemingly hundreds of hands tried to seize hold of her luggage or grasp her arms to propel her in the direction of the exit. Then, out of the mêlèe, she heard her name being called and a tall, dark-skinned man pushed through the crowd towards her, casting expletives at the stocky porters and taxi-drivers around her who immediately began to skulk away in the face of his authority.

He bowed slightly. 'Ms Jenner, my name is Hugo la Torre. Philip Blakemore asked me to meet you on arrival in Peru. Welcome to my country.'

'Senor la Torre. Am I glad to see you.' Sophie flashed him a relieved smile. 'I was beginning to think seriously about turning around and heading straight back home!'

'Please, this way.' Hugo smiled back pleasantly. 'I have a car waiting to take us to your hotel.'

Outside there was a light drizzle falling, so fine as to be almost invisible, but nevertheless a welcome relief from the airless surroundings of Lima's international airport. Hugo escorted Sophie briskly out of the airport building and guided her towards a large black Mercedes parked near the exit. Relief at being taken care of was enough to drain Sophie of any remaining energy and she followed Hugo obediently, letting him take over the irritations of baggage transport and the warding off of the last few persistent street vendors.

Once they were seated in the back of the car, Hugo leaned forward to the driver and directed him to take them to 'Avenida La Paz.' The powerful car moved off smoothly and as they joined the increasingly busy flow of early-morning traffic heading towards central Lima, Hugo turned again to Sophie and offered her a glass of champagne from the mini bar set into the back of the driver's seat.

'A little early in the day I know,' he smiled, 'or late, depending upon your particular time zone, but Mr Blakemore insisted that you be given every attention.' Accepting the sparkling glass of amber liquid, Sophie smiled inwardly at Hugo's comment. If only he knew what Pip's attention to her usually meant these days, a glass of champagne would be the last thing on his mind right now.

They settled back into the soft leather seats and Hugo talked easily about the sights on offer in Lima and elsewhere in Peru. He was, he told her, taking her downtown to the smarter area of Miraflores. It would take about forty-five minutes, but the hotel there would be most suitable for her needs, far nicer than some of the central locations, prone to smog and other inconveniences. Sophie nodded, simply relieved to be with someone who knew the area well. He suggested that after her business had been settled, Sophie should take time to stop over in the Spanish colonial town of Cusco from where it would be easy to arrange a trip to see the world famous lost city of the Incas, Machu Picchu; then again, she must not leave Peru without staying a little while in Arequipa, the country's second city after Lima. She could visit the beautifully peaceful Santa Catalina monastery and from here it would be possible to arrange for her to fly over the mysterious Nasca Lines, deep in the stony desert of Pampa de San Jose.

Sophie sank back into the soft seat of the Mercedes, sipped her champagne and allowed herself to be lulled by thoughts of exploring the sights of this huge country with an attractive man by her side as a guide. Listening to his voice, she could almost believe herself to be here for a minor business meeting, after which she could relax and pay attention only to her own pleasure.

All too suddenly however, her pleasant reverie was interrupted. Hugo laid his hand on her arm and she saw that they were drawing up at the front of the imposing façade of Hotel César. Within seconds, her bags had been transported into the hotel by eager porters and she too had been guided into the cool, hushed interior.

'I will leave you here, Ms Jenner.' Hugo was at her side, smiling as his dark eyes looked into her own. 'The maitre d' will see that you are well looked after. I will let you get some sleep and then tomorrow we will meet and discuss your plans for your trip.'

'Perhaps we could talk now . . .' she began, but Hugo cut her off with a determined wave of his hand.

'Ms Jenner, you have had a very long flight and there is no need to exhaust yourself. I will be here at twelve-thirty, perhaps we can discuss your plans over lunch?'

She nodded, only slightly reluctant to be packed off to bed like a child, aware of her exhaustion, which the trip from the airport had exacerbated rather than reduced. 'I will see you for lunch.'

Hugo took Sophie's hand and bowed slightly. 'Hasta luego,' he said, swivelled on his heel and set off through the quiet marble foyer, leaving Sophie to be escorted to her room by the maitre d', her luggage preceding her.

The room proved to be a suite, large, luxurious and sumptuously appointed, with a huge bathroom and a lounge with a bar and a light buffet laid out on a side table. Sophie, however, was now so tired that she did nothing but throw off her clothes and sink into the soft, cool bed where a deep sleep soon overtook her exhausted body.

It was eight hours later when Sophie woke with a start as the curtains to her bedroom were swept aside by a maid.

'Buenas dias, senora. Good morning.' The maid smiled at Sophie as she placed a breakfast tray with croissants, squeezed mango juice and strong black coffee by her side on the bed. 'It is eleven o'clock. Senor La Torre will be waiting for you in one hour and thirty minutes. I have unpacked your bags and put away your clothes in the dressing-room closet.' The maid nodded goodbye and left the room.

Sophie lay back in the bed, trying to shake herself awake; her body still felt like lead and she could do with another six hours asleep, she thought, reaching groggily for the coffee. She sipped the intense, strong brew, and started to come back into the world. She was, she realised, hungry as well as thirsty, and soon she was working her way through the croissants as well. By the time she had emerged from the shower she was raring to go, and determined to get to the bottom of this puzzle. She phoned India, but there was no reply, so she left her phone and fax numbers on the answerphone in the US and carried on preparing for lunch with Hugo.

She emerged from her room fresh and clean in a plain cotton shift dress, lime-green and embroidered with white daisies. Not her usual business wear, admittedly, but then again, this wasn't London, she reminded herself. It was a different society, and one in which many, if not most of the middle class and wealthy women did not expect to work, a belief bolstered by a casual study of the elegant, Gucci-clad South American women who strolled through the hotel, laden with shopping, apparently visiting the hotel to lunch with their friends. Or lovers, she thought.

The dining room was large, high-ceilinged and reminiscent of an earlier time, the chandeliers gold and crystal, the floor the ubiquitous dark green marble, spreading out onto a wide-covered balcony that looked out over the hotel's grounds. Beneath them were lush green gardens within which smaller dark shapes scurried to and fro, clearing tired flowers, unobtrusively clipping hedges and clearing paths.

She was shown to a table on the terrace where a light breeze, although not enough to ruffle the hairstyles of the grande dames around them, was slightly less chilly than the air-conditioning. To her surprise the terrace and dining room itself were well patronised, and not just by lunching ladies; a number of tables were occupied by couples, some whose disparate ages suggested a clandestine meeting, and also groups of men in dark suits, whose bodyguards occupied the next table, each one tense and alert, constantly scanning the surrounding area for any unexpected action that might threaten their boss.

As she walked across the room, following the head waiter, Sophie realised that both she and her lunch companion were also the object of some considerable interest from the other tables. She smiled. They probably all thought she was his new lover.

Hugo rose to his feet, elegantly dressed in pale beige and a crisp white shirt, and greeted her with his now customary bow. 'Senor la Torre.'

'Good afternoon, Miss Jenner.'

'Sophie,' she told him, taking her seat opposite.

He inclined his head. 'As you wish, but I also insist you call me Hugo.' The waiter held out a menu which Sophie accepted and a second produced a silver ice bucket containing a bottle of wine. 'Will you join me?' asked Hugo, indicating the wine. She nodded. 'Excellent.'

'But we do need to talk about work,' she said, 'I'm afraid I can't get used to feeling like I'm on holiday.'

'We will no doubt give ourselves a serious case of indigestion,' Hugo commented, 'but, nevertheless, we will discuss work and your business here.'

The waiter poured him a little wine to taste, but Hugo, to Sophie's well-contained amusement merely deigned to sniff it delicately, and then nodded, leaving the man to fill Sophie's glass and his own in turn. He raised his glass. 'Then, if I cannot wish you a pleasant stay, might I suggest we toast a profitable meeting and a successful visit.'

Sophie smiled. 'I think we can run to that.'

'Would you like to order?'

'Why don't I let you do that for the two of us? My spoken Spanish is up to a conversation, but I could get very bogged down in the intricacies of a Peruvian menu!'

Hugo nodded. 'Something light?' He spoke to the waiter rapidly in staccato Spanish before returning his attention to Sophie. 'So, Sophie, please tell me how I can help you.'

Sophie took another sip of wine before answering. 'I need to visit Madre de Dios, discuss the banking systems with the local managers and view the forestry, plantings and village development sites.' Hugo made no indication of surprise.

'Can you tell me why?'

'Not in detail, no.'

'But you think it's important.'

'Yes. Very.'

He sighed. 'Sophie, Deschel Chesham have put a lot of money into the regional economy.' She nodded her agreement. 'But it's not easy for foreign investors to get into Madre de Dios and the regional towns. We have had a lot of bad experiences with foreign businesses making promises about investment, then falling for the opportunity to make a quick profit and failing to clear up behind them.' She nodded again. 'And then there are the loggers, the illegal strip mines.'

'You're not suggesting . . .'

'I simply note that because Deschel Chesham have been very forthcoming with hard currency they have been given access to the country and its people and they stand to make a great deal of profit.'

'In the long term.'

'But I wonder what it is that's brought you out from London, and how you think the so-called "autonomous" local managers will feel when you appear, asking questions and demanding answers.' He paused and looked at her from under dark brows. 'They will wonder whether it has to do with people wanting a quicker return of profits and the taking away of their control.'

The reappearance of the waiter with a large salver stopped the flow of conversation. 'Ceviche,' Hugo said, 'our local delicacy, fish and lime, but beware of the red hot chillies.' The two of them ate for a while until Sophie broke the silence.

'All I want to find is everything working as agreed and as reported, Hugo. I'm not looking for change, simply confirmation.'

'And you cannot accept the confirmation from me?'

She shook her head. 'Not from anybody long distance, I have to see it for myself.'

Hugo gazed at her. 'You will only believe the evidence of your own eyes, yes?'

'Yes. I have my reasons.'

'And you must travel to Madre de Dios.'

'And further into the rainforest if necessary.'

'It will be uncomfortable, difficult and possibly dangerous.'

'How dangerous?'

'Bandits.'

'Oh come on, Hugo!'

'Sophie, it is a poor region, with poor people, and many unscrupulous operators.' Hugo finished his ceviche and the waiter poured the end of the wine into their glasses. 'Not everyone can afford to be so trusting or –' he paused – 'may I be quite frank?' Sophie nodded. 'Few people can afford to be so naive.'

'Me? Naive?'

'You are out of your own environment. You do not understand my country or our culture. You have no idea of the conditions in the rainforest.' He leaned forward. 'Once you have passed through Puerto Maldonado you are in unexplored territory. You think Madre de Dios is a park, but it is not. It is a wild untamed jungle. You think Puerto Maldonado is a town? It is a frontier village, a shanty town. I know what is out there. You have no idea.'

'Nevertheless,' said Sophie, 'I am going to make my trip. Will you help me?'

Hugo gazed at her for a long moment. Then he shook his head in despair. 'Philip Blakemore told me you were stubborn, but I was sure I could convince you.' He nodded slowly. 'Very well, it will be as you wish.'

Their flight from Lima to Cusco in the company's private Lear jet was accomplished seamlessly with Hugo pointing out areas in the high, heavily forested mountain ranges where ancient Inca settlements were reputed to lie.

Now that he had accepted her decision Hugo could not have been more positive or helpful, and although Sophie had tried to persuade him to return to his office, leaving her to make the journey alone, Hugo had insisted that they make the first leg together. It was, he told her frankly, to ensure her success as well as her safety that he would travel as far as Puerto

Maldonado with her, after which he would leave her with responsible and well-instructed guides.

At Cusco, they transferred to a helicopter to complete the last airborne leg of the trip to Puerto Maldonado, a frontier town to the east of the National Park. Here, Hugo left Sophie in the shady interior of a local bar whilst he went in search of a guide for her trip into the rainforest. She was aware of being the subject of intense scrutiny by local Peruvians and reminded herself that it would be best to push her long blonde hair into a baseball cap in future if she was to have any chance of moving around as a private citizen. At long last, Hugo returned with a guide it tow.

'Sophie, this is Juan. He has agreed to be your guide into the Madre de Dios. I have paid half his fee, the rest will be payable on your safe return from the rainforest in two weeks time. He knows the route to Chesham's timber project; he has escorted other Western travellers and business people in the past and is a very experienced rainforest guide. You will be in safe hands.' He paused. 'But it still not like walking through a London street. You must know that. Even now, these are remote areas and wild people live in the forests.' He paused. 'Are you absolutely determined to go?'

Sophie hesitated momentarily. It was not too late to call the whole thing off. She could return to London and let Pip know that he was right, that her suspicions had been wrong. But with a flash of spirit, Sophie put aside her doubts and took a deep breath.

'Yes, Hugo, absolutely determined.' Hugo nodded gravely and for the first time since deciding to set off for Peru, Sophie faced the enormity of her undertaking. She was going to place herself in the hands of complete strangers with whom she would only be able to communicate using schoolgirl Spanish, if at all. She would be journeying deep into the unexplored regions of Peru's high jungle and she really had no idea what was waiting for her in there. Taking a deep breath, Sophie fixed Juan with a full stare.

'Buenas dias, Juan. Mi llamo Sophie.'

The stocky Peruvian stared back impassively. 'Buenas dias.'

'If you are content,' Hugo broke in, 'we will go immediately to the landing stage. There is no time to be lost if you are to reach your first campsite before sundown.'

'Right,' she said. 'Let's get this show on the road.'

The next two days were spent in a motorised dug-out travelling steadily north-west from Puerto Maldonado along the Rio Madre de Dios. Juan was accompanied by two wiry porters responsible for lugging their camping and travelling gear, setting up camp, cooking meals and keeping watch for caymen, the Peruvian equivalent of the crocodile. Sophie was initially unsettled, even scared at times, both by the men's silence and the way she would regularly catch them staring at her as she looked up from studying a map or when eating her meals. At night, she retreated thankfully to her solitary tent but found it almost impossible to sleep, listening to the strange sounds of the jungle as well as the low murmurs of her guides as they talked into the early hours of the morning in incomprehensible Spanish.

As she prepared for sleep on the third night of their trek, Juan indicated to her that tomorrow they would reach their destination. Sophie felt the tensions of the past two days fall away as she realised what Juan was saying; they were actually near to the project camp and she would be able to talk to someone and see what the position was. Telling herself that she had been unfairly suspicious of Juan and his team, she readily accepted a cup of chicha, a fermented Peruvian drink renowned for its restorative qualities when taken in small quantities, and its ability to knock out a horse if imbibed too heavily. Several cups later, Sophie excused herself from the company of her guides and crawled back to her tent where she sank into a dreamless sleep.

She awoke with a start, knowing something was different,

wrong. Confused and with a blinding headache, Sophie struggled to take in her surroundings and comprehend her situation. As she slowly regained consciousness, she heard the whisper of voices and felt hands tugging at her clothes, but it was hearing the rip of material that brought her to her senses and vainly she tried to reach at the hands which, she now realised, were tearing her shirt from her body. Only then did she realise that her own hands were restrained, tied tightly behind her back and, attempting to kick, she found that one of the porters was holding firmly onto her ankles.

'Lie still, gringa, or it will be the worst for you.' She recognised Juan's voice and turning towards the sound she saw that he was seated a few feet away and watching as the two porters stripped the clothes from her body. With a final rip, her shirt was torn from her chest and the men gazed eagerly at her breasts encased in the sheer white cotton of her sports bra, heaving with the exertion of her struggle. 'Take it off,' Juan commanded and the porters immediately obeyed, tugging open the front fastening and pushing the cups of the bra aside to expose her breasts. Sophie knew that her large nipples were hardening as they met the cool night air of the rainforest and she struggled against them once again.

'Stand her up,' Juan snapped. The porters manhandled Sophie to her feet and moved aside, one of them grabbing her long hair and pulling her head backwards. Sophie stood, her feet a little apart for balance, her naked breasts thrust forward with her arms tied behind her back.

'You'll be sorry for this, you bastard,' she hissed, glaring viciously at him.

Without responding to her challenge, Juan barked out another order to the porters. 'Take her trousers down.' He smiled. 'I want to see the goods.'

Immediately, the two porters tore at the fly of Sophie's chinos. The zip was violently ripped apart and the men pushed her trousers unceremoniously over her buttocks and hips to her knees. All three men gave a gasp of surprise as they gazed at Sophie's shaven pubis and one of the porters reached to grab at her breasts with one hand while undoing his own flies with the other.

'Stop,' Juan shouted, striding forward and pushing the porter away, throwing him to the ground. 'She is not for you just yet.'

Standing so close to Sophie that she could smell the faint scent of coca on his breath, Juan reached down between her legs and poked an exploratory finger between the folds of her labia. Holding his gaze, Sophie felt her sex contract at the invasion. 'You have two choices, woman,' he said, rubbing his finger around her clitoris. 'You can lie with me tonight and tomorrow I will show you the way to the site you are seeking. Or I can let them have their way with you and when they are finished – it may take some days – they will leave you here to die.'

Swallowing deeply, Sophie could feel his masculinity against her semi-naked body. Her clitoris had hardened involuntarily against the stroking of his finger and she was becoming undeniably turned on by her situation now that the immediate danger to her life had apparently receded. And in any event, what choice did she have? 'How do I know you'll let me go tomorrow?'

Juan stepped back, a look of mock surprise on his face. 'You have the word of a descendant of the Incas. I only wish to show you great pleasure.'

Sophie wanted to smack him, to tell him what she thought right now about the word of the Incas, but again, she didn't have much choice. Making her decision, she nodded her acquiescence and immediately Juan reached down and helped her step out of her trousers which he tossed to one of the porters. 'In case you try to escape,' he said with a sneer. Then he released her wrists from their restraints and pulled her shirt and bra from her shoulders. Completely naked now, Sophie shivered slightly as the three men stared at her body.

'Lie down on the ground, spread your legs and show yourself to us,' Juan ordered. Sophie complied, reaching between her legs and pulling her labia apart to display the pink flesh between the shaven lips. Both the porters were standing a little way off but Sophie could see that they had released their cocks from their trousers and were masturbating furiously at the sight of her in this prone position. Juan sank to his knees between her spread legs and stared intently at her sex. After several long moments, he stood again and pushed his trousers from his hips to expose his still flaccid cock. 'Get on your knees and suck me, then I will show you what a real man can do, rather than one of your white boyfriends.'

Sophie scrabbled to her knees and took his cock in her hand; it was quite short and thick and its pale flesh sprouted from a thick dark bush of pubic hair. As she touched it, she felt it twitch and begin to grow in length but even more so in diameter. Taking his member in her mouth, Sophie ran her tongue around the bulbous head of the shaft and then began to rock to and fro, sucking the whole length of his cock into her mouth before releasing him again and teasing the head with sharp flicks of her tongue. Holding his cock at the base with one hand, she felt it thicken until it was about twice the original girth.

She could sense the throbbing of his orgasm and she intensified her rhythm as he placed his hands at the back of her head and began to thrust into her mouth. With a groan of release, his come spurted suddenly into her mouth and she tasted the flood of salty liquid as he thrust strongly two or three times before pulling back and pushing her away from him.

Raising her head, Sophie saw the two porters had moved closer to watch her fellatio, their eyes gleaming with desire as they continued to masturbate their cocks and, pulling his trousers back on, Juan looked at them before turning back to Sophie. He smiled. 'Not bad. Now I need a rest but my friends here are in need of your services.'

Sophie stared at him. 'But I thought the deal was you would keep me for yourself.'

'Well, I changed my mind. You will service them as a bitch dog. On your hands and knees.'

She glared at him. 'Fuck you.'

'Do it!'

'I can take you all,' she spat at him, 'and you'll still end up sorry you messed with me.' Sophie turned over and knelt on her hands and knees; she sensed one of the men kneeling down behind her and felt him parting her buttocks to gain access to her sex. Jabbing his penis wildly between her bottom cheeks, he failed to find her hole and pushed her shoulders roughly to the ground so that her cunt became more accessible as her arse was thrust skywards. Jabbing again, he slipped easily into her hole and proceeded to pump in and out of her body. Within seconds, he had reached his climax and his come flooded into her sex. He gave up his place quickly to the second porter who had little difficulty slipping his small penis into her wet hole and repeating the rapid ejaculation of his partner. As he withdrew from Sophie's body, she lay for some moments, panting from their onslaught, her sex dripping with their come mingled with her own juices.

'Tie her to the tree.' Sophie realised there was more to come as she heard Juan bark out his next order and the porters each grabbed one of her arms to raise her to her feet. Dragging her to a nearby tree, they tied her wrists together with one end of a length of rope and slung the other over a branch. One porter kept hold of the free end of the rope, pulling Sophie's wrists above her head and her body against the trunk of the tree.

Juan approached her and this time started to undress slowly with Sophie watching from beneath her long fringe. His torso was hairless, heavy muscles straining under dark skin and when he removed his trousers his short, incredibly thick cock leapt forward, ready again for action. At his sign, the first porter released the tension on the rope, allowing Sophie's arms to fall slightly and Juan reached out to massage her large breasts roughly, bending to take first one nipple than the other between his lips and sucking hard on the tender flesh. As he nipped at her with his teeth, Sophie felt a responsive tingling between her legs and she butted her pubis involuntarily.

'I told you,' said Juan, 'you will thank me for this later.' Pushing her thighs apart by the simple expedient of thrusting his hand between them, Juan began to rub her slit, sliding his fingers high into her vagina. Her sex muscles ached with the onslaught and, impaled on his hands and his mouth, Sophie felt her legs become weak as instinctively she bent at the knees, spreading her sex apart and providing him with access. Taking his cue, Juan also bent his knees and grabbed hold of her thighs, lifting her off the ground and, with a swift movement, lowering her wet hole directly onto his throbbing cock. Sophie gasped with the sensation. He was so thick that even his fingers had not prepared her hole for the width of his entry and she cried out with involuntary pleasure as he began to lift her up and down on his tool. The orgasm swept through her body with the sheer intensity of his stubby cock stretching her cunt wide and she slumped blindly against him. With several more thrusts, Juan released his come and the men cut the rope, letting her body slide to the ground. Stepping aside, he ordered one of the porters to tie her up and the other to bring fresh chicha.

Bound at the wrists and ankles, Sophie was laid on her side at the back of the camp and the three men settled down to drink after their exertions. She listened hard to their murmured conversation but found it difficult to make out much of their meaning as they returned to their native Spanish language. She understood that they were talking about the next day but then she thought she caught the Spanish word for mine, or were they talking about her project site? She was desperate to know what they were planning and when Juan finally turned in her direction, she couldn't stop herself from blurting out, 'What are you going to do with me?'

Standing up and coming over to where she lay, Juan initially made no response to her question. Instead, he untied the rope around her ankles and pushing her over onto her back, he motioned the porters to take hold of her legs and pull them apart.

'I think the question is what are you going to do for us?'

Juan said, stepping back and looking quizzically at her spread body. 'Stand her up again.' On her feet, Juan told her to turn around slowly and when she had done so he seemed to make a decision. 'You will understand that we cannot let you go back now if we are to keep our liberty. You are very beautiful, senora, and I had thought about keeping you for myself. But there would be too many problems and so, alas, I have decided that it will not be possible for me to do that.' Juan paused and took one dark nipple between his thumb and forefinger. Giving it a painful tug, he released her flesh and smiled at the sight of the now puckered teat. 'But it would be a shame to leave you here to the wild animals in the forest. And you have a body which should be used for giving pleasure. So tomorrow we will take you to a place where you will be safe and where you will have many men to please. And who knows but we will meet again when I pass this way in the future?'

He shrugged regretfully and she spat into his eye. The porters to one side chuckled and for a moment Sophie thought Juan would strike her. They glared at each other in silence, then Juan shrugged again and, turning to the porters, told them to tie Sophie to the tree. 'There are three hours until daylight and we should all get some sleep,' he told her, 'although it will be less comfortable for you now.'

'I don't give a fuck,' she snarled, but Juan was immune to her anger.

'Very well, but it will be a long trek tomorrow.'

With her wrists still bound behind her back and her ankles firmly attached to the tree to prevent her escape, the porters draped a thin rug across Sophie's naked body and retreated back to the fire. Her mind was racing to understand the meaning of Juan's words and inside she was raging, but one thing was certain in her mind. Whatever she had to put up with, she was going to get out of here; whatever she had to do, even if it meant she had to crawl through this jungle by herself, she was going to make it out alive. And when she did get out, Sophie told herself, Juan and his friends were going to pay.

Chapter Six

Retribution came quicker than she could possibly have expected.

Sophie awoke with a start; she had been asleep for what seemed only minutes but her mind was razor sharp and all her senses were in overdrive. For a moment she struggled to perceive what had caused her to awake so suddenly and then she tensed as she made out the dim shapes of humans emerging from the depths of the undergrowth around the camp. Some instinct prevented her from crying out and she remained motionless as she watched the men encircle the group of her sleeping guide and his porters. She watched in horror as the invaders pulled out long knives and with silent stealth slit the throats of her captors. The murder was over in seconds.

Cringing back against the shelter of the tree, Sophie was appalled to see the murderers let their victims' lifeless bodies fall to the ground and then, without hesitation, turn in her direction. Without a sound, two of the men approached her, where she was cowering under the thin protection of the rug, and she closed her eyes as she prepared to meet her own fate.

She was surprised as she was pulled to her feet and her ankles were untied. She was surrounded by a group of five or six dark-skinned men who she immediately recognised had the flattened features of the Peruvian Indian. She knew that the Madre de Dios area was home to a number of the remaining tribes of indigenous people, some of which had yet to be contacted by the outside world, but as she opened her mouth to speak, one of the men raised his finger to his lips in an international signal which needed no further explanation.

Wrapping the rug around her naked body, the men motioned her to start walking and pulled her past the corpses of her erstwhile guides into the undergrowth of the rainforest. Dazed and unbelieving of her luck, Sophie did as they bid, stumbling along amongst the group as they cut a swathe through the creepers tugging at her feet and head. They seemed to walk for hours, the men constantly encouraging her to keep up with their brisk pace with prods and tugs, and, as the temperature started to climb steadily, sunlight began to pierce the thick leafy canopy of the forest roof.

Sophie was starting to flag, emotionally and physically, when the men suddenly stopped. Without the crashing noise of their passage, Sophie became aware of the stillness of the rainforest around her in the midday haze, then slowly she made out the faint noise of falling water.

With a shout, the men pushed her forwards and they picked up the pace of their march in the direction of the sound. Minutes later, Sophie was being manhandled down a narrow path carved into the stone sides of a deep ravine. The sound of running water suddenly became much louder and with a rush they emerged from the lush plantation hanging over the sides of the gully to a green clearing, one side of which was taken up with a high waterfall tumbling into a deep, clear pool.

A camp had been set out in the clearing, small huts made from dried rushes fixed with twine and manufactured from the aerial roots of plants growing in the ravine. There was an air of quiet industry about the settlement and, as she took in her surroundings, Sophie saw several men and women at work, cooking and weaving. But their arrival had an almost immediate effect as her captors let out a high shriek and all faces were turned towards them. More people crawled out from the huts, and in all about thirty people came to stand in a circle around Sophie and her captors.

Speaking in a guttural language which Sophie could not understand, the leader of her captors delivered a rapid speech to the assembled crowd after which the onlookers all started to clamour at once, shouting and pointing at Sophie and pressing closer, tugging at the rug which was still covering her nakedness. Suddenly there was a shout from behind the group, which instantly fell silent, turning away from Sophie as if she was forgotten. She saw a tall man standing by the door of the largest hut which was placed by the edge of the pool. He walked slowly over to the assembled group which fell aside to let him approach her. For a long moment he held her gaze. Sophie saw that his features were finer than the Indians around him, his skin paler and his face sharpened by an aquiline nose which spoke of a hint of Spanish ancestry in his Peruvian blood. He barked out a command in the harsh language which Sophie assumed was the incomprehensible Quechua of the indigenous Peruvian Indian race and immediately one of her captors stepped forward to pull the rug from Sophie's body.

There was an audible gasp from the crowd as they gazed at Sophie's voluptuous body, her heavy breasts with their huge dark nipples, her narrow waist accentuated by the curve of her hips, the tiny arrow of golden pubic hair pointing towards her sex, its fleshy lips clearly visible in her shaven state. Sophie still looked straight at the tall Peruvian, trying to ignore the whispers from the crowd around her, but she saw his eyes rake over her body, lingering on her breasts and pussy before returning to her face. He gave another guttural order and a woman moved forward from the crowd, brandishing a long knife. Sophie shrank back in fear; surely they had not brought her all this way just to kill her?

'Stay still.' She froze as the tall man spoke to her in heavily accented Spanish. 'I am the shaman in this place. Do as I say and you will not be harmed.'

The Indian moved behind her and Sophie felt her sawing at the bonds which fastened her wrists. Released, she rubbed the weals on her wrists with a grimace. 'Gracias,' she said softly.

Without responding to her voice, the shaman snapped his fingers and two more of the women in the crowd stepped forward, their eyes lowered. Giving another order in Quechua, he turned and walked away from the group, stooping to re-enter the large hut from which he had emerged minutes earlier. The two women each took hold of one of Sophie's arms and pulled her in the direction of the pool. The rest of the crowd hung back, mesmerised by the sight of her naked, white-skinned body but seemingly wary of following too closely as Sophie walked between the two women to the edge of the water.

Leaving Sophie standing alone, the two women stripped off their rough shifts. Underneath they only wore short wraps around their hips and their dark breasts stood out proudly, free of any support. They both stepped into the water and held out their hands to Sophie, indicating that she should follow them. Realising that she was about to be washed, Sophie eagerly stepped between them and they guided her into the pool which deepened gradually until the water was at waist height. Then the two women began to splash the cool, clear water gently onto Sophie's body, her nipples hardening involuntarily with the refreshing sensation. Pulling her even further into the pool, the women indicated that Sophie should stand on the ledge beneath the tumbling waterfall. The shock of the icy water falling onto her body set Sophie's senses tingling and her dark nipples hardened even further, puckering almost painfully.

Sophie closed her eyes and tilted her head up, letting the freshness of the water re-invigorate her body, shaking out the dust and grime of the past few days. To her surprise, she felt hands start to stroke and caress her body and, as Sophie opened her eyes, she realised that the attendant women had lubricated their hands with oils from stone jars lodged in the recesses of the waterfall. She began to luxuriate in their touch as one woman rubbed the musky scented oils firstly into each of her breasts then over the rest of her torso. The other started at her toes and smoothed the oils into the skin of her feet and legs then, encouraging her to widen her stance with a gentle pressure at the top of her legs, one knelt, quite unashamed, to carefully massage Sophie's sex with her slippery fingers while the other gently prised the cheeks of her bottom apart and rubbed the oils into the tender inner flesh of her ass. It was bliss, and she found herself relaxing and letting her worries ease away. She could have let the sensations of massage and gentle arousal go on for ever, but eventually the women finished their task. First they stood back, letting the waterfall rinse the excess oil from Sophie's body for a few minutes, then they began to coax her down from the ledge and back into the pool. She followed them out of the water, once more central in the gaze of the crowd, now gathered by the water's edge.

She walked forward, fully aware that her body was gleaming, her pale flesh shining with the oils with which the women had lubricated her skin, her long blonde hair already drying in the heavy heat of the afternoon sun that filtered through the trees and into the clearing. With the crowd closing in behind her, Sophie trustingly followed the women in through the door of the large hut by the water's edge. It was gloomy inside and it took several moments for her eyes to adjust to the low light provided by a number of flickering torches at one end of the large circular room. She saw that there was a dais at that end of the room and the shaman was seated there on a large, heavily carved wooden chair. The two women walked forward and, taking off their wraps, knelt naked and on all fours before the dais, touching the ground with their foreheads and pushing their bottoms into the air. Snapping his fingers, the shaman barked an order and the two women rose again, turning back to Sophie and bringing her towards the dais where the torchlight flickered on her pale skin. Behind her she heard the murmur of voices as the tribe crowded into the room after her, but her gaze was held by the shaman's eyes, glittering with the reflected firelight.

She felt dizzy, almost intoxicated and it crossed her mind that the oils had contained some drug, something that was making her this willing to stand here, in front of all these strangers. Then the thought passed; she could do nothing, she was in their power after all.

The two women had moved to cup Sophie's breasts, raising and pushing them together as if to demonstrate the fullness of her flesh, then they turned her round so that she was facing the crowd and, with a gentle pressure on her shoulders, made her bend slightly while easing her buttocks apart to expose her ass to the shaman's inspection. Pulling her back round to face him again, the women each poked a finger between the lips of her shaven pussy and parted the flesh, one of them dipping a finger along her slit to her hole. Withdrawing her finger, the woman placed it in her own mouth, closing her eyes and moaning slightly; the murmuring in the crowd grew louder and Sophie sensed their bodies pressing closer around her.

Silence fell on the crowd as the shaman raised his hand and stood up from the chair. As he stepped from the dais and walked towards Sophie, the two women stepped aside and the crowd fell back again. Suddenly Sophie felt a physical chill and with the drop in temperature the dizzy sensation faded away, leaving a rush of adrenaline in its place, very aware of why she was here and the dangerous position she was in.

'Now you are cleansed. You may speak again. Who are you?' The shaman spoke to her in a low voice.

Sophie hesitated. She was unsure how to play the situation. So far the tribe had seemed to be well disposed towards her but she was still fearful of making a wrong move and her imperative had to be how to get out of here alive.

'My name is Sophie,' she said. There was a sharp intake of breath behind her and the two women attendants fell to their knees beside her along with several people in the crowd.

'How did you come to be in the Madre de Dios?' The shaman ignored the evident consternation of the tribe and continued to question Sophie quietly.

'I know that white men are doing wrong in the rainforest and I came here to try and stop them.' Sophie decided to try and align herself with these people who must surely be opposed to the destruction of their environment.

'Why were you with the traitors from the city?'

'They had captured me and had taken me hostage. Your people rescued me. I am grateful, they would have killed me.'

The shaman looked at her for several minutes without moving his eyes from her face. Then he turned and walked back to the dais, motioning for her to be brought to kneel before him.

'My people think you have been sent by the ancient gods,' he said in a low voice. 'The old ones tell that a woman with hair the colour of the sun will one day come to save them from danger. She serves the gods with her body and she has the power to make the men strong and the women fertile.'

He snapped his fingers as Sophie's mind raced to keep up with what he was saying. One of the women ran from the hut and came back moments later holding a figurine carved from stone. She held the statue up first to the shaman and then before Sophie's face. Sophie saw that the carving was of a woman with long flowing hair. Her heavy breasts were lewdly accentuated as was her incredibly narrow waist; her hips and buttocks were out of proportion to the size of her waist and Sophie could clearly see that there was a tiny bush of pubic hair sprouting above her sex which had also been heavily accentuated, the unbelievably fleshy labia open to reveal the folds of a long cunt and a large, deep hole.

With a shock of understanding, Sophie realised that she must seem to these people to be this figurine brought to life. Looking again at the statue, Sophie saw that the figurine's legs were carved from one piece of stone, her feet moulded into a rounded shape. The attendant stroked the figurine's sex lovingly before placing her feet apart and Sophie watched wide-eyed as the woman plunged the statue feet first into her own hole. Moving her hips rhythmically, the attendant moved the stone dildo in and out of her sex with one hand while rubbing her clitoris with the other. Fine beads of sweat began to break out on her body as she closed her eyes and began to masturbate herself towards a climax under the gaze of the attendant tribe. Sophie felt her own juices starting to flow in her groin as she watched the woman's growing excitement. The woman moaned loudly as she continued to pump the dildo into her sex and a rhythmic chant started up in the crowd. Suddenly, the woman shuddered with the release of her orgasm and she collapsed to the ground, working the dildo back and forth as the waves of her climax subsided.

The shaman stepped from the dais and removed the dildo from the attendant's grip. He held the statue to his nose and then licked the juices of the woman's orgasm from the length of its legs and feet.

'The juices of a woman's arousal are very potent,' he said, handing the dildo to the other attendant who proceeded to pass it round the men in the watching crowd, each repeating the shaman's actions. 'But the juices from the sex of Sofa, sex slave to the gods, are the most potent of all.' Moving close to Sophie and taking hold of her long hair, the shaman pulled her head back so that she was forced to look at him. 'They think you are Sofa.'

Sophie swallowed. 'And what do you think?'

'It does not matter what I think. The will of the people is all. I only serve their needs.' The shaman released his hold on Sophie's hair and stepped back to look at her again. 'There is a ritual tonight at which you will be required to officiate. A first coupling will take place by the waters and you will ensure that the union is a fertile one. I am sure that the gods' slave will not fail them.' His face twisted in a sarcastic smile. 'But now, I must prepare myself for the rite. You will be brought to me as the moon rises.'

With that, the shaman left the hut followed by the now silent tribe. Sophie found herself suddenly alone except for the two female attendants who signalled for her to follow them to a smaller hut near the edge of the settlement. There she found piles of animals furs which she sank into, exhausted by the events of the day. One of the women brought her a cup filled with water drawn from the spring and Sophie drained the clear liquid gratefully, realising too late that once again her refreshment had been doctored by the tribe. The soporific effect of some narcotic was seeping into her body as she sat there, leaving her no alternative but sleep. With a sigh, Sophie fell back on the furs and sank into a deep sleep.

She was woken much later by a gentle hand shaking her shoulder. Sophie stretched her long body luxuriously before focusing on her female attendant who was holding out another cup.

'What is this?' she asked, instinctively wary, but the woman just smiled and nodded, then as Sophie continued to shake her head the woman dipped her fingers into the cup and tasted it, nodding to encourage Sophie to drink. Reluctantly, Sophie took the cup; there was little she could about it, and the liquid was actually surprisingly refreshing, ice-cold with the scent of herbs and something else, something indefinable. Moments later she felt a fiery, stimulating sensation in her belly and she inhaled deeply.

It was only as she handed the cup back to the attendant that she noticed the two females had braided their hair and painted their faces, their eyes heavily outlined with kohl and their dark lips and cheeks rouged. The nipples on their firm dark breasts were rouged and had small gold studs placed at the tips, and in addition they each had a thin gold chain fastened around their waists from which a fine thread was passed from front to back, stretched tightly along the slit between their labia and the cleft between their buttocks. They were still barefoot but gold bands encircled their ankles and a fine gold chain shackled the bands together, with just sufficient slack to allow the girls to walk with small paces; gold bands were also fixed around their wrists and each girl wore a heavy worked collar of the same metal.

Pulling Sophie to her feet, the women indicated that it was time for her to dress. First they brushed her hair, leaving it mainly flowing free but tying two long braids on either side of her face and fixing them together at the back of her head to prevent her hair straying over her shoulders and concealing her breasts. Then they painted her face with make-up similar to their own, outlining her large eyes with kohl and accentuating the fullness of her lips with deep rouge. Next she was adorned with a collar of finest gold, minutely worked with designs which, on closer inspection, proved to be men and women copulating in various positions. From the collar hung many gold threads weighted with precious stones, falling to her navel, leaving her breasts protruding from between the shimmering bands.

One of the women leaned forward to pinch each of Sophie's nipples with fingers that had been dipped into an icy-cold liquid. As Sophie watched her nipples harden she realised that they had also become slightly numb; the reason for this soon became clear. The second attendant eased her to the floor, indicating that she was about to add more make-up and that Sophie should close her eyes. As Sophie obeyed she felt a sharp tingle and gasped with shock, rather than pain. The woman was clipping two rings into each puckered nipple, piercing the skin slightly as she worked the tiny bands of gold through the tender flesh. Sophie stared down, stunned, then watched, completely acquiescent while the attendant smiled and nodded and fixed a small diamond weight onto each ring, ensuring that Sophie's nipples retained their distended shape.

Then, while Sophie was still adjusting to the feeling of her weighted breasts, the females carried a long gold skirt over to her. The skirt had a waistband which sat low on her hips and from which many gold threads hung to the floor; two loops hung from the waistband at each of her hips and the attendants demonstrated how the threads could be pulled aside and attached to these loops to expose either her slit or her buttocks or both. For now they left the threads hanging loose with the effect of a shimmering veil which parted to reveal her long slender legs as Sophie walked about.

Bending Sophie over, the attendants rubbed more of the musky oil into her sex and Sophie felt her tender flesh tingle as the spicy lubricant soaked in. Standing her upright once more, each of her attendants bid her shackle their wrists together with fine gold chains attached to their wrist band. Then, lowering their eyes, the females walked out of the hut, pausing at the door to crook their fingers, making sure that Sophie had understood to follow them.

It was dark outside and the moon was just rising above the rim of the ravine. Sophie saw watching figures in the shadows as she walked behind her attendants towards the large hut. She knew that the threads of her skirt were shimmering as she moved slowly through the settlement.

The tribesmen and women threw themselves to the ground as she passed and Sophie felt a growing feeling of excitement as she sensed the sexual tension in the air. Leading her into the large hut, the women stood aside to let Sophie pass through the room towards the dais where the shaman was once again seated, flanked by two stocky tribesmen.

The shaman stood at her entry and Sophie stepped forward, lowering her eyes as she had seen the other women do earlier. From beneath her lashes, she saw that the shaman had also donned a finely crafted outfit for the ritual; his hairless chest was naked except for two rings piercing his nipples, replicas of her own. A thick gold belt was tied around his waist from which a string of gold braids hung over his groin. His cock was already semi-erect as she approached and had started to poke through the threads; even from this distance Sophie could see that it was thick and long and that he was circumcised, the bulbous head already clearly visible at the end of his shaft.

She cast her eyes to one side, alarmed by her response to the sight and looked instead at the tribesmen at his side. They too were almost completely naked except for gold bands at their wrists and ankles and thick gold collars by which, she realised, they were leashed to rings set in the floor of the dais. Then she saw that their cocks were fully erect, pulling their balls tight, and that gold rings had been fixed at the base of each solid shaft, presumably to ensure that they maintained their erections. Sophie felt the juices of her own arousal beginning to run from her hole at the sight and taking a deep breath to calm herself she was vividly aware of the tug of the diamond weights on her nipple rings and her lips parted involuntarily at the painfully pleasurable sensation.

The shaman stepped down from the dais and moved closer to Sophie, snapping his fingers at the female attendants. Sophie could see that his eyes were slightly glazed, his pupils dilated and his full lips had slackened. One of the attendants brought a cup which she offered firstly to the shaman and then to Sophie. There was a thick, clear liquid in the cup which had no aroma and Sophie hesitated before drinking, only taking a tentative sip when the shaman said, 'You must drink. It is the juice of the gods, the sacred extract from San Pedro. It will help you perform the rite which is expected of you.'

There was a faint sweetness to the liquid and after the first sip, Sophie swallowed the remainder of the draught in one gulp. Seconds later she felt a familiar fiery glow spreading from low in her groin, her brain started to buzz and she felt the room sway. Attempting to recover her senses, Sophie focused on the shaman's penis which was now fully engorged and standing out insolently in front of her.

'A young virgin of the tribe will take a husband tonight. You will share the sacred juices of your arousal with each of them to ensure that their union is fruitful. Your juices will only be potent if you have coupled with the gods as their slave first and for that I will be there to assist you. We have both drunk from the cup of the gods; they are close by. Come. It is time.'

Sophie took in the words of the shaman as if from a distance. At that precise moment all she really wanted to do was to lie down and sleep for a hundred years. But she also had a sense of her body floating weightlessly and made no move to stop him as he tied a leash to her collar and proceeded to lead her from the hut through the silent tribe, waiting expectantly, and down to the dark pool outside. Leaving her by the water's edge, the shaman turned to address the tribe in their own language. As he spoke, they set up a low chanting and Sophie watched as her attendants now brought forward a young man, whilst the shaman's assistants led a young woman, both of them completely naked, to stand on either side of her.

Instinctively, she turned to the woman and caressed her full breasts. Then, placing a hand over her belly, Sophie poked an exploratory finger into the girl's slit. She felt the young virgin tense at her invasion. 'Don't worry,' Sophie said softly, even though she knew the girl could not possibly understand. 'Relax and it will not hurt so much.'

She kept up a rhythm with her finger, alternately circling the girl's small bud and then dipping into the tight little hole of her virgin sex. Slowly she felt the girl relax against her finger and feeling suddenly in control, Sophie signalled to the shaman who brought over a cup of his San Pedro draught. Sophie took a sip and after encouraging the girl to follow suit, she turned her attention to the young man.

He was standing at her side, his eyes staring rigidly ahead, but Sophie knew from the stiffness of his young cock that he was not unaroused by the ritual which was now underway. She took his member in her hand and started to rub her long fingers up and down its length, increasing the pressure of her stroke each time. At her touch the boy groaned and started to buck his hips and Sophie turned to the shaman who stepped forward and snapped a gold cock ring around the base of the boy's eager penis. Momentarily startled, he looked down in panic at his engorged cock, the blood now trapped in the shaft until Sophie should allow him to be released. She ran her finger along the length of his shaft which twitched responsively.

Stepping back, Sophie smiled at the young couple, the girl staring with fascinated excitement at the erect shaft of her husband-to-be and the boy looking at her with equal eagerness as he took in the flush over her full breasts caused by Sophie's stimulation and the effects of the hallucinogenic drink.

Moving closer to the pool's edge, Sophie indicated to her attendants to rearrange her skirt and they stepped forward to draw back the fine threads from front and back and attach them to the loops at her hips. Thus exposed Sophie widened her stance and raised her hands high, throwing her head back in abandonment. The chanting in the crowd increased in pace and loudness and Sophie noticed that several tribesmen were slowly masturbating as they watched the sex scene being played out before them. Lowering her arms, she moved towards the shaman and knelt before him, prostrating herself in the manner of a slave; she knew that her buttocks would be exposed to the crowd in this position and she was rewarded by another increase in the strength of their chanting as the tribe became increasingly excited by her show.

Getting back up onto her knees, Sophie glanced up once at the shaman before taking his huge penis in her hand and guiding it fully into her mouth. She felt him tense and his penis begin to pulse with arousal as she slid her tongue around the velvety head, teasing his tiny slit and sucking hard to extract the first drops of his pre-come. He gave a low moan and moved his hips slowly backwards and forwards, his hand holding the base of his shaft steady as she increased her stroke. As she sensed his orgasm building, Sophie slowed her stroke and reached beneath the shaman's balls and pressed hard to prevent his ejaculation. He let out a deep sigh and pulled his phallus from her mouth, grimacing slightly with the effort and the painful sensation of blood leaving his member.

Helping her to her feet, the shaman held Sophie's gaze for a long moment. She smiled faintly before turning towards the tribe and massaging the mounds of her breasts, pulling slightly on her nipple rings and savouring the sensation which had the direct result of increasing the sense of arousal in her cunt. The shaman gestured to her attendants who moved towards them carrying what Sophie realised was a large dildo fashioned in solid gold. Supported by the shaman's assistants Sophie placed her feet apart and squatted, the lips of her sex pulling apart and exposing her cunt to the watching tribe. She threw her head back again and closed her eyes as the shaman rubbed the dildo along the length of her slit, the cold metal making her clit spring into life from within its fleshy hood.

Dropping to his knees, the shaman dipped the dildo into her hole and Sophie gasped as she relaxed to take its girth within her flesh. Slowly working its shaft in and out of her hole, a little deeper with each stroke, the shaman soon had the dildo buried deep inside her where he let it rest as his assistants allowed her body to slide to the ground. Ordering his assistants to pull her legs apart and back towards her chest, the shaman invited the young couple to come closer and look at the sight of the huge dildo stretching Sophie's pink swollen sex flesh, her clit clearly visible at the top of her slit. He guided the young man and woman to stroke her sex and Sophie moaned quietly at the pleasure of their touch, then the shaman ordered the young man to kneel between Sophie's spread legs and the young virgin to lie down by her side, her legs similarly pulled apart and back by the female attendants. Extracting the dildo slowly from Sophie's hole, the shaman invited the young man to slip his shaft inside her in its place. At the same time, the shaman started to push the dildo, which was dripping with the juices of Sophie's arousal, into the tight hole of the young virgin.

The boy directed his engorged penis at Sophie's cunt and, with a groan, sank his member deep into her swollen flesh, now so stretched by the dildo that she had no resistance to his entry. He started to thrust in and out of her dripping sex, his mounting orgasm prevented from coming to fruition by the ring at the base of his cock. Sophie panted loudly as his groin bumped against her clit, bringing her on towards a climax, but his penis was just a fraction too small to allow her stretched hole to grip him tightly enough.

Meanwhile, the young virgin jerked with the stab of pain as the shaman eased the dildo through her hymen. Removing the dildo as soon as the job of deflowering her was completed, and not wanting her to be disappointed by the size of her husband's cock in comparison, the shaman continued to stroke the inside of her hole with his finger, feeling her relax as the pain died away and she started to move against his digit, mutely asking for more as she tensed the muscles of her sex instinctively.

After a few more minutes, the shaman stopped his masturbation of the young girl and pulled the boy from Sophie's cunt. Releasing his cock ring the shaman led the young man to his new partner, lying expectantly with her legs apart, exposing her swollen sex flesh. The man fell upon her eagerly, and thrust his solid penis into her hole, finding no resistance. She gasped with pleasure at the sensation of his shaft stretching her sex for the first time and they started to thrust energetically together, his buttocks pumping backwards and forwards as he quickly reached his orgasm and flooded his come into her body.

Watching their coupling with a smile of satisfaction, the shaman turned back to Sophie who was still lying prone on the ground. Kneeling between her legs, he ran a finger lightly along her bare slit and thrust his fingers into her hole, feeling the sticky juice of her intense arousal and ignoring the orgy around them as the tribe fell upon one another in a sexual frenzy fired by the ritual they had just observed. His eyes dark with desire, the shaman pulled Sophie to her feet and ordered his assistants to support her into the large hut. There they placed her on her knees before the dais, the torchlight playing on the pale smooth flesh of her buttocks, then left to join the increasingly frenzied coupling outside, leaving Sophie alone with the shaman who seated himself on the dais before her kneeling form.

'That was well done,' he said softly. 'You played your part excellently, Sophie.' Startled by his use of her name, Sophie jerked her head upwards to look at his face. But his expression was hidden in the gloom at the back of the dais. 'However, your credentials as sex slave to the gods are still on trial. The virgin will be isolated from the tribe with two women helpers and we will wait for another full moon to see if your juices have been potent enough to fertilise her husband's seed in her belly. You will wait with them.'

'And if she is pregnant . . .?' Sophie was desperately trying to understand where all this was leading.

'Your status as the gods' ritual sex slave will be confirmed.

120

You will stay with us and serve the gods' every need. Of course, you will be well looked after and protected from any harm.'

'And if she isn't . . .?' Sophie hardly dared ask the question.

'You will be exposed as a fraud. The tribe will decide your fate. I will be unable to help you then.'

Sophie stared at the shaman for a long moment as the meaning of his words sank in. So going along with the ritual had only served to make her position even more precarious, or so it seemed.

'And how are you helping me now exactly?' she asked bitterly.

The shaman shook his head slightly. 'Your appearance . . . there was very little I could do. My people follow the old paths . . .' His voice trailed away again. 'If I could do more for you I would, but I have already told you, I am a servant to the tribe and our gods.' His voice hardened. 'As you now are.'

They sat in silence for long minutes. 'So what can I do?' asked Sophie.

She thought he was smiling again, although his voice was also sad. 'You can only do what the gods desire.'

Sophie studied him, lost. He seemed to have changed greatly from the hard, controlled man in charge of the ritual outside. Maybe he felt he couldn't do much, but surely if he was more sympathetic towards her . . .? Moving into an upright kneeling position, Sophie arched her back so that her breasts were fully on display. She shifted her position slightly so that her knees were spread apart, exposing her cunt to the shaman's gaze. 'My magic has not yet reached its fruition,' she said, easing one finger between her labia and rubbing her clit back to its erect state. 'I need to achieve an orgasm for the gods before the virgin can conceive.'

She could not see the expression on the shaman's face but the twitching of his cock told Sophie that her words and body were having the desired effect. Standing, she approached the dais slowly and mounted the steps to stand before him. Sophie untied the collar from her neck and laid it to one side. Then

121

she repeated her action with the gold beaded skirt. Naked now except for her nipple rings and their tiny weighted chains, Sophie stood for a moment allowing the shaman to feast his eyes on her pale, slender body, then, climbing onto the chair so that she was kneeling astride his seated body, she took his erect penis in one hand and started a slow massage along its length. With a small groan, the shaman took the offered nipple between his lips and tugged slightly on the weighted chain attached to her nipple ring. The response in Sophie's groin was immediate and she felt her sex juices starting to flow again. As the shaman started to suck hard on her whole puckered nipple, Sophie directed his enormous phallus at her sex and sank onto the erect member, impaling herself on his hard shaft and driving him deep into her body with one long stroke. She let out a sigh of contentment as she felt his flesh stretch her hole wide open and she remained seated there for several moments, savouring the feeling of fullness in her cunt. Squeezing her sex muscles tightly, she was rewarded as his eyes glazed and his head fell back, releasing her nipple from the exquisite torture of his lips and teeth. Sophie began to move her buttocks up and down, allowing his cock to slide out of her hole almost to the tip before clenching her muscles again and driving him back inside her with a downward stroke. As she heard his breathing become laboured, she increased the pace of her rhythm and closed her own eyes, concentrating on her own pleasure and working towards her own climax. Her breasts began to jiggle with the frenzy of their coupling and the shaman took hold of her hips, encouraging her to increase the length and speed of each stroke of her sex along his shaft.

With a shout of triumph, Sophie's orgasm flooded through her cunt and outwards to her belly and breasts, her mind exploding with the burst of pleasure as her sex muscles spasmed against his throbbing cock. Grunting, the shaman forced Sophie's body deep down onto his shaft, grinding his hips into her spread cunt and she felt the rush of his orgasm pulsing into her body as he came with a long moan of pleasure.

Spent, they moved their bodies together in a slow rhythm, extracting the last ounces of pleasure from the contact of their sex flesh, sticky now with the juices of their orgasms. Then, reluctantly, Sophie rose, the shaman's rapidly deflating cock slipping easily from her hole.

'Stand up,' she heard him say and obeying, she climbed down from the chair and found herself face to face with her lover as he also stood up from the chair. Tilting her chin up with one finger, the shaman looked deep into Sophie's eyes before lowering his lips to her mouth and parting her lips gently with his tongue. His kiss was deep and long and Sophie's head buzzed with the sensation of his tongue exploring her inner flesh. Releasing her mouth and raising his head at last, the shaman took a step backwards. 'I hope that your magic works, Sophie,' he said quietly. 'You will leave me now and go to your charge.'

As if by telepathy, Sophie's two female attendants of earlier in the evening appeared from the darkness behind the dais and Sophie wondered if they had been present throughout her lovemaking with the shaman. They led her away through the camp which was now silent after the frenzy of the sex orgy, to a hut placed at a distance to the rest of the settlement. Behind them a guard materialised, an old man, apparently immune to the effects of the rite, but one who held a long, vicious spear. Sophie was not to escape; neither was anyone else to enter apparently.

One side of the hut was laid out with piles of animal furs and the young woman on whose fertility Sophie's immediate survival depended was already fast asleep among this soft bedding. Taking Sophie to the other side, the two females washed her body carefully with cool spring water, paying particular attention to her cunt, making her squat while they washed the sticky juices of her orgasm away, cooling her tender, stretched sex flesh. Then they led her to the piles of furs where all four females lay down to sleep.

However, Sophie's mind was too active to sleep immediately.

She felt that she had done the right thing by making love to the shaman, and maybe his kiss before dismissing her had indicated that he had not been unaffected emotionally by her. If only she was allowed to work on him over the next few weeks, there could still be a chance she would survive her young companion not being pregnant by the time of the next full moon. Still musing over how precisely she was going to get the shaman to make love to her again, Sophie eventually fell into a deep sleep.

She was woken by the sound of female giggling close by, deep in the animal furs. The light of early morning was filtering through the half open door of the hut, and Sophie shifted her position to see what was causing the humour. Her eyes widened as she realised that the female voice had been joined by the immediately recognisable sounds of a rutting male. Sure enough, the female giggles were stifled and turned into small moans of pleasure as Sophie noticed a pair of hairy buttocks bouncing up and down between the spread legs of her young female charge. Their climax was reached quickly and the sounds of young eager sex subsided as the couple kissed quickly and the boy extracted himself from between his lover's legs, heading for the door and melting into the early-morning half-light, the guard nodding his approval as he went. Sophie smiled and turned back on her side to doze again until morning. If last night hadn't done the trick, she could at least hope the determination of the two young lovers would make sure that the tribe celebrated the next full moon with a pregnancy!

After breakfasting on mango juice and warm flatbread, Sophie decided that there was no time to lose if she was to push home her advantage of last night. Her attendants had dressed her in a finely woven, almost transparent white shift, cinched at the waist with a broad gold belt that pulled the material tight against her full breasts. Knowing that she would be irresistible to any full-blooded male in this outfit, Sophie indicated with signs that she wished to be taken to the large hut but she was momentarily confused when her attendants began shaking their heads. Raising herself to her full height, Sophie repeated her request with as much authority as she could muster. As the girls continued to shake their heads, finally drawing pictures in the ground with a stick, signing and using what few words of halting Spanish they could muster, Sophie eventually realised that they were telling her the shaman had left the camp early that morning.

She closed her eyes and sighed deeply. It seemed that these females did not know when the shaman would return. Rest, they were telling her, rest and be content. They would make sure she had everything she wanted; the shaman had ordered that it be so. She glared into the wall of the tent. Well, it looked like her plans would have to be put on hold until the shaman returned from wherever he had gone. Meanwhile, she would make damn sure that her young charge had every opportunity to let her lover get in between her legs. Some insurance policy!

Chapter Seven

The sun was high in the sky and inside the hut the temperature was becoming uncomfortably hot. Like much of the rest of the tribe, the newly married Shipa and the two unnamed attendants were having a siesta, snoring gently, their arms and legs sprawled out in unconscious abandon, storing up their energy for the remainder of the day.

Sophie eyed them carefully until she was sure they were all deeply asleep, then quietly crossed the hut, stepping across their supine bodies with as little noise as possible. She lifted the cover that hung across the entrance to look out into the stern, impassive eyes of a new guard, sitting ten feet away, watching her intently. She glared at him for a moment but he stared back steadfastly and she retreated inside reluctantly, letting the curtain fall back down. This one was younger and infinitely more attentive than the old man of last night; if he was on duty this evening she had no doubt that Shipa's young husband would be barred from access.

Copying the other women, Sophie lay down and tried to relax. Time to go over her options again; there was no telling when she might need to make a move to get out, even if it obviously wasn't going to be today.

So, what could she do? Well, firstly, could she try bargaining her way out with the men? That thought was almost laughable; there was no way this bunch were susceptible to the promise of sexual favours from their gods' slave; they'd expect to be struck down at the very least.

What about the women? Shipa would probably be scared

witless, if she knew Sophie was aware of her husband's night-time visits. But would she help her get out? Or could she be blackmailed into helping? That was a whole different question.

Could she bribe her way out with anyone else? Unlikely. The tribe all seemed devout and convinced of the gods' existence. All, that is, except for the shaman. Sophie stopped for a moment; he seemed so different to the rest of the tribe. She had replayed their conversation a dozen times now and she was more and more convinced that although he was in control of the spiritual activities of the tribe, his devotion to the faith was less than rigorous. Perhaps it was linked to his ability to speak Spanish, perhaps he had been living outside the tribe at some point, perhaps . . . with an effort Sophie dragged her wandering mind back to reality, fighting to concentrate against the debilitating heat. It didn't matter what the shaman thought about his gods, or where he had been in the past, she had to focus on how to use any knowledge she could scrape together. And to stop drinking anything they gave her; unless it was water straight out of the pool she wasn't touching it, no matter what they said.

She focused on the problem again; she had a month before things turned nasty if the boy had been firing blanks, and surely Pip would be organising a search for her. So, the chances were that she would be rescued, if she could find a way out and into another part of the jungle.

She had to work harder with the shaman, get to know his name, if he had one. He liked screwing her, that was for sure, and more than that, he liked her, she was certain of it. She thought back to their time alone together; he was gentle when he wasn't performing for the tribe. Surely she could use that to get round him somehow and use that to get out.

Because you are getting out of here, Sophie told herself. You are getting out of here no matter what! She pushed to the back of her mind the knowledge that much of the rainforest was inaccessible or simply unexplored. And enormous. She had to start doing something. There was no way she was sitting around waiting to die in the jungle. She turned over in the bed, her mind spinning. Surely, if she could just get out then there would be bound to be search parties? English banking executives didn't disappear into the bloody Peruvian rainforest every week, for God's sake!

The eighth day dawned the same as usual, clear and bright. The weather at this time of year was hot and dry, but soon, in less than ten weeks in fact, Sophie knew it would change and the rainy season would reassert itself. For seven months.

She certainly wanted to be out of here by then.

Sophie emerged from the tent, dressed in the tribe's typical day-costume of a short woven wrap around her hips. She had quickly got used to the tribal habit of walking around either near-naked, or at least topless, and now she was comfortable with her breasts hanging free, although the contrast between her own large rounded bosom, and the smaller flatter teats of the tribal women was enough to make children and grown men stare at her. Even after a week they still hadn't stopped staring. Occasionally she had wandered up to a guard and asked a question in Spanish, pretending to be desperate for some information, letting her breasts brush against him, stretching her arms up to let him get a good look, but her initial instincts about their behaviour had been correct. They might find the sight of her exotic and stimulating, and she had caught more than one with a steadily growing erection as he watched her, but their fear of the gods was such that they would not willingly touch her.

She wandered through the camp, eyes following her wherever she went as usual, and as usual she stopped in front of the shaman's hut. 'Is he back?' she asked the impassive tribesmen standing guard, even though she knew they couldn't understand English. 'Is he back?' She tried again in Spanish but there was as little response to this as to the English and she simply couldn't work out how to ask the question in native Quechua. She turned away in disgust and started her walk to

129

the pool when a voice from the hut stopped her in her tracks.

'Si,' said the voice. 'Yes, he is here.' Her head jerked up to see the shaman emerge, tall, handsome and very controlled. For a moment Sophie was left speechless, and irrationally delighted, then she got a grip of herself.

She put her hands on her hips, noting the way the tribesmen had to work to ignore her nakedness. 'I was wanting to talk to you –' she jerked her head – 'but they didn't know when you would return.' He nodded. There was a long pause as they studied each other.

'So. You wish to talk with me.'

She nodded impatiently. 'That is what I said,' she muttered to herself in English.

The shaman smiled. 'Patience is a virtue,' he told her in perfect English.

Sophie stared at him, the impact of words leaving her speechless. 'You speak English!' He didn't respond, and she knew that his words were something he was already regretting. 'Why didn't you say anything? And how . . .?'

'It is not important,' he replied in Spanish once again, turning towards his hut. 'But if you wish to speak with me, you may.'

She glanced around at the guards. 'Alone.'

He turned back to face her once again, a shadow of irritation crossing his face as he spoke loudly in Spanish and Quechua, for the sake of the guards she was sure. 'You belong to the gods. You cannot be left alone with any man.'

'That's crap,' she snarled in English. 'Complete crap and you know it.'

For a moment there was the glimmer of amusement on his face, then the haughty patrician features settled back into their usual stern line. 'My absence has made you bold, Sofa.'

Sophie's temper flared. 'My name is Sophie as you bloody well know. And maybe I'm bold because I've been cooped up here, watched by everyone around me. And maybe I don't give a damn what you do to me any more.' She stormed towards

130

him. 'You think you can keep me here? Waiting to see if some poor stupid kid gets pregnant, waiting to be strung up when she doesn't? Well, you can just piss off, you and all your tribe.' Her voice sneered. 'You're just a bloody bunch of savages and you can all fuck off for all I care.'

The shaman turned and strode back towards her, grasping her chin in his fingers and tilting her head up to his. 'My people are not savages,' he hissed.

'From where I'm standing they are,' she snarled back.

'I didn't see you putting up much of a fight at the ritual,' he sneered at her. 'Not with anyone, or anything.'

'Stuff enough drugs in the drink and you'll get anything what you want,' she spat at him, anger making her fearless.

'There were few drugs, Sophie, it was just your own real nature at work.'

She flushed and they stood, glaring at each other until he released her, almost pushing her over in a convulsive movement. He gestured sharply to the tribesmen, but they began to argue. With an angry expression, the shaman snarled an answer and they fell silent, dropping back and allowing Sophie to join the shaman at the entrance to his hut. 'Join me.'

She took a deep breath and re-entered the hut for the third time since her arrival. The dais was there, but the room was fresher and lighter; however the shaman ignored the dais and guided Sophie to two stools in the corner of the room.

He watched Sophie carefully. 'What do you want to talk to me about?' He had reverted to Spanish.

She stared up at him. 'Why must you keep me here?'

'You know why. You are the slave to the gods.'

She shook her head. 'Please, you don't believe that, I know you don't.'

He stood. 'There is nothing I can do for you at present. Do not try to test me, Sofa.'

She looked up at him and reached out to take his hand. It was warm and smooth; these were not the hands of a working tribesman, she thought.

131

'Please, you're the only one who can help me.' He stared down at her, his pupils dilating, and she let her fingers run up his arm towards his shoulder. The hut was very silent, and the sexual tension between them was growing. She could feel her own desire, unadulterated by any drugs, and beneath the kilt she could see the shaman becoming seriously aroused.

She reached up and kissed him, his cheek, then his lips; his body was stiff and strong beside hers, rigid, the muscles locked as she ran her fingers across his chest, and then down, to where his cock quivered and she ran her fingers down the length of it, his breathing stilted and tentative under her touch.

Then he drew away. 'I cannot help you.'

'Please.'

'No, you are Sofa.'

She stroked his face. 'My name is not Sofa, it is Sophie Jenner. I have a home and a life in England. I came here to help your country, and now you're threatening to keep me here, to kill me.' He walked away from her, shaking his head. 'Please,' she tried again. 'Talk to me. Tell me your name.'

He stared out of the window. 'I have no name. I am the shaman.'

She shook her head. 'I don't believe that, you speak Spanish, and you speak some English too. You have a name people use outside the tribe.' She stopped abruptly as sudden knowledge overwhelmed her. 'That's where you've been, to the town, to civilisation.'

It was the wrong thing to say. His face contorted. 'Civilisation? This life is civilised; you and your kind, you are the barbarians. You strip our land, my land, of everything and leave it, polluted, wrecked, open to the elements whilst you go back to the West with a fat profit.'

Sophie shook her head. 'No. That's why I'm here, why I was travelling in the jungle. We're working with your people, trying to make things better, set up proper projects where your people can control their own destiny, without leaving the land in a mess.'

132

'And who is "we"?'

'My business. Deschel Chesham.'

He stiffened. 'You know the name,' she said eagerly, 'then you must know what we are doing. What we stand for.'

'Who do you work with?'

She took a gamble. 'My boss, he is also my lover. We belong together. I want to leave and go home to him.' The shaman didn't seem interested in her plans to describe a happy home life however.

'Your partner, you think he will come and rescue you? That is why you wanted to talk to me? To warn the stupid savage of his arrival.' Sophie blushed again.

'No, I just want to convince you to let me go. Pip will look for me yes, but . . .'

She gasped as he gripped her wrist. 'Who?'

'My boss, Philip Blakemore.'

The shaman glared at her then threw her back on the stool, all intimacy lost. 'Your plans stops here.'

'What?'

'I know what you're up to.'

'I don't understand, I just want to get out and go home.'

He leaned across her, very masculine and very close. 'You will stay; if the girl is pregnant the tribe will let you live, if not I will personally see that you die!'

He strode to the door and summoned the guards, snapping orders in Quechua. Then he turned back to Sophie. 'Your plan has failed, but your words have alerted me. We will move and your lover –' his words dripped with venom – 'your lover will never find us in our new camp.' He motioned to the guards. 'For now you will remain in the hut, you will not leave. You will not participate in the ritual of cleansing. You will stay there until we depart this place and if you try to escape you will be killed.'

Sophie stood. 'I don't understand.'

'I think you do.' He drew away and as she passed him she knew he was deadly serious. She walked, her head held high, confused and uncertain, hearing harsh orders given from behind her. Even before she reached her little hut it was clear that the camp was in a flurry of activity; men, women and children were running to and fro, collecting bowls, implements and brushwood, collapsing huts, crushing some parts but saving others. It was all organised, and everyone knew their place, it seemed. She was the only outsider. She crossed the threshold of the hut and heard the cover drop down behind her, but when she looked about she was all alone.

Shipa and the attendants were clearly all outside joining in the preparations for the departure or the impending ritual of cleansing. Adrenaline rushed through Sophie's body and she opened the cover a fraction of an inch. The guard was there in front of her, but his attention was somewhat distracted by the ordered chaos and unusual noise and activity behind him.

She closed the cover and crept to the back of the hut; the shaman had not intended to have her left alone, and who knew how long it would be before Shipa was sent back or the noise died down? She looked at the back of the hut; it faced onto the wall of the ravine. There was a path to one side, she knew it well enough, she had studied the entire camp every day for the last week. Once she got onto the path she could hide behind the aerial roots, she just needed a few minutes' grace to get out and away and then she could start running. She cast a glance back through the entrance, and with a determined effort started to beat her way through the wattle wall.

Pip looked out at Daria Williams, sitting in the middle of the front row of analysts and reporters. She was sitting demurely, legs crossed at the heel, reading her notes and ignoring the mêlèe around her. She seemed to come from another world, a very different place to the rest of the journalists around her; no plain grey suits or casual dress for Daria, she wasn't interested in blending in. She was wearing a striking jade suit, a move designed to enhance her colouring and her red hair, and one that made her stand out, like the only colour picture in a book of black and white photos. The few other women in the room looked plain, dowdy and insipid in comparison, and were giving her flickering glances of loathing from their less obtrusive positions on the edge of the crowd.

Daria knew all this and didn't care. As Pip watched, she uncrossed and re-crossed her long slim legs, now allowing her skirt to expose rather more thigh, her blood-red nails flashing to and fro, flicking through her notes. What she was thinking was unclear, but when she looked straight at him, into the camera and through the wall, he suspected she was thinking about sex. She had that distant look in her eye.

The question was, why was she here? She had no interest in City announcements, she was a features journalist for a woman's magazine. Was it him she had come back for? Or did she know something about what he was going to be saying? He scanned the room, studying the other journalists; finance hacks mostly. No more than he had expected; he had been dropping hints for a few days now. Nothing serious, just enough to suggest uncertainty about Sophie's whereabouts, amongst other things. But still, none of that would have got back to someone like Daria, would it? He pushed his chair away from the monitor. Finding out why she was here would be an interesting experience.

When he walked into the conference room the place erupted.

'Mr Blakemore! Are the redundancy reports true?'

'Mr Blakemore! Sarah James, Videonews. World-watch and eco-groups are boycotting your business. Is it true?'

'Mr Blakemore.'

'Philip!'

'Mr Blakemore.'

He ignored them all and headed for the dais, where he stood waiting for the noise to subside. He avoided everyone's gaze and simply waited, calmly, until the room was completely silent. Then he looked at his audience. Before any of the usual hacks could speak a female voice piped up.

'Mr Blakemore?' It was Daria Williams. 'What do you have

to say to reports of widescale embezzlement and the channelling of ring-fenced funds into strip mining?'

Even Pip was caught off guard for a moment. Bitch, he thought furiously. He stared at the reporter, sitting elegantly attired and relaxed in the front row, smiling up at him with a beguiling, teasing look on her face. His own expression was all the answer she needed and the room erupted again. Vainly, Pip tried to calm the questioners. 'Just a minute. Please. Please!' The noise subsided again.

'I have a statement and that is all I will say at the present time.' There was a subdued muttering from around him as he took the paper out of the folder; he knew what he was going to say but as he looked at Daria Williams, Pip wondered what was going on in her head.

'I have called this meeting to resolve some unsubstantiated comments and rumours. Ms Sophie Jenner left England on an unauthorised visit to Lima, Peru three weeks ago. She has not made contact with the business or any member of the senior management team since that time.' The buzzing was starting up again and Pip had to raise his voice to get the rest of the statement heard. 'We are, of course, extremely concerned for Ms Jenner's whereabouts, but in light of her disappearance we have begun a private investigation and suspended business in the meantime.' Chaos broke out, people were asking questions and sticking microphones on his face. Pip turned to leave, catching sight of Daria Williams' face. How the hell did she know anything about embezzlement? And why her? 'I am sorry I have nothing more to say at the present time.'

But the reporters weren't giving up that easily.

'What about the embezzlement?'

'Do you think it was Sophie Jenner?'

'Is that why the fund is closed?'

'Are you going to call in the receivers? The SFA? The fraud squad?'

They were really running with the idea now, and determined to get more information.

'Do you think Sophie's safe?' Once again Daria Williams' contralto cut through the noise.

Pip stopped and turned, sad and distressed as only a betrayed mentor could be. He sighed and looked into the cameras, apparently forced to make a comment he had fully intended to withhold. 'It is our belief that Ms Jenner is safe and has no intention of returning to the UK.' Bravely holding back the emotion, he continued towards the door. 'Now I am very sorry but we have nothing more to say.'

It took a while, but eventually the security department managed to get the journalists to leave. All except one.

Daria came in through the door of Pip's office, smiling at his secretary. He stood up to greet her, suave, attractive and charming. 'How are you, Ms Williams? It's a pleasure to see you again.'

She took his hand and shook it firmly, waiting until the door closed behind her. 'Let's cut straight to the chase, Mr Blakemore.' He raised his eyebrows. 'Your minions asked me to come and visit and I thought it would be interesting. I hope you don't disappoint me.' Pip said nothing, sat back in his seat and waved her to a chair in front of the desk, but she stayed on her feet, studying him. 'That was quite a touching little speech you made back there.' Pip remained silent. 'You two were screwing, I assume?' No reply. She smiled. 'Fine. I hope you don't mind if I make myself comfortable.'

Apparently at ease she slipped off her jacket, unbuttoned the top three buttons of her silk shirt and strolled across to the refrigerator in the corner. She pulled out a bottle of beer, snapping the top off with ease and tipping her head back to let it pour down her throat, one hand on her hip, her thick auburn hair falling down her back; an exercise in studied and deliberately provocative behaviour. Pip watched silently from the depths of the black leather armchair behind his desk. Daria's breasts were unrestrained beneath the shirt and he could see the swelling of pale, pale skin, even paler than normal against

137

the soft cream of her blouse. She watched him watching her and strolled back over to his chair.

'You've been thinking about me,' she said. 'I saw you watching me. The last time I was here as well as when you were out there.' Pip's lips twitched. 'So,' Daria teased him, taunting him with her words and her body as she sat down in the chair opposite. 'Shall we have an interview? A little discussion? You could give me an exclusive on the background behind Sophie's strange disappearance.'

'I've said all I want to say about Sophie.' Pip kept his temper under control and gave her a charming smile. 'But we can get on with our interview if you like.'

Daria re-crossed her legs and slid them sidewards, exposing as much of her thighs as possible. She finished her beer before answering. 'I've got lots of questions for you, Mr Blakemore.'

'Like?'

'Like why you are booked on a flight to Lima?'

'Obviously I'm going to look for Sophie.'

'With no return date?' He shrugged. 'Not exactly your area of expertise, is it? Flying off into the unknown.'

'Lima is hardly the unknown.'

'Oh? I assumed you'd follow her into the jungle.'

'Why would Sophie have gone into the jungle?'

'You tell me. In any case,' Daria went on, 'it's interesting, the world is such a small place, don't you think?' Pip shrugged, somewhat nonplussed. 'Well, first I interview Sophie, now you, and in between I had a long chat with that other woman, what was her name? Oh yes, India James.'

Pip stiffened. 'I believe Sophie uses India James for various –' he paused – 'minor business analyses.'

'Really? I thought it was something rather more important. However, back to our interview.' She smiled, the vague hint of threat dissipating. 'Please, tell me about yourself.' Daria slid out of the chair and perched vampishly on the side of the desk. Pip ignored it.

'I'm just an ordinary guy.'

138

Daria laughed. 'Oh come now, Pip, I may call you Pip, mayn't I? That's hardly true. You're wealthy, clever and sexy.'

'I've worked hard to get here,' he acknowledged.

'So what do you do at home?'

'I think that's my business, don't you?'

'Do you make a habit of screwing your business associates?'

'Do you make a habit of screwing your interviewees?'

She laughed. 'A habit? No. But if I see someone I like I might see what they're made of and really do some proper investigating.' She paused and leaned forward to draw her red talons down across his chest. 'And the first time we met I thought, "I should do a little digging into his personality and find out what it is that hard bastard is made of". That's why I'm here.'

Pip raised his eyebrows. 'And this is digging into my personality?' He stretched out a hand and stroked her thigh. 'I don't think you're here looking for questions and answers. I think you're here to get a good screwing.' His fingers moved up her thigh, a single finger sliding up to the warm open cleft between her legs. He could see the thin line of a cream silk G-string and, when he slid his fingers further, her pussy hair was soft and long, hiding the damp hole within. 'What happened?' he asked with a smile, 'Did your boyfriend let you down last night? Leave you gagging for it?'

She took his hand off her thigh and slowly ran her lips around his index finger, sliding it in and out of her mouth. She leaned forward as though to kiss him, both watching the other's responses, both playing the game.

'You bastard, I told you to meet me in Room 106.'

Pip shrugged. 'Sorry, something came up in the office.'

'Yes,' she answered, putting his fingers back on her thigh. 'I saw her at the desk as I came in. Pretty little thing, I bet she gives good head.'

'Probably better than you.'

'You should have come around to find out!' Daria's face was contorted into rage and she leaned forward again, running

139

her nails down his cheek, waiting for him to flinch. He didn't. 'You really are a hard bastard, aren't you?'

She stood up and walked back to the fridge, leaning down to pick out a bottle of champagne. When she stood up her face was clear again. 'Do you like the look of my ass?'

'Very trim.'

'A bit big, but men like big asses, don't they?'

'Like I said, it's very trim.'

'You're in a mess, my boy. That business is fucked. If you couldn't see it the media boys definitely could.'

'With your help.'

She shrugged. 'That's a matter of opinion. Can you take the pressure?'

'I do my best.'

'Did you send Sophie abroad?'

'You heard my statement.'

'Yes, but I didn't believe it.'

'That's an odd thing to say.'

'I know what a good liar you are.' She stopped and leaned towards him, making a claw of her fingers and placing it directly over his crotch. 'And I wonder what's really going on out there. Where Sophie really is.' She smiled. 'And I know other people are asking the same questions.' With one finger she started to tease the cock inside the trousers, apparently probing it for a response. 'Just checking for stiffness,' she explained, 'in case it was terminal flaccidity that stopped you from meeting me last night.' Daria eased the notch on Pip's belt and drew it out of the restraining loops. She slid it out and threw it into one corner of the room as Pip reached out to the answerphone.

'I'm in a meeting. No calls.'

'Shall I leave the shirt on or off?' Pip looked up into her eyes and Daria leaned over and gripped his head, long red talons cradling his face below hers, drawing him up to her lips to kiss him hard, leaving dark red lipstick on his lips when she withdrew. 'Not bad,' she said, predatory claws drawing across his cheek as she walked around the chair to the window behind.

As she walked she caught the chair and swivelled it to face her. She really was quite magnificent, Pip thought, and dominating. And she knew it, the slut. She stood in front of him, at least five foot ten in her bare feet, that incredible hair falling in waves over her shoulders, almost as far as her breasts, hanging loose of the blouse, hidden by the silk, but with the darkness of her aureolae visible through the sheer material, the nipples brushing against the fabric, just rough enough to make them erect.

His body was dying to grab her and screw her right there, straight up and without waiting, ripping that little G-string off and fucking her until she screamed. Daria watched him, an amused little expression on her face. 'I know exactly what you're thinking,' she told him, leaning back against the window ledge and gently arching her back, playing with the open edge of her shirt, undoing another button.

'Do you?'

'Oh yes, you'd be surprised how often men get that dimwit "let's have her now" expression on their faces. But I like to take things slowly.' Pip flicked a switch on the desk and the door lock turned. He stood up and joined Daria at the window, tentatively reaching inside the blouse to cradle a pale, creamy breast. Daria unzipped his trousers and felt inside, raising her eyebrows. 'Well, well. So the rumours are true.'

'What do they say?'

'Some of them say you're a total bastard who'd sell your mother for a deal.' She cocked one eyebrow. 'Or were they saying you'd sell your girlfriend without a second thought? I can't quite remember.'

'You shouldn't believe everything you hear.'

'Others say that you've got a stud-sized cock and a huge appetite for sex hidden beneath that business head.'

'They're right.'

'Confident, aren't you?'

'That's how I got to be here.'

She smiled and slid her finger between the folds of his jockey shorts, teasing the swollen cock out of its resting place. 'We'll just have to see where you sit on the scale of things.' She ran a finger down the substantial length of thick male member. 'Brown, aren't you?'

'I like to sunbathe in the nude.'

'Do you? Well, that's something my readers don't know. Yet.'

Daria pushed him back into the leather chair, dropped to her knees and exposed Pip's cock. Full and hard, she surveyed it carefully for a moment, then slid her ruby lips around it and sucked gently. There was a sudden intake of breath, a slight soft hiss as Pip tensed, then relaxed at her touch. His hands reached out and grasped her hair, playing with the curls, absent-mindedly grinding the locks into a tousled mop.

She was very practised at fellating a man, he knew that immediately. Her fingers held him in check, and her mouth sucked him into her, then released him and slid back to let him slide from her grasp; almost but not quite. Then she deliberately began to tease him, massaging the head of his cock and running her tongue around the ridge, the widest part of him, down to the base and up again, holding the folds of skin back with care and running her tongue around the tip, the rim and finally into his slit, tasting the semen and the textures of all parts of his cock until Pip was ready to let himself go into her mouth. With determination he pushed her back slightly.

'Now,' she pouted, staring up at him from beneath dark thick eyelashes, 'what's the matter with you? Can't you take it? Surely you're not going to tell me I'm too much for you?' He glowered at her, and then a smile broke across his face.

'You bitch, you were trying very hard to make me come, weren't you?'

She smiled back. 'Perhaps I was being just a bit of a tease.' She rocked back onto her high-heeled shoes and Pip pushed her flat on her back and dropped out of the chair to straddle her chest, kneeling across her.

Daria smiled up at him and stretched out her glorious body, letting him see the round, upturned breasts exposed in full at last, as her blouse fell to each side. Her eyes watched his expression, but her big luscious mouth fell open slightly, just as if she knew what he was planning.

Pip leaned over her, pulled his trousers down and rammed his cock in her smiling, teasing mouth, pushing it deep into her. At first he pushed it so far inside that he was sure she would start gagging and for a moment he thought she was about to choke, but then she relaxed and obediently let her mouth go slack, accommodating all of him. Daria wrapped her arms around his thighs and began to suck at him once again, but Pip didn't want her working him any more. He grabbed her arms and pulled them away, stretching them out above her head. For a moment she wriggled in surprise, but Pip's fingers gripped her wrists tightly and held her there, stretched out beneath him, keeping her firmly in place while he started pumping his cock into her soft, hot mouth, moving steadily and rigorously while she lay there watching him.

Pip had thought of fucking Daria for a few minutes and teaching her a lesson by coming into her mouth when she wasn't expecting it. He'd already had enough and her taunts had annoyed him; the thought of seeing the milky fluid dripping out of her mouth, of watching her gag and swallow was stimulating. But looking into her glazed expression, he quickly realised that this woman would probably beg him to pump it into her, no doubt eagerly swallowing it all down. He also realised that there was no way he wanted to give her the chance to tell him she hadn't been shafted long enough or hard enough.

He took control of himself and withdrew from her reddened mouth, leaving her lipstick smeared sluttishly around her lips and dark red stains on the side of his cock. Daria stayed flat on the floor, rubbing her wrists. She licked her lips. 'More?'

'You're incorrigible. A real whore.'

She pouted again. 'Don't be a spoilsport, Pip, you've only just started.' She slid her fingers down and into the front of her cream silk G-string. 'Can't you tell? I like getting fucked.' Brown curls were just peeping over the edge of the material and he could see the springy mass beneath. She slid a finger in, and then out, licking the tip. 'I'm hot and sweaty and wet down here.' She grinned. 'And I'm still gagging for it.'

Pip laughed out loud. 'All right, you randy bitch,' he told her, 'you're so eager, what do you want?'

'Hmm.' She thought for a moment. 'How about we check out your chair?'

He shook his head. 'I've got a better idea.'

'Oh?'

He pulled her to her feet, her hair completely dishevelled and her eyes slightly glazed with desire. Daria leaned against him and kissed him, her mouth tasting of salt and sex. 'Well?'

He pointed to a door in the wall opposite. 'After you.'

Daria went through and Pip shut the door behind them. They were in his boardroom. She looked quizzically at him. 'Doing it on the big desk, Pip? That's a little *passé*, isn't it?' He pulled her over to the enormous boardroom table and pushed her on top. 'Still, I don't mind, but I'm a little disappointed; you'll have to perform well to make up for being boring.' Pip stripped in silence. 'Well, your cock is pretty big, and at least your pecs are as good as they get.' She was sitting on the table and struck a pose, her hand behind her head, her bare legs crossed at the thigh. 'I can get naked too, if you want? Do you want?' He shook his head.

'Get rid of the panties.' She nodded and slid them down her thighs, kicking them over her shoes, in his direction. 'Now put your hands on your hips and turn around.' Obediently, she pushed her blouse to either side of her breasts and swivelled slowly about, leaning against the table in front of her. Pip pressed a console button and with a whirr the blinds came down across the windows and on each opposite wall a bank of TV screen came to life. A ten-foot picture of the near-naked Daria was projected onto the screen. She looked at herself in admiration, and then glanced back at Pip.

'Better,' she murmured. 'Are we going to do it on camera?'

He nodded and reached out a hand to her, swivelling her around to face him once again, hoisting her gently onto the edge of the table. She sat down and reached out her hand, taking his cock and drawing him in towards her, placing him at the base of her pussy.

Slowly he slid his cock inside, feeling the surprisingly tight pussy ease apart under the relentless pressure. Beneath him, Daria spread out her hands across the table and groaned with pleasure, never taking her eyes off the picture in front of her. Pip reached the full depth of her pussy and started to pump his cock into her. Grunting with the exertion he pulled her closer to him, supporting her.

Daria seemed almost hypnotised by the picture of them together on the screen behind his shoulders, whilst on the screen in front of him Pip could see her face, tilted upwards, watching his buttocks tense and relax as he moved in and out of her vagina. Her legs wrapped around him, crossed at the ankles, her high-heeled shoes grazing his skin, her eyes blank with lust.

Abruptly he stopped and pulled himself out, turning her around, pushing her across the table to enter her from behind, finding the wet, juicy hole and easing himself back inside her. Daria groaned, the sound echoing back and around the room from the speakers, and he pulled her roughly upright; wrapping his arms around her he plunged inside, his fingers grasping for her tits, squeezing them hard as he moved inside her, releasing them as he retracted, watching with pleasure as she groaned again, a panting, begging noise then became a whimper when he squeezed and pulled at her nipples.

Daria's head tilted back and for the first time she closed her eyes, reaching down to rub at her clit, knowing he was watching her, watching her clit swell and darken. As she carried on playing with herself he could feel himself coming; he felt like he was going to explode, holding himself against her, determined to outdo her and not to give in to the near-overriding impulse until she came.

At last Daria gasped for breath, groaning and panting, and as her eyes flew open she watched herself finally surrender to spasms of pleasure. Rocking helplessly against Pip, her pelvis butted back onto him, grinding herself onto him as her orgasm consumed her. With relief, Pip gave in to the demands of his body. In the final moments he fucked her as hard as he could, falling forward, pushing her down into the table top, his penis thrusting with a life-force of its own, pushing in and out of her until at last his shuddering orgasm obliterated any further thought.

Sophie stopped and doubled over, panting helplessly as she gripped her knees and tried to catch her breath once again. In the silence of the forest her breathing sounded like a loud rasping, loud enough to wake any sleeping animals and birds and certainly loud enough to alert anyone who might be tracking her path.

As the exhaustion receded slightly, she dared to look back over her shoulder and straightened up, ready to defend herself if the need should arise. The forest, she realised, with a sudden panic, was deadly quiet. The past few weeks had made her realise just how much life was out there in the jungle, and this was far more quiet than she had become used to. Why? Could it really be just her presence?

This was not the time to panic, she told herself, trying to calm down, trying not to let her fears consume her. She was not going in a circle and she not going to head back towards the camp. Unconsciously she bit her lip.

'You are not going in a circle and you are not going back to the camp!'

She cast an anxious look up at the trees; the light was starting to fade and the best thing would be to keep going until dark. She almost chuckled to herself; that was the only thing she could do! That and look for water.

Sophie started to walk straight ahead once again, making her way across the small clearing in the forest. It was strange, she thought again, there really should be more noise around here. She walked carefully and much more quietly now that she was no longer running like a maniac, her bare feet hardly disturbing the forest floor.

She had been walking for nearly two days now; she had spent last night huddled in a tree, terrified of the predators that might be lurking here; the tiny poisonous ones, the snakes and the spiders, and, just as bad, the human predators; the tribe, the shaman. She shivered again as the light began to fade noticeably; he, the shaman, would not allow her to escape from him easily. Of that she had no doubt.

Sophie stopped once again and looked around her. She couldn't stop here, out in the open; the trees were tall and sheer, there was nowhere to hide or make into a safe place. She had no choice, she had to keep moving. She must try and get further before nightfall, find somewhere where she could hide and save herself and try to work out some bearings.

She began moving again, her feet making soft shuffling noises as she worked her way through the dead and fallen leaves, picking her way across branches and lianas. Suddenly she heard a sound far behind her; her stomach contracted in terror and she had to fight against the urge to run like crazy and get away from whatever it was. She listened hard.

There it was again, a whistle and a shuffle. Dear God, it was the tribe! They were behind her. The noise in the distance started to get closer and, panicked, Sophie started to run. There was nowhere to hide, no place to go and crouch in until they should pass so she had only one alternative, to run as fast as possible until she couldn't run any more, to hope they hadn't tracked her and to get away.

She sprinted through the grove, lost in near-darkness as the high canopy of trees spread their branches and sealed her in from the outside world. Now she was breathing so hard through panic that her blood and breath were pounding in her ears. She couldn't tell if her pursuers were following her or not; she didn't dare look back in case they were there and at any moment she expected a hand to fall upon her shoulder, to drag her to a stop and to take her back to captivity.

147

Suddenly a snaking branch caught her ankle. Sophie tripped, was catapulted into the air and flung downwards, rolling down a hill until she managed to grab a branch and pull herself to a stop. She dragged herself to her feet and squealed in agony, her ankle throbbing painfully. She groaned and propped herself up against the tree, and looked behind her, her heart pounding furiously; there was no sound from behind her at all. Maybe she had been wrong and it wasn't the tribe. She turned to face the other direction, into the hollow and almost fell over again as adrenaline surged through her body.

In the hollow below was a camp. An honest-to-God camp. Not a tribe or a village, but a camp with buildings, fences, people. She stared, hardly able to believe her eyes. It wasn't particularly big, but it was clearly there for the duration. Long barrack huts were set out in a series of rows at one end, and then there were a group of smaller huts in the centre, with a large square building, presumably some sort of mess hall, to one side. It all nestled in a fairly secluded hollow and around the whole area was a high fence with, she now realised, guard posts at each corner and lights on top. What on earth would anyone want or need with watch posts? she wondered, before pushing the thought to the back of her mind. Who the hell cared? It was civilisation and that was all that mattered.

She began to make her way down the slope, no longer trying to hide or keep to cover. It must be a logging camp, that or mining. Exactly the sort of bastards she was working to put out of business, but again, right now who cared? They didn't need to know who she was, or why she was here. She could just tell them she was a tourist who had become separated from her group and captured by that bloody bunch of savages. She shivered and limped along as quickly as she could, suddenly fearful that someone might materialise from behind her and steal her away before she could get help. No! She kept moving. With a bit of luck there would be a European in charge. Dear God, she thought, so long as there was someone who spoke English. No, that didn't matter either. She shrugged the thought off, frantically making plans. Even if there wasn't a European there would be a radio and she could talk to someone in the city, Puerto Maldonado, somewhere! Just so long as there was some way to get out of this place.

She was almost at the base of the hill and as she started across towards the gate a group of people emerged from one of the central huts. She had clearly been seen and someone was raising the alarm. She waved and stopped, almost overwhelmed with relief as she looked down; beneath her was the unmistakable gleam of golden blonde hair. Almost certainly a European. Thank God. With difficulty she scrambled down the last bank and into the camp, dragging her tired feet through the gates and towards the group gathering in front of her.

The group of men coming towards her were mostly Peruvian, some almost pure blood Indians but mostly a mixture of races, the misto. They were short, none of them more than five foot eight, but between them, dwarfing them all, striding with longer paces than anyone else was the European, blonde hair, ice-blue eyes.

She stopped in shock as he held his arms out and ran to greet her.

'Pip!' Sophie threw herself into Pip's arms, gabbling like a maniac, as he swept her up and hugged her. 'Pip, how can this be? How can you be here?'

'I've come to find you.'

'But how can you be here?'

He laughed, setting her gently back down to the ground. 'Me? How can you? You're miles away from where you're supposed to be. In fact you're hundreds of miles away from Lima. And that's where I told you to stay.' He shook her gently. 'What the hell's been going on? I should be so mad with you! And look at you –' his face contorted – 'what's happened to you?'

She wrapped her arms around him again and held him close, starting to sob. 'It's been awful, Pip. Indescribably awful.'

He hugged her consolingly. 'Come on, calm down, you're

safe here.' Across her head he nodded to two men and motioned for the rest to scatter. 'Come on sweetheart, let's go and talk. You're okay here. You just calm down and tell me all about it.'

Chapter Eight

Sophie sipped a large cup of steaming hot coffee and looked across the table at Pip, waiting patiently for her to continue with her story. Dressed in a spare pair of his jeans and a clean, white, but enormous T-shirt, with clean hair drying around her face in curls, Sophie looked about fifteen.

'I don't know where to start.'

'How about at the beginning. You were in Lima.'

'I was in Lima and I went out into the jungle.'

'Why? I told you not to go.'

She shrugged.

'Honestly, Sophie, why didn't you tell me everything?'

'I couldn't. You wouldn't have believed me and you would have stopped me.'

Pip shook his head. 'So this is why you wanted to come out here.' He was talking to himself, but then he looked across at her again and gave her an encouraging smile. 'So, what exactly did India have to say for herself?'

'She told me she had a lead on where the money was going. She thought not all of it was being salted away and that some was going into illicit or at least dubious work in the jungle. Which is how they were covering up the supplies and the payments for labour. When it got out here it wasn't for eco-projects or farming at all, it was for mining and logging.'

Pip stared at her. 'Are you serious? India collected all that information?' Sophie nodded. 'What else?'

'Precious little. She pointed me in the right direction, but she was carrying on digging into it in the States.' She smiled.

'India doesn't like leaving the US. She thinks the rest of the world is an uncivilised jungle.' She looked out of the window to where the trees were swaying in a gentle breeze and laughed ruefully. 'Of course, this time she happened to be right on the mark.'

Pip leaned across the table and patted her hand.

'You just tell me everything that happened to you after you reached Lima.'

Sophie looked outside. It had been hours since she had started talking and now that they had eaten dinner and drunk some red wine she was feeling much more relaxed. The whole nightmare seemed to be receding to the depths of her mind.

'That's when I got away.'

'And then?'

'And then I ran.'

'But how did you get away from them?'

She shook her head. 'Honestly, Pip, I don't really know. I just took the chance, there was no-one around for a moment and the door, well, the cover across the entrance, it was open. I managed to tear a hole open at the back and then I crawled out, feeling sick as a pig. When I was away from the camp I started running. I think they were all at some service.'

'A service?'

'A ritual.' He still looked confused. 'A tribal meeting.' She blushed. There were some things Sophie wasn't sure she wanted to discuss with Pip. 'I don't know why they didn't take me along but they all very busy.'

He sat with his arm around her and Sophie cuddled up, relaxed and safe at last. 'Sophie, sweetheart, I need to ask you a few more questions.' She nodded. 'The first one is, where are they?'

'The tribe?' He nodded. 'I don't know exactly. I just started running.'

'How long did you run?'

'I told you, yesterday afternoon, into the night and today.'

'Fifteen, eighteen hours.' She shrugged uncertainly, but he wasn't concentrating on her any more. 'And you only twisted your ankle at the last moment.' She nodded again. 'If we assume you were going in a reasonably straight direction, then they can't be more than what? Ten, twenty miles away, if that.'

'But they've moved.'

'Moved?' His voice was sharp. 'When?'

'Yesterday. That was why they were at the meeting, planning where to go next, I think.'

'And where were they going?' His arm gripped hers.

'I don't know. Pip, you're hurting me. Why do you care where the tribe were going?'

Pip seemed to come back to reality, but his expression was still cross. 'They're a bunch of malcontents. Ingrates! And they need rooting out.'

'I don't understand.' His mind was elsewhere and abruptly he stood and went to the door of the room. 'Jose!' One of the Peruvian men came to the door and Pip started speaking to him, rapidly and in an undertone. When he had finished Jose nodded and ran off, and Pip closed the door.

'I didn't know you spoke Spanish.'

He smiled grimly. 'Lots of things to learn, Sophie. Is that really all you can tell me? That the camp moved on and you don't know where to?'

She nodded. 'I'm sorry, Pip.'

'Well, you haven't been a great deal of use, have you?'

She smiled up at him but then realised he was deadly serious. 'I don't understand.'

Pip turned back to face her and this time his face had lost all veneer of concern. 'You piss about in the jungle, making me answer lots of very difficult questions in London, and screwing up all my plans . . .'

'I don't understand.'

He glanced around him in disgust. 'Do you really think I'd be out here in this shithole if you'd done what you were supposed to do?'

'Stayed at home in London?'

'Stayed in the jungle.'

'I don't understand.'

He glared at her. 'And stop saying that; you always were lacking in imagination, now you're getting to be repetitive as well.'

'Pip!'

'Oh shut up, Sophie, it's too late.'

Apparently disgusted, he turned back to his desk, leaving her shocked. The silence was broken as the outside door was flung open and a stocky man strode into the room, a gun flung over his shoulder. Pip nodded casually, 'El Capitano.'

The Peruvian's eyes roamed round the room, eventually alighting on Sophie. He smiled and Sophie politely smiled back. His smile broadened and coarsened and his gaze slithered over her body; he made her feel queasy and vulnerable all in one.

'He's the camp commander,' Pip said. His voice was bored. Sophie got up with a feeling of misgiving verging on panic.

'What's going on?'

Pip looked at her again. 'You're going to the women's section. Don't make a fuss.'

'The women's section?' Sophie struggled to understand what Pip was saying. 'Why can't I stay here with you?'

He shook his head. 'I can't afford to have you hanging around any more.' He looked across at the captain. 'Do what you want with her but make sure she doesn't get out of here alive.'

The captain grabbed Sophie by the arm and dragged her to the far end of the room where he pushed a bell-button set into a panel on the wall. Sophie tried to pull herself free and looked over her shoulder to where Pip was now sitting behind the desk, his long legs resting on the desktop as he lounged back in the chair.

'Pip, this is not funny! What's going on?' Her pleas were increasingly panicky and desperate as she saw Pip watching her and the captain. She realised that he was enjoying her panic. Enjoying it? He was getting off on it.

154

'Pip,' she demanded, temporarily shaking herself free of her captor and planting her hands determinedly on the desk. 'Answer me!'

Pip shook his head. 'You just don't get it, do you?' She stared at him, still unwilling to believe whilst her brain was telling her the truth. 'Why do you think the porters turned on you?'

Sophie stared hard into Pip's eyes, comprehension stealing slowly into her mind. 'You set me up! Why?'

He pulled himself up and swung his legs off the desk. 'It's your own fault, Sophie! You screwed this up for me. You wouldn't listen to reason and you insisted on coming out here. Of course, then you had to bloody well see the plants, the farms.' He shook his head. 'You stupid bitch, you didn't leave us with any other choice. You could be sitting at home in London, with your gym and your little business trips, but no, you had to start digging away and now I've had to cut my operation short too.'

Sophie stared at Pip. 'I still don't understand, what operation?'

'You must understand, I had no choice, Sophie. I had to make some money of my own. For years I've been supporting those fat cat bastards on the Board . . .'

'But you get paid. You get bonuses, you have for years. Millions. You're rich. I know you are.' She stopped. 'Where is it all?'

He shrugged. 'A few minor ventures here and there. I could have got it all back with the right deal. But the numbers rolled over and I had to keep moving.' He waved his hands vaguely. 'It's no big deal. I've got a high credit rating.'

'You lost it? You lost all your money?'

'It wasn't my fault,' he snarled. 'I had a few problems, nothing too big, but then the East went belly up.'

'You've lost all your money?' She couldn't believe it.

'I didn't lose anything,' Pip thundered. 'It wasn't my fault. I had to keep the business going. I had to bankroll a few more projects than I'd planned.'

'With the bank's money? And this?'

Pip smiled proudly. 'This is a new venture. My new venture. And this is guaranteed.'

'What?' she sneered. 'A strip mine in the jungle? A bit of deforestation on the side? Are you growing coca as well? You're mad.' Pip gripped her wrist and pushed her away in disgust.

'Shut up, Sophie.'

'And what about your partners?' Suddenly, complete understanding sank in. 'Oh my God. Hugo! He's in it with you. That's why he's our agent. He's your bloody partner.'

'Very good, Sophie.'

She stared at him. 'Don't you think you'll just end up dead in a ditch when he's had enough of you?'

'Shut up! You don't know what you're talking about.'

'Pip,' she begged, 'listen to reason. This isn't you. Listen to me! We could go back home and explain.'

Pip howled with laughter. 'Go back home? Are you mad? Anyway, it's not me who needs to explain. It's you!' He stared at her. 'Oh yes, Sophie, didn't you know? It's you who's been embezzling money and ran away to South America.'

'What?'

'Well, you don't think you'd have got that job if I didn't need a patsy, do you?' He straightened up. 'You must be very stupid if you did. Mind you,' he went on, half-talking to himself now, 'you did trace the cash calls and I never thought you'd even find them.'

'Nobody would believe I'd do something like this, defraud the bank, my employers . . .'

His face twisted into a snarl. 'You stupid bitch. They would and they do. As far as the world is concerned you set the whole thing up and I found out. It's just a pity you died when your comrades turned on you.'

'No!'

'Oh yes. Just before I could bring you to justice. It was all very sad, but now I'm here to sort out the problems.' He smiled. 'I'll need to be in South America for quite some time.'

'You're mad!'

He snapped his fingers at the captain. 'Am I? Funny, I seem to be the one in charge around here. She's yours, Miguel, I'm bored with her. She might amuse you and the men for a few days.'

'What do you mean by that?'

Pip smiled, ignoring her. 'Actually, on second thoughts, call me. I might enjoy seeing it.'

'Pip!'

Finally, he looked her straight in the eyes. 'We're out in the jungle, Sophie, and you're not going anywhere. You're not going back to England and neither am I.' He stood and walked away from her, looking out into the camp. 'I'm sorry, Sophie, but you should have stayed at home. I could have let you carry on working and Charles would have entertained you on a regular basis.'

'What are you going to do with me?'

'What do you think people like Miguel do for entertainment in this godforsaken place?' He turned to Miguel and the two of them shared a smile. 'This isn't just a mine, Sophie. Why don't you think of it as –' he paused – 'an entertainment centre. That's it. And you're going to become the entertainment.' His face hardened. 'Miguel, send her to the brothel!'

Her eyes wide with horror, Sophie looked away from Pip as a door at the far end of the room opened and a large female dressed in a figure-hugging leather mini-dress and thigh-length boots walked towards them. The dress was no more than a rectangle of leather laced together down the front; it barely covered her enormous hips and buttocks and her crotch with its thatch of dark pubic hair was clearly visible through the gaps in the laces. The laces were stretched wide at her chest, clearly inadequate to deal with the huge mounds of her breasts which were squeezing over the top of the dress. She had a thick leather choker around her neck as well as leather cuffs on her wrists and she carried a whip in one hand and a variety of cuffs and bonds in the other. Her head was shaven and her face was heavily and grotesquely made up in a parody of a western harlot, although her features were clearly Peruvian.

'Sophie, this is Lola,' Pip smiled, as the female studied his girlfriend carefully. 'She's in charge of the girls here and you will do well to obey her.'

Sophie ripped her hand away as the female took hold of her wrist. 'You can't do this to me, Pip,' she hissed. 'You have to let me go!'

'You're wrong, Sophie, I don't.' Pip stopped smiling suddenly and nodded to the female who flicked her whip close to Sophie's face. 'I would strongly recommend that you do as you are told. Lola is well versed in ways of training her girls if they prove to be too headstrong and misbehave.'

Sophie glared at Pip and was completely taken by surprise when the female moved behind her, grabbing both her wrists and wrenching her arms back to secure them with tight leather cuffs. Next a leather choker was fixed around her neck and a leash attached. As Sophie struggled, the female gave a sharp tug on the leash and the choker tightened, making Sophie's head swim momentarily.

'Don't be stupid, Sophie, there's a good girl.' Pip nodded to the female again who pulled Sophie in the direction of the door. 'If you behave, maybe I'll see you later.' Unable to resist any further, Sophie could do no more than follow the female as she was dragged through the door with the leash, the door slammed behind her and Sophie heard the turning of a heavy key. They were in a small darkened room and before Sophie's eyes had time to adjust to the dim light, she found herself being dragged to one side of the room where her leash was fixed to a ring in the wall and pulled tight.

'Don't move,' Lola hissed in heavily accented English. 'If you do the choker will tighten around your neck even more.' Sophie stood motionless against the wall and Lola unzipped her jeans and tugged them to the floor.

'Stand with your feet apart.' Sophie took a step sideways, aware that the female was scrutinising her shaven crotch. 'You have a high slit for a Westerner. That will be much sought after by the men here.' Lola poked a fat finger between Sophie's sex lips and gently eased them apart, giving her clitoris an exploratory rub. Sophie's bud hardened involuntarily and with a grunt of satisfaction Lola got to her knees and, pushing her face between Sophie's legs, started to flick her tongue over her clit. Despite herself, the little bud hardened even further under Lola's expert cunnilingus and from the tingling in her cunt, Sophie knew that her clit had been freed from its protective hood.

Abruptly, the stimulation of her clit stopped and Lola stood up, putting her face close to Sophie's. Her enormous breasts brushed against Sophie's chest. 'You will serve me well, I think,' she said. Her breath was sour and Sophie had to work hard not to pull her head away, 'But you must remember that you are not here to receive pleasure but to give it. The Western man was right; as you are highly sexed it will not perhaps be so hard for you as for some of the others.'

Taking a knife from the top of her boots, Lola cut Sophie's T-shirt open with one slice and pushed the material away from her breasts, so that the rags fell to the floor. As they dropped away Sophie remembered that she was still wearing the nipple rings from the camp and she was not surprised when the female warder's eyes widened at the sight of the gold, glinting in the dim light. 'Well, well,' Lola laughed quietly, tweaking the rings before twisting them from Sophie's hardening nipples. 'I will take these as an insurance policy. But I may have you wear them when you are entertaining me alone. Would you like that?'

'Get stuffed,' spat Sophie, but Lola just chuckled heavily and, unhooking her leash from the ring in the wall, tugged her in the direction of a second door.

'You must learn to behave, Sophie. Now I will show you around your home and introduce you to your new family.'

Lola opened the door and from beyond Sophie heard the low, rhythmic beat of music. They entered another interconnecting room, this one filled with couches and low tables. Around twenty men were lounging about, eating and drinking and talking to each other in low tones. Sophie scanned the room and saw, dotted amongst the tables, a number of small stages on which females in various stages of undress were moving sinuously to the rhythm of the music. As she took in the scene one of the men stood up and grabbed a dancing female by the wrist, pulling her from the podium and towards a door at the far side of the room. The naked girl made no protest and her place on the podium was taken almost immediately by another female who started to writhe suggestively, thrusting her crotch towards the watching males and kneading her small breasts.

'This is where the men come to relax when they are not working, and to watch the dancing,' Lola said unnecessarily. 'You will have to learn how to dance but I'm sure you will have little problem attracting attention.' She looked appreciatively at Sophie's naked body and reached out to pinch one dark nipple.

'Hey, Lola!' One of the men on a nearby couch leered in the direction of the two females. 'Who's this you've got for us today?'

Lola tugged on Sophie's leash, and started to move through the tables towards the door at the far end of the room. 'She's not for you yet, hands off. She's untrained so you'll have to wait.' Sophie followed Lola through the room and more men spotted the pair, catcalling at them, some grabbing at Sophie's breasts and buttocks as she passed.

'Give her to us, Lola, we'll train her.'

'All she needs is the feel of a cock inside her, give her to me.'

Lola turned Sophie round to face them as they reached the far side of the room. She gritted her teeth and glared at them all as Lola grabbed hold of one of her breasts and palpated the mound of flesh. 'This sort of meat doesn't come cheap,' Lola scoffed at them. 'You'll have to wait until others with deeper pockets have had their fill.'

Turning to open the door, she pulled Sophie into a narrow corridor beyond. One side of the corridor was lined with cubicles, none of which had any doors, and Sophie could see that each one contained only a narrow padded couch.

'This is where the girls do business. I don't allow sex in the dancing room,' Lola informed Sophie as they walked down the corridor. Several of the cubicles had couples in them having sex in various positions and their path was punctuated by the grunts of rutting males. Opposite the row of cubicles the corridor was lined with doors and halfway along Lola opened one. 'Come,' she said, 'see what else we do here.'

The door opened onto a small room which, like the cubicles, contained a padded couch but in addition, there were various instruments of bondage scattered around the room. A female was tied to the couch with her legs spread wide in stirrups and a man was positioned between her legs, pumping his cock deep into her hole. She was blindfold and her large breasts were encased in a tight halter, pushing the mounds of flesh together in a deep cleavage. The man paused and his eyes ran over the two women for a moment, then he nodded at Lola and returned to the matter at hand.

'I expect all my girls to be able to give pleasure in whatever way a man desires.' Lola watched the scene in front of them closely before turning to Sophie with a smile. 'The Western man tells me that you have been training in some of the arts necessary for a successful whore but you will learn many more here.'

The woman on the couch began to moan as the man increased the pace of his thrusts into her open sex and Sophie felt her own cunt tighten in response to the sight of the erotic scene in front of her. Lola laughed quietly as she monitored Sophie's reaction and pulled her out of the room, closing the door on the sounds of the copulating couple within.

At the end of the corridor, they entered a large airy room which was lined with showers and douches. 'I insist that all my girls are kept clean.' Lola pointed to a naked female who was

161

standing with her legs wide apart being douched by another female dressed in high-cut black panties and thigh-length boots similar to Lola's.

'You will be able to recognise my assistants by their uniforms. They help me organise the slaves' work and are also responsible for cleanliness and discipline.'

Sophie watched as the assistant slapped the female's thigh to make her turn round and then proceeded to douche between her buttocks. 'The water is always quite cold so that the slaves are kept tight and fresh.' Lola laughed again, leading Sophie through the shower room.

'Make sure she is ready for the evening shift,' she shouted to the assistant as they passed, adding to Sophie, 'The next shift in the mine will finish in about one hour and there will be many men wanting our services.'

The final room in the brothel contained a large dormitory. There were about twenty girls in the room, some lying asleep on piles of cushions or narrow pallets, some eating or chatting quietly, but all sounds ceased as Lola entered the room with Sophie and all eyes turned in their direction.

'A new girl,' Lola announced, 'but she will not be joining you immediately.' There was a murmur of interest amongst the watching girls as they took in Sophie's pale skin and long blonde hair. 'Come.' Lola pulled Sophie's leash and they walked out of the dormitory onto a rough wooden deck where Sophie was momentarily blinded by the bright sunshine. 'You will be kept separate from the others while you are undergoing your training.'

She led Sophie down from the deck and across an enclosed courtyard. 'The captain has requested that you be kept for the entertainment of him and his guests while you are being broken in and I have agreed. We have never had a Western female in the brothel before and you will be much sought after. We would not want you getting over-used too quickly.'

Unlocking a heavy wooden door, Lola pushed Sophie into a cool room where the only light came from tiny windows set

162

high in the walls. Closing the door behind them, Lola turned to face Sophie with a lascivious expression on her face. 'And I also want you so I will be supervising your training myself.'

With a swift movement Lola released Sophie's hands from their cuffs. 'You'll find a jug of chicha over in the corner. Fetch me a cup.' Giving Sophie a push in the direction of a small table at the far end of the room, she turned to light candle sconces hanging from the walls.

As she poured the chicha from a large stone jug and walked back to where Lola was waiting for her, Sophie had the chance to take in her surroundings.

'This is my room,' said Lola from behind her, as if she knew what Sophie was contemplating. 'Do not think you can escape. Each room connects and the girls would stop you if you tried to leave.' Sophie nodded, her eyes running across the hut looking for a way out, but there appeared to be no other exit.

The walls were hung with various whips, crops and other implements of erotic stimulation which Sophie couldn't even identify. Several large rings were fixed at different heights around the walls and there was a large bed in the centre of the room and a mosquito net hung from the ceiling directly above. Taking the cup from Sophie's hands, Lola drank deeply before tossing the cup aside and placing her hands on her hips.

'Unlace me.' Lola leered at Sophie, breathing out sour chicha fumes. Sophie reached out to untie the laces at the top of Lola's leather tube dress and immediately the material sprung apart and her enormous breasts burst out of the dress.

As Sophie continued to unlace the leather down to her waist and hips, Lola kneaded the bulk of her breasts, pulling on her gigantic brown nipples to make them hard. Letting the dress fall to the ground, Sophie looked at Lola for further instruction, aroused despite herself by the sight of the huge woman, the curves of her belly, hips and buttocks reflected in the luscious flesh of her labia which were protruding from the thick bush of her dark, coarse pubic hair. Taking a wide stance, Lola pulled her sex lips apart and thrust her groin forwards.

'Lick me off,' she said. 'Now!' she snarled as Sophie hesitated before dropping to her knees and starting to lick tentatively at Lola's sex. Impatiently, Lola grabbed the back of Sophie's head and pulled her face deeper into the fleshy folds of her sex. 'Harder, slut,' she snarled, grinding her cunt against Sophie's mouth.

Sophie flicked her tongue experimentally around Lola's clit which was positioned high in her slit and easily accessible as it began to harden under Sophie's attentions. Becoming braver, she began to suck and nibble on Lola's sex bud and the woman moaned with pleasure, rocking her hips slightly and pulling Sophie's face closer into her groin. Continuing her oral stimulation of Lola's responsive clit, Sophie pushed one finger into the slave mistress's hole. It was dripping with the juices of her arousal and, like the rest of this enormous woman, it was huge and fleshy. Sophie replaced one finger with three and began working them in and out of Lola's cunt. She was rewarded almost instantly as Lola began to pant heavily, squatting slightly to allow Sophie easier access to her sex flesh and rubbing herself against Sophie's fingers to increase the depth of their penetration. With a series of surprisingly soft cries, Lola reached her climax quickly and Sophie could feel the spasms of her orgasm deep inside her vagina.

Releasing Sophie's head from her vice-like grip, Lola straightened her stance and stepped back, breathing heavily. 'Not bad for a beginner,' she laughed. 'Bring me more chicha, I lost a lot of liquid that time.'

Silently, Sophie got to her feet, wiping Lola's juices from her mouth. Picking up the discarded cup from the floor, she went back to the chicha jug and poured Lola another cup. 'Bring the whole jug, slave,' Lola commanded. 'You might as well have some too. The alcohol might help your performance.'

Draining another cup of chicha, Lola allowed Sophie to do the same before ordering her to climb onto the bed and to spread her legs. Lola peered at Sophie's sex for several long moments before reaching under the bed and bringing out a box which she placed next to Sophie and opened the lid. Sophie saw that the box contained several dildos of different sizes, some single and some double. Selecting a single dildo of medium length and thickness, Lola gently stroked Sophie's slit with it before pushing it slowly into Sophie's hole. Sophie willed herself to relax but she was unable to stop herself from tensing against the intrusion of the dildo.

'Stop that,' Lola snapped, pushing it deep into Sophie's sex and leaving it there while she selected a larger dildo from the box. 'You will need to learn that you do not own your body any more. You can be bought by anyone and you will allow them to do anything.' Lola gave the dildo resting deep in Sophie's body a twist. 'We'll leave that there for the time being so that you get used to the feel of a cock inside you. Now, masturbate me with this one.'

Lola lay back on the bed and opened her legs wide to expose her massive cunt again. Taking hold of the huge dildo, Sophie knelt between Lola's thighs and pushed the false cock into Lola's hole, at the same time massaging her clit which had hardened again and was protruding at the top of Lola's slit. Sophie was aware of the other dildo lodged in her own hole and, as she masturbated Lola, her sex muscles tensed around the thick shaft inside her.

'Faster.' Lola began to pant again and her hands grasped at the covers on the bed as she concentrated on her orgasm. Sophie pumped the dildo in and out of Lola's hole, roughly rubbing on her clit and willing the woman to reach her climax. She did not have to work for long, with a low moan, Lola butted her hips as she orgasmed a second time and she slowly came down from the peak of her climax as Sophie gently extracted the dildo from her hole.

'Very entertaining.' Both women started as a voice from the door brought them back to the present. 'But I didn't know that you were training her to provide services to lesbians, Lola, much as I appreciate that your appetites tend in that direction.'

Pip was standing in the open door and seeing the bulge in

the crotch of his chinos, Sophie guessed that he had been enjoying the show for some time. 'It's time for you to begin earning your living, Sophie,' he said. 'I'm leaving in the morning and the captain has organised a little farewell party for me. He has agreed that you would be ideal entertainment.'

Looking away from Sophie to Lola who was now standing by the bed, Pip stared at her huge bulk for a moment. 'Get her dressed and bring her along to the captain's quarters,' he said. 'You can come too, it might be amusing to see you together later on.' Turning to leave the room, Pip called over his shoulder, 'Oh, and take that dildo out of her cunt and have her douched. She needs to be tight.'

Half an hour later, after Sophie had been washed and douched, Lola had her dressed in a black cut-away bra and crotchless panties. Lola had laced herself back into her leather mini outfit and she fitted leather cuffs to Sophie's wrists and ankles before reattaching the leash to Sophie's choker. Tying her wrists together at her front, Lola led Sophie back through the brothel to the anteroom outside the captain's quarters.

Knocking on the door, Lola turned to Sophie. 'You will do as they ask and later I will have you again while they watch.' She smiled, licking her lips with anticipation as she looked over Sophie's body. 'If you do not do things correctly, you will regret it.'

'Enter.' Sophie heard Pip's voice from within the room. Lola pushed the door open and, with a squeeze of Sophie's buttocks, led her by the leash into the room. Pip and the captain were lounging on two couches in the centre of the room. Both men were naked except for their jockstraps and it was clear from their attitude that they had been drinking. Between the couches was a podium on which a naked female was dancing in front of the men. As she writhed to the throbbing music, Sophie saw that the female was masturbating herself with a long dildo, moving it in and out of her cunt while she looked at the men from under her lowered lashes,

166

her jaw slack with feigned sexual abandon.

Turning slowly around, the dancer rubbed the dildo along the cleft between her buttocks, teasing the head of the shaft into her bottom hole and wriggling her hips suggestively. 'Sophie,' Pip called. 'Come and watch. The captain particularly enjoys his females from behind as you can see, but you might find that a little uncomfortable at this early stage.'

Sophie didn't reply, but she stared at the dancer who was now moaning and panting in an attempt to attract the men's attention away from Sophie. The captain snapped his fingers.

'Enough, Consuela. Leave us now.' Abruptly the female stopped her gyrations and stepped down from the podium. Before scurrying from the room, she shot Sophie a glance and Sophie saw a mixture of relief and sympathy in the girl's eyes. A feeling of horror began to creep through Sophie's veins as she started to comprehend the daily humiliations that life in this place would almost certainly bring.

'The girls will not be very pleased with you if you keep upstaging them like that, Sophie,' Pip laughed. 'You may come to be grateful for Lola's protection. Now, get up there and show us what you can do.'

'You can't make me.' Sophie glared at Pip.

'No, perhaps not.' Sophie was momentarily surprised by Pip's response to her show of resistance. 'It will probably take a bit of time and much more training before you become properly servile. And I don't have that amount of time although Miguel certainly does.'

The captain nodded his eager agreement. 'Next time you are here, she will have learnt how to dance.'

'But there are many more ways in which you can be entertaining.' Pip stood up and took Sophie's leash from Lola's hand, tugging sharply on the end so that Sophie's head jerked back as the choker tightened. 'And there are things I can make you do, as you well know. Things you like to do.'

Signalling to Lola, Pip dragged Sophie over to one of the couches. Pulling his jockstrap to one side, Pip seated himself on the sofa and Lola pushed Sophie to her knees between Pip's spread legs.

'You were pretty good with your mouth to Lola, as I recall,' Pip sneered. 'Remind me how good you are with a cock.' Stroking his penis from base to tip, Pip waited as Sophie swallowed hard, hesitating as she took in the sight of his engorged cock, twitching slightly with his masturbation. 'Come on, Sophie, Lola can be very sharp with the whip on her slaves if they don't do as they are told.'

As if to reinforce his words, Lola tugged gently on Sophie's leash. Sophie leaned forward and opened her mouth to take Pip's cock between her lips. She flicked her head around the head of his shaft before beginning to move her lips along the length of his cock. If there was one thing she did know, it was how Pip liked his blow jobs to go. She felt Pip relax and looking up, she saw that he had closed his eyes as he concentrated on the pleasurable sensations her mouth was causing in his groin.

'Spread your legs.' Sophie was startled as she felt a hand push between her legs from behind and she realised that the captain was kneeling behind her and was intent on getting access to her cunt. Tied as she was and with her mouth full of Pip's throbbing cock, Sophie had no option but to yield to the captain's insistent probing of her sex and shifted her position to place her knees apart. She gasped as the captain started butting his cock against her bottom hole, but she was too tight and instead he slipped further along to sink his shaft deep into her cunt.

'Keep sucking, bitch,' Pip snarled between clenched teeth, as he started to climax.

Sophie heard Lola laughing as the captain proceeded to thrust his cock in and out of her hole and she continued to fellate Pip with renewed vigour. Her eyes glazed as the feeling of being nothing more than a receptacle for providing pleasure to men began to take hold. With a massive thrust, Pip pushed Sophie's mouth from his cock and Lola pulled her head back with the leash so that Pip's come spurted onto her neck and breasts. At the same time, the captain gave a shout and gripping Sophie's hips tightly, ground his cock into her sex, shooting his come into her belly. As Lola released the tension on her leash, Sophie slumped forward. She was aware that her cunt was throbbing with the tension of unreleased sexual arousal and her lips felt sore and stretched with the effort of fellating Pip's large cock.

Pulling his jockstrap back into place, Pip snapped his fingers at Lola. 'We need some more chicha, Lola. And then I think I'd like you two to put on a show for us while we recover.'

Obediently, Lola fetched another jug of chicha from the corner of the room and then pulled Sophie over to where an iron ring was hanging from a chain fixed into the ceiling. Pulling Sophie's arms above her head, Lola attached her wrist cuffs to the ring before turning back to the men, slowly unlacing her voluptuous flesh from within her leather sheath dress. Moving her hips to the beat of the music which still pounded in the background, Lola reached inside the now familiar dildo box and pulled out a double-headed phallus; the join between the two cocks held two dangling balls and one shaft was much thicker and longer than the other. Standing in full view of the two men, Lola inserted the thickest shaft into her own sex, stroking the other dildo which now protruded lewdly from her groin. Then, walking over to where Sophie was hanging from the chain in the ceiling, Lola butted the dildo between Sophie's legs, forcing her to part her thighs to allow Lola to rub the length of the shaft along her slit. Bending her knees slightly, Lola adjusted the angle of the dildo and with one practised stroke, shoved the shaft into Sophie's hole. As the woman began to move the dildo in and out of Sophie's sex, she took hold of one swollen dark nipple between her teeth and began to suck hard on Sophie's tender flesh.

Despite herself, Sophie let her head fall back as the slave mistress worked at her with the dildo, each stroke producing an equal and opposite effect in Lola's own sex so that her thrusts became ever more frenzied as she strived to reach her climax.

Sophie moaned as Lola continued to fuck her but the other woman reached her climax too soon and Sophie's mounting orgasm was halted in its tracks as Lola pulled away, withdrawing the dildo from Sophie's hole with one movement.

'Not bad,' Pip said from the couch. 'But I think you came too soon as usual, Lola. Sophie generally needs a bit longer than that. Maybe we should let the miners at her.'

The captain grunted. 'Whatever you wish, but maybe you would just prefer some variety, Phillipe. Lola, take her away and have her trained up properly. And send us Conchita and Juanita. They know how to please a man.'

Lola unhooked Sophie from the chain and cuffed her hands again behind her back. 'Goodbye for now, Sophie.' Pip gave a low chuckle. 'I'll be leaving in the morning and I don't expect I'll see you before I go. So have fun!'

'Don't think you will get away with this,' Sophie hissed defiantly as Lola led her away, only to hear Pip's mocking laughter following her down the corridor back to the brothel. She had to admit that it looked like he might have the last laugh on this one.

They passed two females being herded by one of Lola's assistants in the direction of the captain's quarters; both were wearing only tiny micro briefs and cut-away halter bras which supported the weight of their full breasts. Sophie wondered where these females had come from and how they had ended up in this desolate hole, destined to serve men like Pip with their bodies until they were no longer sufficiently attractive. And what then? She closed her mind to the desperate thoughts crowding into her mind. There had to be a way out and she would find it.

Lola placed Sophie in the care of one of her assistants in the shower room, ordering them to clean her up and put her in the dormitory until she was required again; the biting cold of the shower and douche came as a surprisingly welcome relief to Sophie's tired skin and she felt the tender flesh of her pussy responding to the jets of water, the muscles tightening as they cooled down. Sophie dried off quickly with a small, rough towel and the assistant pushed her through into the dormitory, slamming the door as she walked back into the shower room to attend to several more girls who had just emerged from the brothel corridor.

Gazing round the large room, Sophie's attention was caught by the sight of the girl who had been dancing for Pip and the captain before Sophie had distracted their attention. Like Sophie she still wore her rough choker; she was lying on her side on one of the pallets scattered around the room and the bed next to her was empty. Sophie walked over, sat down and the two girls stared at each other for several moments. 'You're Consuela, yes?'

'Si, mi llamo Consuela,' the girl replied in Spanish and then in faltering English, 'I hope they didn't hurt you too much.'

'I'm fine,' Sophie smiled at Consuela. The girl was young; she couldn't be more than eighteen and Sophie's heart went out to her, trapped in this place. 'How long have you been here?'

'A few months.' Consuela lay on her side, crossing her arms over her small breasts.

'And why are you here?' Sophie couldn't stop herself from asking the question.

'My tribe lost its land to the miners and we were scattered. They offered me a bed and food to eat.' Consuela looked at Sophie with dark eyes. 'As long as I could dance.'

'Just dancing?' Sophie probed the girl further, aware that she was treading on very thin ice. Consuela was silent but the pain in her eyes was visible before she looked away. 'Consuela, do you know how to get out of here?' Sophie changed the subject.

'There is no way out.' Consuela looked back at Sophie. 'They guard the camp day and night. And anyway, we have no clothes or shoes. We would not live for long in the jungle.'

'There has to be a way out, Consuela, and you and I are going to find it.'

Sophie smiled at the girl to conceal her misgivings, but she had hardly finished speaking when the door to the dormitory burst open and Lola strode into the room followed by an assistant. She was brandishing a long, thick whip and as she tore around the dormitory, females cowered away from her great bulk.

Sophie stood up, instinctively knowing that Lola was searching for her. Lola stormed over to Sophie's pallet and grabbed her by the arm, clicking her leash into place and handing it to her assistant; Consuela jumped up, desperate to help her new friend and she was joined by other females who rose from their pallets, sensing the possibility of a revolt. But Lola sent her whip into action, scattering the terrified females with its vicious aim.

Turning back to Consuela, Lola smiled softly. 'So you want to be with your friend, eh, Consuela? Well, I will grant your wish.'

Snapping another leash onto Consuela's choker, Lola tugged sharply so that the girl staggered against her great bulk. Taking one of Consuela's pert nipples between her finger and thumb, Lola gave it a painful pinch. 'Come, little one. I need to be entertained.'

Taking Sophie's leash from her assistant, Lola dragged the two girls behind her, turning at the door to flick her whip once more amongst the watching females in the dormitory. 'See they get back to their beds and no noise,' she ordered her assistant. 'Any girl who makes problems will be punished by me personally.'

Then she led Sophie and Consuela through to a side room containing only a bed and a couch. 'Bring me pisco,' she ordered Sophie, slamming the door behind them and turning the key in the lock. 'And, you, help me out of my dress.' Consuela leapt to unlace Lola's leather sheath and, once freed from her restraint, Lola flung herself down on a low couch and spread her legs lewdly. Taking a large cup of the Peruvian brandy from Sophie, she ordered the girls to get onto the bed.

'And I want a real show,' she said, drinking down the pisco and starting to masturbate herself while watching the two females. Consuela looked uncertainly at Sophie and Lola cracked the whip, its tip flicking carelessly against Sophie's buttock. 'Get on with it.'

Holding Consuela's gaze with her own, Sophie reached out and slowly stroked one small breast in a circular motion. The pale pink bud of Consuela's nipple hardened in response to Sophie's touch and, encouraged, Sophie took the other breast in her hands and gently massaged the two pert mounds of flesh. Consuela gasped and arched her back, tightening the flesh of her breasts even further. Then she mirrored Sophie's action, first weighing the heaviness of Sophie's breasts in her hands before kneading the two globes and gently pinching out the large, dark nipples.

'Come here, I want to put these on you.' Lola's voice was becoming slurred as she continued to drink deeply from the jug of pisco, but Sophie saw that she was holding out the gold and diamond nipple rings she had been given in the camp. Sophie climbed down from the bed and presented her tits to Lola who clumsily fixed the rings in place, giving them a painful twist to make sure that they were properly clipped onto Sophie's pointed nipples. 'Now, get back to it, and liven things up a bit, will you?'

Sophie climbed back onto the bed and showed her nipples with their new decoration to Consuela. The girl's eyes widened as she recognised the Inca gold adorning Sophie's body.

'It's okay,' Sophie whispered, reaching to guide Consuela's head towards one of her nipples. 'Suck me while she's watching. She's getting drunk, I don't think she'll be awake much longer.'

Consuela obeyed Sophie's whispered instruction, bending her head to take one of the nipple rings between her lips and tugging gently on it, then moving her lips over the whole of the large dark teat and sucking rhythmically. Sophie closed her eyes. The feeling of the girl's mouth on her tender flesh was exquisite and she felt the juices of her unsatisfied arousal

173

beginning to flow back into her sex flesh. She reached down and carefully moved her hand between Consuela's thighs. Still sucking on Sophie's breast, the girl shifted her position to allow Sophie access to her pussy and Sophie pushed a finger between her warm sex lips, surprised by the wetness which demonstrated the girl's arousal. Pulling the girl's mouth from her nipple, Sophie bid her lie back on the bed and spread her legs apart.

Consuela's pussy was small and neat, the pink sex flesh deliciously folded to hide her tiny hole. Sophie parted the labia at the top of her slit and teased out Consuela's clitoris from beneath its protective fleshy hood with her finger. Consuela's eyes were closed and her breathing was becoming laboured as Sophie gently probed her sex, moving the labia further apart, catching her breath as she revealed the female's entrance deep within the folds of her sex flesh. Sophie dipped her finger into Consuela's hole and was rewarded with a moan as the girl clenched her muscles around the intrusion. Sophie carefully glanced across at Lola who was sleeping in a drunken stupor on the couch; she could wait till later, Sophie thought, turning back to Consuela. She shifted her position until she was kneeling on all fours, her face over Consuela's pussy and her own cunt placed above Consuela's head.

Consuela had opened her eyes and was reaching up to pull apart the folds of Sophie's labia with her fingers. She stroked the soft flesh for a moment, then reached out and pulled Sophie's buttocks towards her face. Sophie settled her pussy over Consuela's mouth gratefully and the girl began to lick and suck her sex eagerly. Giving a long sigh, Sophie turned to regard Consuela's open pussy, as her own body began to respond to the girl's cunnilingus. She sank her mouth onto Consuela's cunt and the two girls moaned with pleasure.

Sophie reached her climax first, rocking her hips as Consuela thrust two fingers into her hole to finish her off. As her groans subsided, Sophie reached for Lola's box of dildos, selecting a long thin member from the assortment. She proceeded to gently masturbate Consuela with the shaft, all the time keeping up

174

her oral stimulation of Consuela's clit until the girl was drenched in sweat and came with a series of sharp cries, her hands massaging her own small breasts while Sophie worked at her sex flesh, her body racked with the release of a massive orgasm.

Chapter Nine

Sophie and Consuela were still lying on the bed, clutched in each other's arms, when Lola finally began to emerge from her deep alcohol-induced sleep. She groaned and muttered to herself, slapping her chops together, but the exhausted women didn't hear her. Then with a roar she came fully awake.

'Hey, you two, get your asses off the bed . . .' She stopped as a dull, but very loud 'thud' sounded in the distance and the next second the room rocked with the force of an explosion. 'What the hell . . .?'

Lola's face was suddenly creased with fear and, ignoring the two girls, she reached under the bed and pulled out a box. She delved inside, dragged out a black shift and pulled it on over her head before heading for the door, still brandishing her whip. Another thud shook the hut to its foundations and Sophie sat up on the bed in alarm; through the open door she could see the other women running to and fro, gabbling in a mixture of Spanish and Quechua, a few screaming hysterically.

She grabbed Consuela's hand. 'Come on,' she said and sprang off the bed to rootle through the box. To her relief it contained a motley assortment of clothes, ranging from the bizarre to the mundane, but fortunately it also included a few shorts, jeans and shirts. Consuela, however, was still sitting on the bed, staring at the walls in a fixed state of terror and Sophie had to shake her by the wrist to make her respond.

'Consuela!' she snapped. 'Concentrate! Get dressed, this could be our way out of here.' Consuela gave her a wide-eyed look and nodded slowly, pulling on the skirt and T-shirt Sophie held out to her, whilst Sophie pulled on a pair of denim cut-offs and a man's shirt, tying it in a knot around her midriff.

She reached out to Consuela and started unbuckling the leather collar from around her neck. Consuela shrank back whimpering, 'Lola will be so angry if we take them off.'

'Fuck Lola,' Sophie muttered. 'Come on, get mine off me.'

Almost in tears Consuela complied and giving her no time to argue any further Sophie grabbed her hand and led her out of the bedroom and into the women's dormitory.

Outside the window the night sky was lit up in a glow of red. As Sophie's brain tried to work out exactly what to do there was another explosion, and the women beating on the barn doors at the far end screamed in unison. She grabbed one of the girls by the hand as she scurried past. 'What's going on?'

The girl stopped. 'Terrorista!' she hissed.

'What?'

The girl nodded, clearly terrified. 'They will kill us all!'

Consuela gripped Sophie's arm and started trying to drag her back out of the room. 'She is right. Come! We might try to hide.'

At the front of the hut the women were still banging on the door, trying vainly to break through.

'Maybe they're coming to save us.'

Consuela looked at Sophie and shook her head. 'They are the Terrorista! They do not save people like us!'

There was a flurry at the front door and as the sound of men's voices came through into the hall the women backed away. Two shots rang out and the heavy wooden doors started to swing inwards, revealing three figures outlined against the blaze behind. For a moment the women fell silent and two of the newcomers stepped forward; they were dressed in uniforms like the guards and they both held guns. As one, the women groaned with disappointment and moved back in a herd, all except for Lola, who cackled and walked forward.

'Hey? About time too! Have you sorted out those pig Terrorista yet? Huh?'

She stopped abruptly as the third, central figure moved into the light. Unlike the others he was dressed in casual western clothes, although he too had a handgun.

'Who are you?' he asked in Spanish.

'I am Lola, I run this place,' she snarled back. 'Who are you?'

The tall impassive figure looked down at her and clearly judged her wanting.

'Get out of here,' he told her, the sound of revulsion in his voice. 'Go with your friends and the camp attendants and leave this place.' His gaze roamed around the rest of the room, flowing over the women there.

'We are the Camino del Or, the Golden Way. We are here to get you out. This camp will be ashes before dawn.' He glanced back at Lola standing in front of him and his lip curled with dislike. 'You and your kind have a choice, you can either be escorted to Puerto Maldonado or you can take back your life with your own people. Either way, you will leave now. Make your minds up.'

'Hey,' Lola spat out, 'who do you think you are? Telling me what to do.'

She yelped as the two guards immediately pointed their guns at her and the stranger's hand whipped out, gripping her wrist and forcing her to her knees.

'I am Eduardo Or,' he told her in a cold voice, 'and I know exactly what you are. You are in no position to argue or to make demands about anything and I promise you this, if I hear of you setting up a business like this again, then I will not offer you the chance to leave. Do you understand me?'

His voice was dark and threatening. 'Most of the rest of you are not here by choice and you are free to make your own decisions. But she –' he looked down at Lola grovelling on the floor in front of him – 'she leaves now for Puerto Maldonado with the guards.' He raised his voice again. 'And if you go to the town warn all who come into the forest that we will not allow places like this to exist any more.'

Still shaking, Consuela put up her arm. 'Please, senor, how can we find our families?'

One of the henchmen at his side answered. 'We will help you.'

She nodded and walked forward. 'Then I will go with you.'

The women started filing out, some heading towards the group of guards who stood, their own holsters empty, surrounded by men in black with guns. Sophie remained silent, tempted to follow Consuela, but loath to draw attention to herself. As the room cleared the central figure turned towards her.

'Sophie?' It was a definite question, as if he recognised her but couldn't quite believe his eyes.

She started. 'What? Who is that?'

'It is I.' He walked towards her and instinctively she backed away nervously.

'Who?'

The figure came forward. 'Your shaman.' She stared. 'Come, Sophie!' He reached out to her and as he came closer she could see that it was indeed the shaman.

'What are you doing here?'

'There is no time for explanations now.'

'But . . .'

'Don't be afraid.' She stared at him warily. 'I won't hurt you, I've come to rescue you.' In the red glow he smiled again. 'Come, we must go. My men are setting fire to the camp, we have only a few minutes.'

She made her decision and took his hand. 'Let's go!'

Outside the hut there were Peruvian Indians, men she didn't recognise, who were setting fire to the huts, and between them and the outer perimeter the scene was one of carnage. With a shout from the shaman they ran away from the camp; in front of her the women were scattering, some running into the forest with the tribesmen, others, including Lola, taking a different direction with the guards and a few of the miners. The captain and Pip, however, were nowhere to be seen.

'This way,' the shaman told her, leading her into the jungle, following the path of the brothel-women and tribesmen. For a moment Sophie resisted. 'You don't have any choice,' he told her.

'I don't want to go back to your camp!' she said desperately. 'Where are they going?' she asked pointing to the others. 'Shouldn't I be going that way?' He shook his head.

'They are going to Puerto Maldonado. You come with me, I will see you get back to Lima.'

She stopped dead in her tracks and stared at him, hardly able to believe her ears. 'What?'

He smiled. 'Cusco first, then Lima. I promise.'

Hours later they were still walking through the forest, the top canopy of trees had closed over them and with a sinking heart Sophie was beginning to wonder where all this was going to end. The shaman's hand gripped hers tightly but no-one spoke to her as they walked in file through the night.

The rest of the small group in front and behind them appeared to be very sure-footed and quite confident of their direction, although Sophie could see no clues or indicators to distinguish one part of the forest from another. Occasionally she would trip and the shaman would take her arm and help her along, and at other times the men would move towards her and speak rapidly in Quechua, casting irritable looks in her direction. The result was always the same; the shaman answered them in staccato terms and they moved back to their positions. Whatever the reason, and whatever the motives, she was once again a prized possession, a prisoner or a guest, she wasn't sure which.

They were deep in the forest before they stopped for a break but when they did they weren't at the tribal encampment, much to Sophie's relief. Instead they paused at a plain rock face with a single cave opening. There was a pool nearby, but no sign of any proper dwellings. The rest of the group gathered together and the tribesmen disappeared into the cave, emerging a few moments later with bundles of food. They shared them out and everyone sat down to eat, Sophie now noticeably excluded from their little group by the other women. She decided she didn't care much, and sat to one side, munching on flatbread and fruit whilst the shaman and the tribesmen muttered together. At length the men called an end to the respite and with a lot of grumbling the group got to their feet once again.

Sophie stood as well but the shaman took hold of her arm.

'We are not going that way, Sophie.'

'Oh?'

'We stay here tonight.' He guided her into the cave and lit a lamp, pointing to a bed in the corner. 'If you are tired you should sleep, we will move again in the morning.'

'Where in the morning?' she asked bitterly. 'Back to the tribe so you can lock me up like the last time?'

He shook his head. 'No, I told you, I will take you to Cusco, but we are still several days' walk away. I know you do not trust me,' he went on, seeing her expression, 'but recall that I brought you out of the camp. Please try to believe me.'

'Okay,' she said, 'I'll try.' He nodded and turned away but Sophie hadn't finished. 'Wait! Don't you think I deserve some explanations?' He didn't reply. 'Oh, come on,' she exploded. 'I'm trying to understand what's going on. And I want some answers.'

'What do you want to know?'

She stared at him. 'What do I want to know? I want to know what the hell's going on. There I am stuffed in a fucking brothel and suddenly you charge in like the A-team with your bunch of toy soldiers, setting fire to everything and hacking people to pieces.' She swallowed, suddenly nauseous at the recollection, but the shaman stood in front of her, apparently unmoved.

'You do not understand.'

'You're bloody right I don't. And what's all this Eduardo stuff?'

'When did you hear that?'

She glared at him. 'I'm not completely stupid, you know, I

182

do have ears. Now will you please tell me what the hell is going on?'

The shaman sighed and sat down in front of her. 'My name is Eduardo Or.'

'And all that I'm-the-shaman, the-man-with-no-name stuff?'

He shrugged. 'When I am with the tribe that is also true.'

'You certainly get around,' she said with more than a little sarcasm, but Eduardo didn't respond. 'Pip called you a bunch of ingrates.'

'Who?'

'Philip Blakemore.'

'Blakemore is a bastard.'

She laughed. 'You got that right.'

'He has abused the trust of my people as well as yours.'

'It's just a pity you didn't tell me that before I handed myself back to him.'

'That is in the past.' Eduardo stood up.

'Hey!' she said. 'I need a little more of an explanation. Like what you thought you were doing holding me in the camp.'

'I am the shaman, Sophie, it is my job to do the tribe's bidding.'

It was Sophie's turn to scowl. 'You imprisoned me.'

'I could do nothing.'

She shook her head. 'I don't believe that. You just set all those people free but you were quite happy to let me be the subject of some stupid test and then keep me captive.'

'It is our religion.' He stared down at her, unfathomable and full of contradictions. 'I was not lying, the people did believe you were Sofa.'

'But you didn't!'

'You fitted all the prophecies.'

'Right!'

'I would have got you out, I would not have let harm come to you.' He sighed. 'I would have found a way to help you, but you told me you were working with Blakemore. I already knew who he was. I thought it best to keep you in the camp until I

183

had a chance to decide what to do with you. Then, when you left like that . . .'

'Like what?' She almost punched him. 'I sneaked out of your bloody camp and ran for my life! What would you have done?'

He was shaking his head. 'I had no choice.'

'So how come all of a sudden you're willing to take me to Cusco?'

'I am trying to make amends. I was wrong. You were not working with Blakemore and his people.'

'You've got that right.'

'Sophie, when I found out the truth, I raided the camp as soon as I could bring enough people together.' She turned around and sat down, trying to ignore him. 'Do you believe that?'

She took a deep breath. 'I'd like to, but you haven't exactly been consistent.' There was long silence. 'How did you find out Pip and I weren't lovebirds any more?'

'We have people in the camp, and there was word from Lima.'

'So where are your people now?'

'Waiting for my return.'

'Do they know about you?' He shook his head. 'And you just come and go? How come you speak English?'

He shrugged. 'My family are wealthy.'

'So why all this?'

'I could no longer bear the destruction of the rainforest; western businesses taking what they wanted and leaving desolation behind. I decided to join a group that takes direct action.'

'Terrorists.'

'The name does not matter. We will not go away. We will reclaim the forest, even if the government is too weak to throw out the malcontents and too poor to refuse the lure of the West.'

'Oh God,' she scoffed. 'Just what I need, stuck in the rainforest with an eco-warrior.'

Eduardo stood up. 'You are hardly in a position to mock, Sophie.' With stiff politeness he walked to the entrance to the cave. 'Imagine what would have happened if I had not come to rescue you.'

'You expect me to believe that the raid was just to rescue me?'

'You are important to the tribe,' he told her simply. 'And to me,' he said, and left the cave.

Sophie glowered at the wall of the cave, more than a little unwilling to believe anything Eduardo told her. Eventually she calmed down enough to go outside; it was the middle of the night and he was sitting on a boulder at the side of the pool. He looked across at her in the moonlight and smiled. Apparently their row hadn't altered his new attitude towards her.

'You look like you could do with a bath.'

'Thanks a lot,' she said crossly, 'that's a really good conversation starter. And exactly where am I going to get a bath?'

'There. Use the pool. We are all alone.'

She looked down onto the pool; there was a break in the trees, the night was warm, the moon was shimmering on the water and it looked inviting to say the least. 'What about the caymen?' The shaman gave a little laugh. 'Well?'

'There are no crocodiles here.'

She looked at him and then at the water again and felt the grime on her body.

'Okay.'

He nodded. 'I will sit guard, just in case.'

Sophie made her way down to the water, pulled her clothes off, and tiptoed through the rocky pebbles that lay around the edge of the pool. The water was cool and gentle on her tired body, and she slid in and under the surface, scrubbing at her hair, her face and all over her body, feeling the grime fall away into the bottom of the pool.

When she looked across to the shore the shaman was there,

sitting on the bank, watching her. 'You look particularly lovely in the water.'

'You've seen it all before,' she told him smartly.

He laughed. 'Not like this. But I do remember seeing you before, under the waterfall.'

His shirt was unbuttoned and she could see his smooth hairless body and well-built chest glistening in the night; she could remember the last time as well, the only time they had been together. And she knew she wanted him again. 'You could come in if you wanted,' she told him. 'I haven't got used to you in clothes yet.' Without another word he slid off his shirt and chinos and slipped in to join her just where she was standing, shoulder-deep in dark blue waters. 'I'm still mad at you and all your people,' she said sharply, 'and I didn't say you could come right up to me.'

'No, you didn't.' He ran his fingers along the side of her face then leaned forward to kiss her gently on the lips. 'But I knew you wanted to.' Sophie closed her eyes and reached up to hold him, to kiss him back; his arms slid down her naked back, reaching beneath the water to caress her and, as the moon started to sink in the sky, they left the water for the riverbank, to lie there clasped in each other's arms.

Eduardo ran his fingers along Sophie's flank, her fingers stroked her hair and teased the strands out of her eyes, running down her wet skin, brushing away the droplets where they collected between her breasts, in her navel, tickling her as his fingers moved around her body.

She rolled him over on the ground and lay on top of him, their bodies entwined, fused together from head to toe; then she kissed him carefully and began to work her way down his body, blowing gently on him as she went, watching his skin ripple in the cool air. His sleek body glistened and shone and he looked completely at peace. She stroked her way to his thighs, and straddled him on all fours, working her way back to where his penis lay, alive and swollen to its full extent, curving gently against his belly.

Then she looked up to see Eduardo's eyes watching her. Before he could speak and break the silence she crouched above him and slid him inside her. Lying flat above him they both savoured the moment; she moved herself slowly up and down, feeling and seeing tremors of pleasure running across his face, his eyes shut tight as he sank into the depths of semi-consciousness.

Sophie lifted herself up, sat astride him and began to rock gently, to and fro, backwards and forwards. Eduardo groaned and her movements increased in speed and depth; she could feel him deep inside her, stretched almost to the point of pain when she rocked back, and eased into relaxation when she moved forward, totally in control.

Eduardo's fingers reached out to her hard, erect nipples, and he placed his hands on her breasts, holding them, feeling them move to and fro, stroking the damp skin, then moving down to her thighs, stroking the new growth of dark golden hair and exploring the crevices between her thighs, touching her clitoris, teasing it into a greater swollen fullness. His fingers matched her rhythm, and they rocked in silence, the faint sounds of the jungle at night all around them.

At last Eduardo's eyes opened again; his hair was slick with sweat and his face was creased with the need for restraint. With a sigh, he rolled Sophie over. 'Now it is my turn,' he told her, pinning her down beneath him. Instead of giving in, Sophie reached up and put her arms around his neck, dragging him down to kiss her once again, rolling him onto his back. Eduardo laughed and the atmosphere of intense, moody sexuality changed into a feeling of fun. They both started giggling like children, their laughter cutting into the fading night, rolling over and over on the ground, dust and twigs getting in their hair, rolling onto and off the pebbles, getting almost as far as the water, where they stopped.

Suddenly they were frantic for each other's body, they were panting with desire and desperate to reach a state of climax. Eduardo pinned Sophie down again and kissed her passionately; his tongue was roaming around her mouth, breaking off only to smother her neck and shoulders with more kisses, the two of them moving and grinding their hips together, their bodies breaking into a sheen of sweat as their climax approached. Sophie cried out in abandon and Eduardo groaned and gasped, thrusting himself into her, his body wrenched into convulsions every bit as desperate as hers until the two came together in a series of intense, fiery orgasms.

They lay entwined in each other's arms, staring up at the trees as they changed from the grey of dawn to deep shades of green with the sunlight flickering through the branches. Howler monkeys started screeching in the treetops and the macaws and parrots took flight, heralding the start of the day.

Eventually Eduardo spoke. 'You could stay here.'

'What and be a slave for the tribe?' Sophie was only half-joking.

'No, be with me.'

'Isn't that the same?'

'No, you know it is not.'

She looked at him for a long moment, then smiled cynically. 'Oh I see, is that what the big seduction scene was all about?'

'I do not understand.'

Sophie's lips hardened into a thin narrow line. 'I am going home and I am clearing my name. No-one is going to stop me doing that.'

'Why would I want to stop you?'

'I don't know,' she snapped, the pleasure of their union dissipating rapidly. 'Perhaps you think I'd tell everyone about your little double life here.'

'No-one would believe you.'

'Oh no?'

He pushed himself up on one elbow. 'Sophie, I know what you really want and that's to stay with me.'

Sophie shook her head. 'Why is it the men in my life are always telling me what I want? That they know what I want.'

She stood up and grabbed for her clothes. 'Well, I decide what I want and what I do.'

Eduardo's hand reached out to run up her thigh. 'You need to give yourself up to your own desires.'

'I've heard that before too,' she hissed.

Eduardo pulled himself to his feet. 'Very well,' he said stiffly, 'you will go home. Will you at least agree to wait in Cusco until I have completed some business before leaving?'

Sophie shrugged. 'I've told you, I just want to go home. Please don't break your word this time.'

Eduardo's face grew hard. 'I think you will find I have never broken my word to you.'

'Whatever you say. Just don't ask me to trust the word of the descendants of the Incas. You might find that doesn't have much weight with me.' She looked about her, their temporary idyll gone for good. 'Okay, let's go.'

They entered Cusco under cover of darkness two days later. Sophie had been expecting another Puerto Maldonado, but it was immediately evident that this was no frontier shanty town; instead it was a lovely city with beautifully kept Spanish colonial architecture.

On the outskirts they were met by a car, a taxi, she assumed, until she saw the way the driver treated Eduardo, part deference, part awe and part fear. Clearly he was well known here. They drove down to the city from the surrounding hills and Sophie glimpsed the huge white stone Christ figure dominating the city skyline, then they moved onwards to the centre of town.

The car deposited them in the Plaza del Armas and, taking Sophie's arm, Eduardo guided her around the bustling square and along the Avenida del Sol, finally stopping at the front of a large hotel.

'The Hotel del Incas,' Eduardo told her. 'It is built on the remains of an Inca temple, the Temple of the Virgins of the Sun.' Sophie raised her eyebrows in disbelief and Eduardo gave a low laugh. 'It is true, in this place the Sun Virgins would brew chicha for the Lord Inca.'

'And?' Sophie gave Eduardo a questioning look, but his expression was inscrutable and he pointed further down the street.

'There is the site of the Koricancha, the Temple of the Sun,' he said, his gaze lost in the history of his people. 'It would have been covered in sheets of gold, blazing in the sun. A testimony to the power of the Inca rulers of Peru.' He turned to face Sophie and smiled. 'And of course, the Lord Inca would keep over two hundred Mamacomas, Sun Virgins, in his household.'

'Not just to brew beer, I'll bet,' Sophie muttered.

'No,' Eduardo laughed. 'Their purpose would be to serve Inti, the Sun God. They would beg favours of Inti on behalf of the Lord Inca and would be expected to give him sexual satisfaction in return.'

'What a surprise,' she murmured and Eduardo laughed again.

'You are tired. Come, I have a room waiting.' Eduardo escorted her indoors, where, true to his word, they were clearly expected. The hotel staff were brisk but pleasant and Sophie was soon in a large comfortable room on the second floor, looking out over the ruins of the temple. Eduardo stood at the door watching her examine the room.

'Seems fine,' she said sharply, trying to ignore his gaze.

Since they had begun to approach the city their conversations had been limited to mundane questions about the distance still to go and the direction in which they were travelling. But while Eduardo had been talking about the history of Cusco, Sophie had found herself increasingly entranced and his words had begun to conjure up disturbingly arousing images in her mind; his hand on her arm as he guided her to her room had caused a frisson of excitement to run along her spine, but the last thing she wanted now was to encourage any further intimacy between them, and she told herself that she was simply overwrought.

At last Eduardo spoke. 'I must leave you here,' he told her, and bowed briefly in a formal farewell. 'If you need anything call the management, they will attend to all your needs. I have some arrangements to complete but I will return later and we will discuss your return to London.'

Then he was gone, off on his mysterious errand.

She knew she could call Lima and have the company arrange for her to travel home, but the thought of the general disbelief her return was going to generate, and the explanations she would have to provide, was suddenly too much to contemplate. At least for now.

Telling herself that she at least owed it to Eduardo to stay put until he had done whatever he had to do in Cusco, Sophie decided to take advantage of the hotel room to wind down after her long, long journey.

Chapter Ten

The best things about the Hotel del Incas, Sophie decided as she lay in the bath, were the refrigerator, the mini-bar and the unlimited hot water. The forest pool had been a pleasant distraction, she told herself, but thank God for a big tub, bubble bath and soft fluffy towels.

Breathing a deep sigh of relief she added more hot water to the bath; it came flooding out of the taps, warming her toes, working its way up her body in swirling currents. Ecstasy, and there was also a glass of chilled white wine at her fingertips and a fresh crisp bed to get into when she was completely clean.

She stroked her cleavage, luxuriating in the scent and sensation of soapy suds flowing over her body, sliding her fingers down through the water to caress her thighs. Delicious sensations flowed over her, and she let her head roll back onto the rest behind. This was heaven and she was floating on a carpet of luxury. She sipped wine, let her fingers slip down her body to where soft bristles of pubic hair were beginning to grow, and allowed her thoughts to wander back to her experiences with Charles and Pip in London. It all seemed so long ago.

Her mind shied away from recalling most of the horrors of her adventure in the rainforest, but she was drawn to remember the intense sexual experiences of the tribal ritual in which she had taken part. And her thoughts inevitably turned to the enigmatic shaman – now Eduardo – and their lovemaking.

What Eduardo was doing right now she had no idea, and

neither did she care, she told herself sternly. But still, he was always there, lurking at the back of her thoughts. In a way, for all their bickering in the forest, she was not looking forward to being on her own. However, she told herself as she rinsed the fluffy white bubbles from her skin, it was only his cock she'd miss, not the rest of him.

Almost without noticing, she had casually teased herself into arousal by thinking about his attentions to her body in his various guises; a little fantasy of life in the jungle began to play itself out in front of her, one where there was no inconvenience like a complete lack of hot water. Still, she thought, if Eduardo was really as rich and powerful as he said maybe they could split her time between Cusco and the jungle.

She laughed, giving herself a mental shake. This was ridiculous. The best, the most intelligent, no, the only thing to do was to go back home and clear her name. She couldn't go through life with people thinking all this mess was down to her; she should get out of this bloody country and never come back.

She paused in her thoughts; it was a pity Pip couldn't be taken back home to face his just desserts. Eduardo had been particularly reticent about Pip's fate and considering some of what she had seen she wasn't sure she wanted any details.

She lay back again, reaching for the wine with one hand, and into the sudsy water with the other. Her body felt reinvigorated and relaxed. Now was the time when Eduardo should come back and caress her, stroke her, get that incredible cock of his out and start teasing her with it. This was the moment when he should tell her she should stay and give in to her desires, she told herself, her fingers running around her flesh, stroking her swollen clit.

This was when she was most weak, when he could persuade her to do anything, particularly if he started easing himself inside her, kissing her and stroking her breasts and teasing her nipples . . .

She jumped as a finger slid over her shoulder and stroked

194

its way through the water, caressing her breast with care. Sophie leaned back against the bath with a smile. 'That's wonderful,' she murmured as her nipples were stroked into hardness. 'Mmm, Eduardo, yes. I was just thinking about you . . .'

'You are mistaken, Sophie. Surely you can tell the difference between your various lovers by now.'

She opened her eyes to see Pip staring down at her. She gasped in panic, but before she could scream his hand was over her mouth and only a muffled squawk came out.

'So here you are,' he sneered. 'I'll bet this is a little surprise you didn't expect.' She shook her head. 'Get out of the water,' Pip snarled. 'And don't start screaming or I'll knock you right back in there and hold you under.'

Sophie nodded her acquiescence and stepped out of the bath, the bubbles clinging languorously to her body. Pip's eyes ran over her and he smiled.

'You know you're in better shape now that when you were in London. A few weeks' work and exercise has toned you up in lots of ways, I'll bet.' He reached out and grasped her crotch, watching for her reaction, letting a finger run around her labia. 'Perhaps you've been working overtime with your new friend Eduardo?'

Sophie reached for a bath towel and tried to summon a little dignity above the panic that had flooded her brain. 'At least he's someone who knows how to do it on his own. He doesn't need an audience to get it up!'

For a moment she thought Pip would carry out his threat and knock her senseless into the bath, but in the end he pushed her aside.

'Just get in there,' he said, indicating the bedroom. 'And get dressed. No tricks. No delays.' She followed his instructions and walked to the bedroom, putting on her jeans and a white shirt Eduardo had left behind for her. Pip never took his eyes off her.

'Where have you been?' she asked.

'What? Worried about me, were you?'

195

'No,' she replied, 'I thought you got fried in the jungle. And it would have been better for you if you had!'

Pip grabbed her and threw her onto the bed. 'Don't talk to me like that, you little bitch. I put up with your lip before but I won't put up with it any more. Understand?'

'Just keep your hands off me,' she spat.

'Oh, Sophie, and we used to be such a loving couple. Look at us now!'

'I should have known you were up to no good after what you and Charles did to me in London.'

'You enjoyed it. And anyway, I think I told you then that I had certain plans for your future.' Pip smiled with the recollection of their evening.

'You just didn't say those plans included setting me up as a thief and a prostitute!'

Pip laughed. 'You know,' he said, 'I probably didn't tell you that bit. Sorry. I should have sent you a memo.' Then his face hardened. 'You got away from me once before, but now –' he grasped her hand and drew her up to him – 'now you're not going anywhere.' His eyes ran down her body again. 'At least you've got some experience and I shouldn't have any troubling selling you on to someone who likes a bitch with a bit of spirit.'

'I'm not going anywhere with you,' she snapped. 'I'm going back to England to clear my name.'

Pip laughed. 'No, you're not, Sophie. You're coming with me whether you like it or not.' He glared at her. 'Normally I don't hold a grudge in business, but I don't have anything to lose any more.'

'I don't understand,' she told him, desperately playing for time, hoping Eduardo would appear.

'You've ruined the operation in the forest and now, you know what? I can't get my money out of Switzerland; that little witch India has managed to tie everything up. My partners aren't happy with me either. They like to keep a low profile and because of you and those terrorist friends of yours their names are all coming to the surface.'

'Good,' she said shortly. 'I hope they suffer.'

'I wouldn't start cheering yet,' he said. 'And you can drop the little princess routine. Forget about stalling, no-one's coming to save you this time.' Pip pushed his face up close to hers and she realised he was holding a knife. 'I need some ready cash to get out of this place and get my money. You're all I've got left to sell, and I'm going to get as good a price as I can. The people I deal with like the merchandise in a reasonable state for transport, but they're not that fussy. They don't really care if there are a few marks.' He straightened up and pointed towards the door. 'Get moving or else I'll have to start kicking you into shape. And I mean literally.'

Sophie set her lips in a thin line and did as she was told, opening the door onto the corridor. Pip pulled her back and, leaning out of the room, he glanced quickly up and down; the way was deserted. 'Come on,' he snapped, 'maybe I can salvage something from this mess after all.' He pushed her into the corridor, and marched her forward, out of the fire door and then down the rickety iron fire escape at the back of the building. At the bottom, Pip grabbed her arm. 'Come on,' he said, guiding her down the backstreets, 'we're going to see the fleshpots of Cusco!'

Pip and Sophie made their way through a labyrinth of dingy streets, finally emerging onto a dirty thoroughfare where neon lights shone unshaded from cheap bars and where hostesses clustered around the doors of every night-club, trying to persuade passing tourists to go inside.

There were lots of people around, and more than once Sophie was on the verge of asking for help, but Pip kept her moving and no-one would meet her eyes. At last Pip stopped at a small tatty-looking door; he knocked and a grille in the door shot open and was almost immediately slammed shut. The door opened and Pip pushed Sophie inside.

Keeping a painful grip on her upper arm, Pip spoke rapidly in Spanish to the huge bouncer behind the door. The bouncer's face remained impassive as his eyes raked over Sophie's body, taking in her long blonde hair and lingering on her chest which was barely disguised under the big white shirt she was wearing. After a few moments he stopped Pip's gabbling by raising his hand and indicated a staircase at the end of the corridor. Sophie could hear the familiar beat of erotic music emanating from the basement and she looked over her shoulder in panic at the bouncer as Pip started to hustle her towards the staircase.

'Down the stairs,' Pip snarled, pushing her ahead of him. Sophie stumbled forward and found herself in the basement where she was momentarily blinded by the glare from lights trained on a low stage at the far end of a tiny, windowless room. As her eyes adjusted to the light she saw that it was packed with men of various nationalities, drinking beer and smoking but mainly sitting in silent contemplation of the entertainment on the stage in front of them.

Two women were dancing, each dressed in different erotic outfits, and each using the music to simulate various sexual acts. The first was attired as a dominatrix in a tight PVC basque with cut-away sections exposing her breasts, crotch and buttocks; she was brandishing a cat o'nine tails and thrusting her hips forward suggestively. The second female was wearing pussy-pouter panties, the lips of her sex pushed outwards by the design of the crotchless briefs; she wore no bra but her large breasts were adorned by nipple studs from which tassels were hanging. She alternately displayed her front and rear and she wriggled her hips as she pulled her buttocks apart to display her bottom cleft to the assembled crowd.

Moving amongst the crowd of men, several semi-naked females were selling drinks and coca. One woman was sitting on the lap of one of the men, clearly engaged in sex, while another fondled her breasts in front of them. As the seated man grunted his climax, the second man unzipped his flies and pulled the female onto his lap, impaling her on his engorged cock. She immediately began to move up and down, her breasts jiggling with the effort whilst other men started to cluster round, waiting their turn.

Suddenly, one of the men in the crowd stepped forward with his arm raised and Sophie saw that he had a fist full of cash. Pointing to the dominatrix, the man shouted a figure and a pimp stepped out of the shadows on the stage, repeating the figure whilst exhorting the woman to carry on dancing. All hell seemed to be let loose on the floor of the room as other men leapt forward, all brandishing money and shouting their bids for each of the women. Sophie watched in horror as the auction finally reached its climax, with the two women being pulled down off the stage and handed over to the highest bidders.

'Now that's what I call trading,' Pip leered, as the next two were pushed onto the stage and the music started again. The crowd again became quiescent, sitting back down and ordering drinks as they prepared to watch the show before the auction started again. 'Come on, it's time to show you off.'

Pip pushed Sophie towards the side of the stage where they were met by another huge man who motioned them into a further back room. Pip pushed Sophie into a spotlight in the centre; she was vaguely aware that there were several other people there but they were hidden behind the spotlight itself.

'Take your clothes off.' Pip snapped the order from behind her shoulder.

'No.' Sophie's voice was quiet but defiant.

'Strip her,' one of the men behind the spotlight shouted and immediately, Sophie's arms were pinned behind her back and a gag pulled over her mouth as one of the bouncers ripped her shirt apart and dragged her jeans to her ankles.

'Not bad. She has a fine pair of tits,' the disembodied opinion came after a moment's pause. 'And you say that no-one in London will miss her?'

'No.' Pip's voice was tense. 'They think she's dead.'

'Let me see her pussy.' Pushing Sophie to the ground, the bouncers pulled Sophie's legs into the air and spread them apart so that she was lewdly exposed to the watching men. She heard shuffling as though the men were moving closer to get a better look. 'And her ass.' Letting her legs fall and turning her over onto her hands and knees, the bouncers shoved her shoulders to the ground and prised her buttocks apart. 'Mmm, but you say she's still a virgin there.'

'Yeah.' Pip's voice again. 'But she can be stretched, surely. And think of the fun doing it.'

'We are not interested in fun, only business.' There was another silence before the buyer spoke again. 'It's extremely risky for us taking European pussy, although I will admit that she would fetch a fine price in the Middle East or even the Far East. Has she been slave trained?'

Pip laughed. 'Well, you can see that she's not exactly obedient but she has worked as a prostitute and I can personally vouch for her if properly handled.' There was an interminable pause as the men murmured together at the far end of the room and Sophie's heart pounded as she waited to hear her fate.

'Very well, you will come with us and we will agree a price. She will have to be trained before being sold on but we can take that into account.' The man snapped his fingers to the bouncers. 'See that she is secured. I will call for her later. I will need the ass dildo.'

The bouncers pulled Sophie to her feet and, as the men rose to leave the room, she managed to struggle free of the restraining hands on her arms and tear the gag from her mouth. 'He's lying,' she screamed. 'They do know that I'm alive and they're looking for me now.'

Pip laughed harshly. 'Pay no attention to her,' he scoffed. 'No-one knows she's here in Cusco. London thinks she died in the jungle.'

'Silence her,' the buyer snapped and the bouncers reached to pull the gag back over Sophie's mouth. 'You will be punished later for this insolence.'

Biting at the bouncer's hand, Sophie struggled free again.

'If you don't believe me, perhaps you'll believe Eduardo Or,' she spat out.

She was as astonished as Pip as the room plunged into silence. Then the buyer snapped, 'Stop. Unhand her.' Sophie could only hear the pounding of her heart and as the silence continued, she bent to drag her jeans back up from her ankles and pull the shreds of her shirt across her chest. 'What do you know of Eduardo Or?' the buyer spoke quietly from behind the spotlight.

'He brought me out of the rainforest and he is in contact with London right now to tell them I am alive,' Sophie spoke softly, adding as confidently as she could, 'And he has personally guaranteed my safe return to Europe.'

Pip broke in, 'She's lying. This Eduardo had it away with her and then he dumped her in the hotel. He has no interest . . .'

'Stop. This is a chance we cannot take,' the buyer spoke quickly, barking out a series of orders to the bouncers before turning back to Pip. 'The deal is off.'

Pip opened his mouth to speak again, but Sophie was being unceremoniously dragged out of the room by the bouncers and pushed up the stairs, out of the street door and bundled into the back seat of the nearest taxi. As the door was slammed shut on her, Sophie realised that the driver was waiting for her instructions, peering curiously at her in his rear-view mirror. Starting to laugh from pure relief, Sophie gathered her wits sufficiently to say, 'Hotel del Incas,' before slumping into the back seat and letting the cab drive her away.

Ignoring the stares of the hotel reception staff, Sophie walked through the Hotel del Incas and took the lift to her room. The door was still unlocked and she passed gratefully into the dark interior, shutting the door quietly behind her.

'Where the hell have you been?' Sophie jumped at the softly spoken question from a dim corner of the room.

'Eduardo?'

'I've been waiting here for you. Where have you been?'

'It's a long story.' Sophie was suddenly weary and she staggered over to the bed and sat down heavily, putting her head in her hands as the enormity of her escape swept across her. With two strides, Eduardo was by her side, his hands on her shoulders.

'Are you hurt? What happened?'

Sophie raised her head to meet his anxious gaze. 'Pip came here. He forced me to go with him to some sort of sleazy auction. He was intending to . . .'

Eduardo laid a gentle finger on her lips. 'It's okay,' he said quietly, calming her mounting hysteria. 'I was afraid of something like this. Come, I will take you to a safer place. I should never have left you alone.' Gently, Eduardo pulled Sophie onto her feet and guided her to the door. Without question, she followed him, happy to let someone she trusted take control. And she realised with a start of surprise that she did indeed trust Eduardo Or; she trusted him with her life.

A limousine was waiting outside the hotel foyer and, after speaking hurriedly to the reception staff, Eduardo led Sophie out of the hotel and helped her into the car. They drove only a short distance, arriving suddenly in the quiet Plaza San Francisco.

The driver turned off the Plaza and they went down another backstreet, coming to a halt outside an imposing mansion, the wooden balconies declaring its Spanish origins. As they stepped out of the car, the ornate front door opened up and Sophie and Eduardo stepped into the cool interior of the house.

'This is my home,' Eduardo answered Sophie's unspoken question. 'You are welcome here.' Signalling to a maid who had appeared at the back of the large, airy hall, Eduardo turned his dark gaze on Sophie. 'I will answer all your questions in good time,' he said with a smile, 'but first you must rest. I will have some food brought upstairs.'

Feeling curiously calmed and excited at once, Sophie nodded and followed the maid up an elaborately carved staircase. She was shown into an enormous wooden-floored bedroom, the whitewashed walls hung with tapestries of Inca design and a huge king-sized bed laid with crisp white cotton sheets and soft pillows. The maid showed Sophie to the beautiful tiled bathroom where Sophie looked longingly at the double tub but reluctantly decided that a shower was the most expedient way of freshening up at this late hour.

Half an hour later, Sophie emerged refreshed from the shower room, wrapped in a fluffy towel and rubbing her long hair dry with another. She smiled as she saw Eduardo lounging on the bed. He had changed out of his shirt and chinos and was wearing a pair of light white cotton drawstring trousers, his chest naked and bronzed in the light of several sconces of tall candles placed around the room

'This is your bedroom, isn't it?' Sophie stopped towelling her hair and shook her locks loose.

'It's the best room in the house and I wanted you to see it.' Eduardo's eyes were impassive. 'Would you like champagne, Sophie, or is it too late an hour?'

'Champagne would be lovely.' Sophie turned to appreciate the various *objets d'art* which were skilfully displayed in cases about the room. 'There are beautiful,' she said to Eduardo as he handed her a glass of sparkling wine. She took a sip. 'So, are you going to let me know what's going on?'

Eduardo returned to the bed and lay down, propped up on one elbow with his head resting on his hand. 'It's quite simple,' he said. 'I am the first son of a wealthy Peruvian family of high class and heritage. Our Inca blood was mixed with that of Spanish noblemen many generations ago. I was given an excellent education, but I have no need to work.' He paused. 'I have travelled extensively in North America and Europe searching for a reason for my life, but I never lost my roots, my love for my people or for my country. When I cam back to Peru I spent time in the Amazon, studying the shaman's art from the great masters who practice there. I brought those skills back to the Madre de Dios to help the people who are struggling against the destruction caused by outsiders. I spend my time now in the rainforest and in Cusco where my family still live, and where I have my contacts in the professional and business world.' He looked intently at her. 'I am making a difference, Sophie. One day we will succeed.'

'And why were the men in the auction bar so afraid of your name?'

Eduardo shrugged nonchalantly. 'I am well known. I am not one to be crossed.'

Sophie realised as he spoke that she would never know this man; his history, his upbringing, his overwhelming love for Peru and its mysterious culture. But he had a hold on her which could not be broken and she wanted him so badly that she was almost in pain with the longing.

Letting her towel slip to the floor, Sophie stood for a moment, allowing Eduardo to gaze at her slender body before walking slowly to the bed where he was lounging. Eduardo sat up and held out his arms as she approached, pulling her close to him and drinking in the scent of her freshly washed skin as he pressed his face to her belly.

Gently, Eduardo pulled Sophie down onto the bed and they lay a moment looking at each other before he covered her mouth with his own, suddenly urgent in his desire to taste her flesh and explore her tender parts. Rolling on top of her, he pushed her legs apart with his thighs and devoured her exposed sex with his eyes before pushing her legs towards her chest and sinking down to take her hardening clit in his mouth. Sophie closed her eyes and moaned as he sucked hard on her clitoris, licking the emerging juices of her arousal and poking his tongue into her hole as he teased her towards a climax.

Kneeling back, Eduardo invited Sophie to look at his penis as he stroked it to even greater length and thickness while she lay supine and waiting for his invasion; she could see the droplets of his arousal sneaking out of the tiny slit in the engorged head of his cock. Sophie reached up to take hold of his cock and drew him down towards her sex. Steadying himself with his arms, Eduardo held her gaze with a long look from his dark eyes before plunging his penis into her hole.

They both let out a sigh of pure pleasure as they coupled; Eduardo started to move within Sophie's body and she set up an equal and opposite rhythm with her hips, drawing him deeper inside her and bringing him swiftly to a climax with her motion. Letting out a low moan, Eduardo pumped his come into Sophie's belly, throwing his head back, his eyes tightly closed as the waves of his orgasm pulsed through his body.

They rolled over onto their sides, Sophie keeping Eduardo's softening cock inside her hole and wrapping her legs around his thighs.

'Sorry,' Sophie laughed softly. 'That was unfair of me. I should have made you wait.' As she spoke, she felt Eduardo's cock twitch inside her hole and she squeezed her sex muscles to encourage his recovery.

'It just means I will be able to last longer next time,' Eduardo responded, moving his hips slowly against her groin. His cock gradually regaining its erection inside her, Eduardo rolled back on top of Sophie and began to work her sex again, pushing her legs over his shoulders so that her cunt was pulled tight, the tingling nerve endings in her clitoris screaming for release.

Sophie reached her own climax quickly this time but there was no rest for her. Eduardo maintained the rhythm of his sex in hers and no sooner had one orgasm begun to fade than he brought Sophie to another peak, her cries of pleasure sounding through the quiet house.

At length, Eduardo orgasmed with a grunt of relief, shooting his second climax into Sophie's hole with a series of mighty thrusts and then slumping down on the bed beside her. They lay quietly for several minutes before Eduardo raised himself on his elbow again to look down at her and stroke her flushed cheek tenderly.

'Sophie, we have to discuss what happens next.' He paused, 'I love you.'

Sophie looked at the handsome man beside her. 'I love you too,' she whispered.

'Then it is settled,' Eduardo kissed her lovingly for a long moment. 'You will stay here with me.'

Sophie closed her eyes and allowed herself to imagine again what life with this man, in this country, would be like. 'It would be all I ever wanted,' she said stroking Eduardo's limp penis gently. 'But I don't know whether it would be possible.'

Eduardo sat up briskly and poured them both another glass of champagne.

'Sophie, you must listen to me,' he said, looking at her earnestly. 'I have been waiting for you all my life. You are part of my mind, part of my body. You are meant to be here, with me, in Peru.'

For a second, Sophie told herself to give in to her desires. With Eduardo, her life would be full of unexpected challenges, that was for sure. She would get India to clear her name in the UK and then she would be able to add her knowledge of the business world and her contacts to Eduardo's. Eduardo watched her inner struggle anxiously. He let his hand reach out to touch her beautiful body and to tip her face towards his.

'Stay with me,' he whispered. 'Please, Sophie, I beg you.'

As Sophie returned his gaze, Eduardo was shocked to see the pain in her eyes. 'I'm sorry, Eduardo.' He could barely hear the words. 'I can't stay with you. It would never work.'

Epilogue

Sophie picked up her briefcase and let herself out of the office. Turner looked up at her from his desk and raised his eyebrows.

'Yes, Turner,' she told him with a tired sigh, 'I'm going home early, I am exhausted.' To her surprise, he nodded; it was only four-thirty and she had fully expected him to tease about leaving the office this early in the day.

'You look like you need it,' he said instead.

'Thanks a lot!'

'I mean it, Sophie, you really look like you need a break,' he said again. 'You've been pushing yourself too hard over the past couple of months. You should take more care of yourself.'

'So are you looking for a night off as well?'

Turner laughed. 'No. Anyway, you know I'm right.'

Sophie nodded. 'Yes, I guess so, and that's why I'm going home early.'

'With your computer?' he asked slyly.

'I'm just going to review some reports at home.'

'Mmm. Not very convincing, Miss Jenner. You know,' he went on, waving a card in front of him, 'the Swiss Partnership Christmas Party is on tonight. You should go for a few hours; it would do you more good than sitting at home with your PC.'

Sophie shook her head. 'I'm not in the mood for parties.'

'Sophie, it's nearly Christmas,' Turner reminded her in an exasperated tone. 'You need to get out and have some fun.'

Sophie smiled. 'I guess I'm just not much of a fun person these days.' She paused at the door. 'Thanks though, I appreciate the thought.'

'Think about it,' Turner called after her. 'You need a break.'

'Yeah, yeah.' She waved goodnight and made her way outside. Turner had a point, she admitted reluctantly; she had been working a lot of hours and suddenly Christmas was less than a fortnight away; even here in the City, people were rushing about with bags of shopping and the party season was definitely in full swing. On a sudden whim she caught a taxi and directed the driver to take her down through Regent's Street to look at the lights and the shop windows. At the top of Regent's Street she abruptly changed her mind; it was just too tacky and depressing. She knocked on the panel separating her from the driver. 'Let's cut the tour, can you just get me back home as quickly as possible?'

'Sorry, love,' he told her, 'we're a bit stuck now.' Frustrated, Sophie sat in the back of the car watching people milling about and emerging from department stores; kids hanging around Hamley's looking in the windows; an electric Christmas tree covering Simpson's and, worst of all, a Santa Claus standing outside the Ritz to welcome people in. She groaned out loud, but fortunately by then they were picking up speed again, making their way through the underpass at Hyde Park Corner, up into Knightsbridge and on to South Kensington.

The mews was a blessed, quiet relief in comparison. 'Sorry,' said the driver again, as she gave him a big tip, 'but you know what it's like at this time of year. Traffic's murder.' She nodded, holding her temper in check; it wasn't his fault. The taxi turned around in the road and she let herself back inside her house.

In the months since her return to England the mews had been a safe haven; even after the media scrum had broken out she had still been able to find some peace there, if only because Daria had taken her under her wing, letting Sophie hole up at her own flat for a few weeks. Somehow, over that period the two women had become good friends, strengthening tentative bonds that had outlasted Pip's manipulation.

It was only when she actually reached London that Sophie

realised how truly naive she had been in thinking she could easily clear her name, or that people would even believe her patently absurd story. In the face of the Board busily covering up their own incompetence; coping with Pip's disappearance and her inconvenient re-appearance; minimising complaints from Peru's finance administration and desperately massaging the figures from Pip's illicit ventures, she was in danger of not only being thrown out on the streets, but of having her name blackened as well.

For a time it seemed she was destined to take the rap for Pip's actions and she had felt very alone but India James had suggested that she contact Daria Williams, of all the unlikely people. India was right; it needed a more experienced operator than Sophie, someone with the right connections and the nose for a story, to take the millstone of Pip's actions from around her neck, even though she and Daria had mutually agreed to produce a vastly streamlined version of events for the general press. The resulting publicity was enough to enable Sophie to keep her job, if only because the Board wanted less, rather than more, publicity from a high-profile termination, but she was still tarred with the inference that only an incompetent manager would have allowed such embezzlement to go on without her knowledge.

At first, Sophie was ready to accept the results of her inadvertent complicity, but at length she tired of being the Board's whipping boy and struck back, threatening to tell the press a fuller story and release more information from India's private files. The result had been a negotiated agreement; she kept her position and they stopped trying to force her out. She was cleared, if not completely exonerated from blame, and now here she was, working on a new project for the bank, albeit barred from doing anything with South America, and wondering why on earth she had fought so hard to be treated like this. It was more than just the boredom and mundane nature of her new project, redesigning database systems for the business. That in itself was an insult, a definite sidewards shunt, but she continued to work hard, determined to prove her ability to her bosses, even if they didn't seem to respect her for her integrity.

To her surprise, Turner had been one of the few people to accept her word completely and offer to come back to work for her. She was determined to see he didn't suffer for his loyalty and next year, when her position was more secure, she would get him a promotion and move him on, whether he still thought she needed him to take care of her or not.

Sophie stripped off her suit, changing into jeans and a soft cotton shirt, and sat down in the living room. She opened up her notebook computer and tried to concentrate on the reports, but there was little of interest in front of her. At length, she made her way into the kitchen and pulled open the fridge door, but she wasn't really hungry and it was a bit early to start drinking. Instead she started running through her answerphone messages, another task she had grown bored with once it became clear she was never going to get a call from Eduardo.

The first call was from Daria, suggesting that they write a joint article on women in banking. The next was from a man, an American. She struggled with the name, Andrew Something. Who the hell was Andrew Jameson? Recollection suddenly dawned on her. Andrew! American fling from the summer. God, that seemed like a long time ago.

'Hi, Sophie, I'm back in town for a few days and I thought you might like to have dinner. Heard about your adventures in the jungle, you even made the American press and you know how insular we can be! I'm free if you want to go out, so if you're around page me on Andy 525, or call me at office . . .'

The phone clicked off and Sophie sighed, looking around at her empty house. She had precious few Christmas cards, no decorations and no life; this had to stop soon or she would end up in the nut-house. 'Right,' she said out loud. 'This is the best offer you've had all week. All month in fact. Get yourself together.' And with a look of grim determination she picked up the phone and called 'Andy 525'.

The party was on the top floor of a hotel off Piccadilly; once again the traffic was busy and by the time the taxi deposited her at the door Andrew was already there waiting for her, smiling as he saw her face through the glass. She just hoped he wasn't too disappointed; she had a suspicion she looked wan and depressed, but his face was shining with pleasure.

'Hey,' he said, giving her a warm hug, 'you look fabulous.'

Startled, Sophie looked at her reflection in the mirrors around the lobby. She realised with surprise that she didn't look awful at all; she was thinner and leaner than she used to be, but her face belied the stress she felt; her dress was very simple, she couldn't face fuss these days, just a straight, floor-length black gown, severe and finely cut, a single black satin band below the bust, with jet earrings and a simple matching necklace. She looked more than okay actually. She allowed herself a little smile; beneath the austere gown she was still wearing her diamond nipple rings, but no-one here was going to get a look at them!

The party was already in full swing, and it was only as she recognised the people around her that Sophie remembered with a sinking sensation that this marked the half year since it had all started. She was greeting people and walking towards the dinner table with Andrew at her side, trying very hard to ignore the stares she was getting, when it swept over her in a wave of recollection and she couldn't imagine how she could have forgotten. It was the Swiss Partnership's summer bacchanal that had set the whole chain of events into motion; it was then that Pip had dragged her into the alcove. Her mouth dried up at the recollection. The week after that she had gone to his flat and then she had gone to the US to see India. It all stemmed from that party!

Fortunately, this occasion was a more traditional affair. She forced down an excellent, if standard, Christmas dinner, and although she was quiet no-one seemed to notice. Probably because of the booze that was flowing in vast quantities, she told herself, accepting Andrew's offer of a dance. It was late, the music had slowed to a romantic pace and he took her in his arms, apparently enjoying himself immensely.

'You look amazing,' he told her.

'Thanks.'

'Are you going to tell me about your adventures?' She shook her head. 'Too scary?'

'You'd never believe it,' she assured him.

Andrew laughed and swung her around. 'Hey, but you got out of there okay, and you're back at work, right.'

She nodded, then stopped. 'Oh, what the hell. Actually, Andrew, I'm in such a crap job you wouldn't believe it.'

'How come?'

'They've shunted me as far to the side as it's possible to go and still be called an employee. You could say I'm there on sufferance.'

'So why have you stayed?'

She shrugged. 'I need a job and I don't have the energy to persuade new people I can still cut it.' She allowed herself a little smile. 'In case you hadn't noticed I'm a bit of a figure of prurient interest.'

'Some of the stares are a bit obvious,' he admitted.

'Well, I'll show them all. They're not getting rid of me that easily.'

Andrew smiled again. 'I didn't think you were a quitter.' The music drew to a close. 'Come on,' he said, 'let's get you home.'

The car drew up at her house and they both got out. For a moment, Sophie was going to send Andrew directly on his way, but it was late and she had to admit that she was enjoying his company, so instead she led the way indoors. In the kitchen she pulled out a bottle of chilled champagne, but when she got back to the lounge she found Andrew looking around in bemusement.

'What, no sign of Christmas at all? What's your name? Miss Scrooge?'

She smiled. 'I'm only just getting into the spirit. Come on, can you open this?'

He popped the cork and filled two long crystal flutes. 'Here's to Christmas spirit.' The glasses chinked together and Andrew leaned forward to kiss her lips. Sophie closed her eyes, felt his touch and tried to enjoy it, but it was no good, it meant nothing.

She drew back and Andrew studied her carefully. 'Well,' he said, 'I have to admit I don't always get such a poor reception.' Sophie blushed deep crimson. 'Whoever he was, I clearly don't measure up.'

'I'm sorry. I didn't mean to mess you about.'

'*C'est la vie.*' He smiled regretfully.

'I should have hung on to you when I had the chance.'

Andrew laughed. 'As I recall, you were busy hanging on to your swimsuit in case you got done for indecent exposure in a Jacuzzi!' He picked up his coat. 'I guess I'll just be getting back to my hotel. I'm probably going to have to walk, no way I'll pick up a taxi with all these parties going on.'

'I'm sorry,' she said again, but he was shaking his head.

'Stop that or I'm going to have to make you feel seriously guilty. Your British weather is nothing compared to Chicago's, it won't kill me.'

Sophie kissed him on the cheek and shut the front door behind him, locking it up for the night. 'Great,' she told herself. 'Just great.'

The champagne bottle was still there; she refilled her glass and made her way upstairs, picking up a throw from the sofa as she went. She by-passed her bedroom and made her way to the patio doors of the top-floor conservatory, looking out into the night. The summer flowers had long since been replaced with tubs of winter pansies and baby conifers, and the subdued lighting was lit up with patches of colour. Andrew was right, the night was crisp, but not unpleasant; she opened the doors onto the terrace, wrapping the throw around her.

'Well, you really screwed it up this time,' Sophie told herself out loud. 'Another chance gone, another good time ruined. I only hope you're pleased with yourself.' The night remained resolutely silent, with only the hum of traffic to keep her company.

She drank the remains of her champagne in silence and turned to go back inside to find her path blocked by a tall shape. Shocked, she dropped the glass to the floor where it shattered instantly, slivers of crystal scattering across the deck.

Eduardo stood watching her. He held out his hand, 'Sophie. I've come to take you home.'